INCREDIBLE
ABERRATION?

INCREDIBLE
ABERRATION?

Robert E. Bonson

Library of Congress Control Number: 2007904926
ISBN: Hardcover   978-1-4257-7455-4
                     Softcover   978-1-4257-7435-6

To order additional copies of this book, contact:
Xlibris Corporation
1-888-795-4274
www.Xlibris.com
Orders@Xlibris.com
41813

In the end,
it is not what the eye sees,
that counts;

it is what the mind perceives.

ONE

The Envelope

Erickson stood at the side of the road, watching the departing mail truck throw up a whirlwind of dust in the hot summer afternoon. The thick manila envelope he'd been handed by the postman could only portend trouble, he thought.

He looked at the hand-written label again, hoping that it really wasn't addressed to him, but there it was in a strong, masculine script: "Lt. James J. Erickson, RR15, Fresno, California 93706." There was no return address and the postal cancellation showing the point of origin was blurred beyond recognition.

He stiffened slightly and grasped the envelope tighter. No one called him Lieutenant anymore, much less sent mail addressed to him that way. Warily, he held the envelope at bay as he slowly walked up the dirt road back to the main house of his small ranch.

With each step, his mind churned up old thoughts of anger at the Army for what they had done to him when he really was a Lieutenant.

As he reached the front steps he stopped, silently wishing there was someone inside to talk to, but there was no one around he trusted enough to confide in; certainly no one he could talk about what had happened.

The two ranch hands he employed knew how to run the place and left him alone. He liked the solitude, yet he was beginning to realize that he had to get out of the silent obscurity into which the Army had forced him.

Their treatment of him had been unfair and he wanted desperately to have the truth come out. But, would it? Could it? Hell, he wasn't even sure what the whole truth was – but he knew he hadn't lied to the Board of Inquiry.

Every detail of his testimony was still as fresh in his mind as it had been when the Officers on the Board had heard and rejected his words – often it seemed, as soon as they came out of his mouth.

Remembering those days on the stand, he felt the anger well up inside again. Agitated, he found himself being thrust once more into the bizarre events involving his platoon in the summer of 1976. The scenes began to rush through his mind, full of vivid sound and color, grabbing him, holding him, as he sought once more a rational explanation as to what had happened.

By now he was seated on the stoop of the porch, but his mind was firmly in the campground to which his platoon had been banished after the run-in with the MPs.

The images of that first morning were still so real he could smell the pine trees. He remembered how he and Corporal Putnam had started down the hillside trail from their campground to Jockey Hollow in search of the rest of their unit so they could join the Bicentennial activities. Within moments, all awareness of the porch and the ranch were gone – he was now fully engrossed in the scenes cascading before his eyes.

He led the way, holster gently flopping with each step. Putnam was close behind; holding the same pace, hand on his holstered .45, ready for anything. They both felt apprehensive, especially after the strange circumstances that had greeted them upon awakening. He had agreed to their carrying the weapons, more to placate Putnam's foreboding, than as a means of personal protection. Yet, it did give him a sense of security that he found appealing.

At the base of the hill, they came upon a wide, thick grove of tall black willows, partially obscuring the large pond beyond. As they began their trek around the grove, an armed man suddenly bolted towards them from the nearest clump of trees.

"HALT!" he demanded.

Startled, Erickson and Putnam stopped and stared. Dressed in a red coat covering a white blouse, with white pants tucked into knee-high black boots, the man was an impressive sight. Ominously, the bayonet-tipped muzzleloader in his hands was pointed directly at Erickson, the man's finger poised at the trigger.

Erickson quickly assumed the man was practicing his part for the Bicentennial celebration and asked, "What part of the 76th are you with?"

There was a puzzled look on the man's face as he answered. "We serve under his Majesty in the 16th Light Dragoons." Then sternly, he added, "Who *are* you? What *are* you doing here?"

Erickson didn't like the soldier's demeanor and told him so with his tone of his voice. "Private, I'd appreciate it if you would show us the way to the Officer in charge, so we can get our Platoon set up before the celebration starts tomorrow. That's the 4th of July, you know!" He emphasized the "4th" hoping it might add some urgency to the man's cooperation.

"I am not a Private. I am a Sergeant. The 4th was Thursday past. Tomorrow is July 7th."

"OK, Sergeant," Erickson responded disdainfully, not willing to join the game. "We'll find our way without you." Shaking his head, he and Putnam started to walk towards the pond.

"Seize them!" the Sergeant yelled over his shoulder towards three similarly clad soldiers emerging from the trees. With their bayonet-tipped muzzleloaders at the ready, they rushed towards Putnam and Erickson, who promptly stopped.

The Sergeant took a few steps to close the gap and, pointing the muzzleloader directly at Erickson, touched the tip of its bayonet just at the left side of his chest.

"Hey! Watch that bayonet!" Erickson exclaimed, scowling at the Sergeant. "You put that damn thing down, or I'll take it away from you!"

"You are very brave for an unarmed man," replied the Sergeant, oblivious to Erickson's sidearm. Then, prodding him again, he pushed Erickson closer to Putnam, who was defiantly facing the other three soldiers.

Erickson's jaw took a firm set. Looking the Sergeant directly in the eye, he emphasized each word that angrily burst from his mouth. "I don't know what you're trying to prove, but back off and we'll try to forget we ran into you."

"You speak a strange tongue," replied the Sergeant. "The Captain will want to talk to you. March around the trees and the pond, towards the smoke. The camp is just beyond."

"NO!" Erickson's jaw was like steel. In response, the Sergeant put more pressure on the bayonet.

"Ouch! Watch that bayonet, Sergeant!"

"Then march!"

Angered at what he saw happening to Erickson, Putnam lost his temper and reached for his .45. Reacting, the Sergeant quickly thrust his bayonet towards Erickson, just as he twisted to the right to get his own automatic out. The movement saved him, for as he turned, the bayonet tore through his fatigue blouse. With nothing to stop his momentum, the Sergeant lost his balance and fell forward, jamming the bayonet into the ground.

Alarmed, Putnam fired his .45, the loud discharge cascading off the trees as the bullet hit the right ankle of the Sergeant. Shuddering from the shock of the impact and with eyes bulging, he looked at the .45 in Putnam's hand and then started a long, gut-busting scream as the pain of the vicious wound slammed into his brain.

Taking advantage of the distraction, Erickson shoved the closest redcoat into the other two, sending all three to the ground.

"Let's get the hell out of here!" he shouted as he turned and started running up the trail. A sharp 'click' reached his ears from behind, followed immediately by a muffled retort and a zinging sound past his head.

"They're shooting at us," he yelled over his shoulder to Putnam, running close behind. "The bastards are shooting at us!"

Reaching the temporary safety of a tree, Erickson turned and saw the three red-coated soldiers standing near their Sergeant, loading and firing their muskets up the trail towards him. In the distance, he saw another dozen red-coated troops riding hard to join them.

As he and Putnam started running up the trail again, he could hear the pounding hooves in the distance and knew the horses were being spurred after them.

In desperation, he called to the rest of his platoon in the campground above. "HELP!" he yelled, "We need help down here!"

TWO

Colonel Lester Gets His Orders

Colonel Benjamin Lester stood before the desk of his boss, Brigadier General Eznik Xetrel, and listened as the General explained why he had called him in.

"I've been told twice in the last few days," he said with concern in his voice, "that questions are being asked around the Pentagon about Erickson. Seems somebody here in Washington is intent on digging something up. I understand the questions being asked indicate they believe Erickson's story. Now, that's insane! What Erickson experienced was not real; it was all in his mind. And I sure as hell don't need somebody out there trying to prove otherwise!"

Lester nodded his head in agreement.

Obviously annoyed with the prospect that someone might actually believe Erickson, Xetrel fumed on, emphasizing each sentence by stabbing the air with his bony right index finger.

"You and I sat through the entire Board of Inquiry and heard the whole story. He never produced a shred of evidence to counter the Army's charge that he and his platoon went AWOL. Nor did he provide any proof of what he claims happened to them while they were gone! My god, the way he lead his platoon was unforgivable; he deserved to be sent packing."

"Where is he now?" Lester asked, curiously.

"Still in California, as far as I know. On his ranch." Xetrel was becoming calmer. "He's kept quiet ever since the Board reached its judgment. But, I think he'd love to get back at the Army and prove us wrong. With all these questions being asked, he may have a chance. Somebody's started to stir things up and that means Erickson could get stirred up, too!"

"Who's asking the questions?"

"I don't have a clue. The people who told me about it said the guys didn't give their names. They were just a couple of fellows asking questions.

Whoever they were, they had access to the inner reaches of the Pentagon and knew who to contact."

"FBI? CIA? NSA?"

"Not the right kind of people for those organizations; less sophisticated in dress and manner. More like spooks, but out of their element. Not the normal kind of spooks we've known. That's what makes it so threatening! Check it out, Colonel. Use your talents and connections. I want to know who has an interest in Erickson and why – *before* it gets out of hand. We've got to make sure Erickson doesn't get any ammunition to start something or get some Congressman's attention. That could be a political disaster for the Army. Think of the careers that could go down the drain – including yours and mine!"

"Yours and mine? Why us? All we did was attend the Board of Inquiry!"

"Don't be an ass, Colonel. The very fact that *we were there* makes us vulnerable. The senior members of the Board have all retired. We're all that's left of the Army's proceedings against Erickson. If those proceedings come into question, I can assure you, you and I will be among the *stuckees* when it's all over!

Pointing his finger towards his office door, Xetrel barked his order, "You find out what's going on and control it!"

Lester knew much of Xetrel's anger was for show, but he also knew that if pressed, Xetrel's full power as a Brigadier could be brought to bear. He surely wasn't going to cross him if he could avoid it; he learned that in the years since meeting him at the Erickson Inquiry.

* * *

After returning to his office, Lester searched the Pentagon phonebook for the number of his old friend Admiral Funston. It had been years since he'd seen 'Funny,' but Lester knew if anyone could tell him who was stirring up the Erickson ashes, it would be the proud little Admiral; his organization had a way of keeping tabs on things like that.

He soon found the number and dialed. When it was answered, he got put through quickly. Funston was delighted to hear from him, but told him he was tied up then and for the rest of the day, as well. They set a time to meet the next day.

* * *

Lester originally met Funston in 1974 when they served together on a Tri-Service Team. Lester had been a Captain then and Funston a Navy Lt. Commander. They had taken to each other instantly, sharing the same humor, southwestern upbringing and values, and a keen interest and insight into things cryptic and unusual.

The Tri-Service Team had been created after covert sources reported to Naval Intelligence that the Soviets were working on an exotic technique to obtain U.S. military secrets.

The cold war was very tense then, with the Vietnam experience still fresh on both sides. The Soviets desperately needed to know what the United States was doing and planning. Any avenues available to help them achieve that purpose were actively pursued.

One technique the Soviets devised, while far-fetched in concept, offered an opportunity to revolutionize their clandestine operations. The scheme involved channeling the power of known Russian psychics via ultra high-powered laser beams and satellites into western military nerve centers.

The system was simple in concept and construction. They built a copper screen to capture and collect the energy transmissions of a proven psychic seated in the center of a small enclosure. The energy was then fed to a simple, but sophisticated laser fabricated from highly purified amethyst. Powered by a small nuclear source, which produced the required ultra-high burst rates, the collected psychic energy was then fired at Cosmos 778, already in stationary orbit over the eastern United States. With a 12-year life, the 2-meter diameter satellite was the perfect tool to disperse the laser beam into energy paths all over the East Coast. The psychics had only to follow a path towards whatever informational pot-of-gold they might find.

Astonished at this application of the Soviets achievements in laser technology, Naval Intelligence quickly shared the information with their rival services and requested immediate coordination of counter-measures. Following a series of high level and sometimes heated meetings, a Tri-Service Team was created to implement the U.S. response. Funston had been selected to lead the team, inevitably known as TriST.

TriST soon received several disturbing reports of Soviet minor successes using their new technique. A few months later, they received another report, this time about a Russian psychic having 'observed' a conversation between the Soviet Ambassador and the American President at a State Department dinner. They were in awe when they learned the psychic had tape-recorded what he 'heard' during the conversation, which was later verified by the Soviet Ambassador.

Funston and Lester stepped up their efforts to scour the United States for psychics of their own. As pressure to stop the Soviets mounted, Lester and Funston finally selected eight proven candidates.

Their immediate goal had been to develop techniques for not only sensing incoming Russian psychic energy, but countering it, as well. It had been a slow and exacting process, frequently hindered by frayed tempers. The pressures of trying to keep up with the frequent Soviets excursions simply collided at times with the realities of human endurance. And, the fact that the Soviets were conducting their experimental excursions at all times of the day and night only compounded the need for TriST to be constantly on the alert.

With practice, TriST operatives became successful in finding and stopping a few, but not all of the Russian missions. While elated with their success, Funston and Lester began to realize the magnitude of the effort they would have to mount to fully control the Soviets and what it would cost. Knowing the three Services would not pay for such expenses out of their budgets, another means to defeat the Soviet threat had to be created.

Thus was born the Psychic Research Agency (PRA) with a charter from the National Security Council to investigate all feasible aspects for the military application of psychic phenomena. Its efforts were so highly classified that few outsiders held the necessary clearance to access its results.

While the PRA's initial thrust had been to find and repel the Russians, the abilities of its psychics to gather intelligence, as well, had not been ignored. Bypassing the cost and time to develop a laser transmission capability like the Russian's, Funston's people had opted to concentrate on expanding the powers of their psychics to simply roam at will within the Soviet Union using their own talents and energy.

While theoretically sound, the approach had suffered from one major drawback: positive results could not be continuously repeated. And, without repeatability, Funston knew he would not have an intelligence-gathering program of value to the military. Left to operate only in the counter-measures mode, he had little hope of promotion.

Concerned about the lack of repeatability, Lester had talked to the psychics in private. They told him their energy would flow much better in relaxed circumstances. The secret laboratory-type conditions and tightly controlled mission aspects existing in the back rooms at the PRA frequently overwhelmed their efforts, they said, despite extraordinary exertion to keep a mission on track.

Lester had just starting the process of easing the burden on the psychics when, without explanation, he had been pulled off and assigned as an observer at the Erickson Board of Inquiry. It was a jarring reassignment that, while typical of the Army, left him bewildered.

He often wondered what had gone on after he left, but concluded that Funston's promotion to Admiral said it all.

His immediate reaction when he heard about the promotion was to feel jealous. But, he'd maintained momentum, too, reaching full Colonel just as he finished a long tour of duty in Europe with General Xetrel in more mundane and immediate forms of intelligence work.

*   *   *

When he arrived for his meeting with Funston, Lester was ushered into the walnut paneled office from which the Admiral directed his activities.

The Admiral came around his desk and walked across the plush sea blue carpet towards him, extending his pudgy hand in hearty welcome. Lester grabbed it in warm friendship.

"It's good to see you again, Admiral," he said. "If this office is any indication, you have certainly done well since the old days."

"I've done very well, my boy. Very well, indeed," Funston responded. "For a landlubber from New Mexico to reach this point; well, it's been an extraordinary experience. You've done well for yourself, too, I hear. Still working for Xetrel?"

"'Til he retires."

"Come," the Admiral said, pointing to the oversize chairs in front of his huge desk. "Sit down, enjoy one of these wonderful leather monstrosities." As he sat down in one himself, he added, "So, when do you think that will be?"

Lester seated himself in the chair next to Funston's, then answered. "Oh, I suspect the General will be leaving the Army by the end of the year. He wants to stay long enough to earn maximum retirement pay, but not a day longer."

"And you?"

"Looking for a star, if I can catch one. It may be hard to do without the Soviets around."

"You could always come back here," the Admiral said, with a slight, knowing smile in his eyes.

"Take your place when you go?"

"Probably."

"Interesting thought."

They went on talking for over an hour, enjoying the time bringing each other up to date on their lives. As they became re-acquainted, Lester decided to take the direct approach in asking about the Erickson matter.

"You remember that Board of Inquiry I was assigned to, the one that took me away from here?"

"Yes. I was sorry to see you go. I needed you here."

"I was sorry to go, too. It was quite an assignment, though. A Lieutenant and his platoon disappeared during the Bicentennial. The Army charged them all with being AWOL, but then concentrated only on him. Because of the circumstances and the potential for press attention, they called it an Inquiry and kept it very quiet."

"What kind of circumstances?"

"Said he found himself at the start of the Revolutionary War, fighting Redcoats!"

"Oh my! That's quite a set of circumstances. No doubt they found him loony."

"The rest of his Platoon told the same story."

Funston started to chuckle, his full belly jiggling up and down as he tried to control his mirth. "Well, I assume they didn't put the whole lot away in the brig. What happened?"

"They discharged them all. Told them to keep quiet, or else they would get them for desertion. Now, after a quarter century, somebody's digging around in the ashes, asking questions. You can *imagine* how unhappy that makes the Army. Got any ideas on who or why?"

"I'll keep my ears open for you."

"I was hoping that maybe some of your boys might have picked up something."

"I'll check them out. But, they've been pretty busy since the President lit a fire under all of us in this business. You know – to come up with more and better intelligence capabilities for less money in a world of terrorists."

"I'd appreciate your checking with them," Lester said, knowing the meeting was over. "I'll leave my card so you can reach me."

After exchanging good-byes, Lester returned to his temporary office at Fort McNair. His own office in the Pentagon was a shambles after a ceiling pipe had burst and he was grateful to his friends for getting him assigned to McNair while it was being repaired.

Realizing that his work was going to be more difficult now that he couldn't count on Funston's immediate help, Lester decided he could use another pair of hands. And, legs too, for that matter.

Picking up the phone, he dialed a number at the Pentagon. "Carl," he said, when it was answered, "I need you. Get your butt over to McNair, pronto."

He hadn't waited for a reply. They'd been working together since Lester had returned from Europe and Carl knew how to find him.

THREE

Another Copy

A few mornings later, the heat of the July day was already shimmering through his window as Lester sat at his desk and looked at Captain Carl Treppello standing before him. He fingered the thick report Carl had laid in front of him five minutes earlier. It was about Erickson.

"Where the hell did this come from?" he said, challenging the hefty young officer standing before him.

"I don't know, Sir. It was on my chair yesterday afternoon when I came back to the office. I looked around, but didn't see anyone suspicious. Came to show it to you then, but you'd gone for the day."

"This in very strange, Carl. We start probing into why someone's asking questions about Erickson and the next thing we know there's a fat report about him on your chair. My wits tell me this smells of a set-up." Lester stroked his chin. "I assume since you got it yesterday, you've had time to read it through?"

"Yes, Sir. Last night. I got so absorbed with it that I didn't get around to eating. It's fascinating. Full of facts and assumptions tied to what happened to him."

"It's gotta be a set-up, then." Lester screwed up his tanned, rugged face, letting his deep brown eyes and the sarcastic tone of voice convey his thoughts to his assistant. A moment later, though, he changed his tone. "You say it's full of facts, Captain. What are they? What conclusions do they reach?"

"Conclusions, Sir?"

"Yes, conclusions. I'm sure it contains conclusions, or it wouldn't have been sent to us."

"Well, the report says there *is* substance to the story Erickson told the Board of Inquiry in 1976 – in spite of the Army's denials that any Soldiers disappeared in New Jersey during the Bicentennial celebration."

"Well, I know what I think about Erickson," Lester responded scornfully. "I was at the Inquiry." Moving to pick up the report, he added, "Who put this thing together?"

"I think it was the PRA. Let me show you why." The dark-haired Captain leaned his 5'10" frame over the front of the Lester's oversize desk to pick up the report. "See these black streaks and marks?" he said, pointing as he flipped through several pages. "The copier was set too high and it copied every detail, sometimes right through the slips of paper that were used to cover up the markings in the top and bottom margins of the pages."

"Yeah, I see the bleed-through," Lester responded.

"Now look at page 17," Treppello said, handing the book back.

Lester flipped to the page. At the bottom, surrounded by the outline of the paper that was supposed to cover them, were the words: "PRA – Sensitive." At the top of the page in similar faint letters was the remnant of a bold stamped legend: "Restricted Access – Level II."

"Goddamnit!" Lester said, as he jerked upright in his chair. "What the hell's going on here? When I talked with Funston, I asked him if he knew about the Erickson inquiries and he said he'd look into it. Now this shows up. Nothing gets done in that organization without him knowing, so he had to have known about it at the meeting. That sonofabitch lied to me! Why? What's he up to?"

Treppello remained quiet, knowing a response wasn't expected. After a moment, he cleared his throat and made a suggestion.

"Colonel, there's a lot of meat in this report. Why don't I make a copy for you? Then we can go through it together."

Lester nodded his head in agreement, then leaned back in his chair. As Treppello left his office, he couldn't help but think, *yes indeed, this whole thing smells of a set-up.*

FOUR

Saturday, 26 June – Friday, 2 July 1976

The boxcar jerked violently, then shuddered. Erickson sat up instantly, the fog of his sleep clearing from his eyes. A deep sigh welled up in his throat, but it was drowned out by the squeaking wheels and brakes of the train as it worked its way around the sharp bends in the track, slowly moving down the long grade.

He became more awake now, getting a grip on his surroundings. Moving his lanky legs over the edge of the bunk, he adjusted his six-foot frame to accommodate the limited space as the converted boxcar began to take on a familiar shape. Three soldiers in fatigues sat around a wooden table in the middle of the car playing an endless game of cards. Surrounding them were four stacks of three bunks bolted into the corners. Other men in their bunks had also been awakened, but had closed their eyes to their circumstances and tried to regain the oblivion of sleep.

Erickson's eyes came to rest on the small Private seated at the left side of the table, adjusting his cards. Answering the stare, the Private said, "Hope the trucks stay tied down all right, Lieutenant. Don't feel like getting out on those flatcars to retie them or any of the rest of the equipment."

Erickson continued his absent-minded staring and answered half-heartedly, "They'll be OK. The transport people in L.A. knew what they were doing when they loaded us on board."

Another pair of eyes was staring at the Private as well, but for a different purpose. Tapping the table and pointing his finger at him, Corporal Putnam called the errant player's attention back to the game. "Come on, Lee, quit worrying about the trucks and start worrying about how light you are in this pot." Putnam thought Lee worried too much about everything, exaggerated everything, and didn't mind telling him so.

The conversation at the card game picked up as the train continued its tortured, twisted descent. Erickson mentally took inventory of his command: two more olive-drab bunkcars; a flatcar carrying his three Army troop trucks;

another carrying a large trailer containing their uniforms, combat clothing and various weapons and ammunition; and, a third flatcar carrying the portable kitchen and his jeep. He and the 4th Platoon, J Company, 76th Special Services Battalion were enroute from Los Angeles to Newark, New Jersey.

Lee got disgusted with his luck, threw in his cards and left the game, moving over near Erickson. He hesitated for a moment, then screwed up his courage and asked the question he had asked everyone else without getting a good answer. "Why did they put us in these cars and send us East, Sir? I mean, I know we're all Reservists and the Army can send us where they want during summer camp, but why New Jersey?"

Erickson looked at the short, baby-faced Private and took an instant pity on him. "6th Army Headquarters picked us from our regular units to represent them in a special job at the Bicentennial celebration."

"Why us? Why New Jersey?"

"There were two reasons. You, I, all of us here have colonial ancestry, either as descendents of colonists during the War for Independence, or of the soldiers who fought on the British side. And, we're all supposed to have better than average knowledge about the weapons and gear of the World War II foot soldier. We're going to a place called Jockey Hollow, near Morristown, New Jersey, to participate in a Bicentennial program. There'll be a lot of other units there, too, depicting the various weapons, uniforms and fighting gear of the American Army from 1776 through 1976."

"That kinda fits, I guess. I do know a lot about World War II weapons since my father was in it and got me started by talking about it so much. I'm not sure about any of my ancestors being in the Revolutionary War, though."

Erickson smiled at Lee. "If you're here, it's because the Army thinks you had some. Anyway, it's got to be different from what you've done before in summer camp and should be fun."

Lee was enjoying the opportunity to talk directly to the Lieutenant and sputtered out his next question. "Someone said we're carrying live ammo. Is that right, Sir?"

"Yeah, that's right. We're going to use it in a daily event called the mad-minute, where each unit will fire the weapons of their time. The muzzleloaders of 1776 will go first, followed in order by improved weapons of later generations, on through the weapons of the modern Army. Each group's weapons will be faster, louder and more dramatic than the previous. The whole thing will take about 10 minutes, with a rising crescendo of noise, that will be culminated with a mass presenting of arms salute to the flag while the Army band plays the Star Spangled Banner in the background."

Lee looked puzzled. "Live ammo with people around?"

"Hard to believe, isn't it? I understand that blanks were favored by the Army Brass for safety's sake, but some exuberant Colonel finally convinced them that blanks didn't sound or act the same way as the real thing. Apparently, they found the right location with the right kind of hill to point the weapons at. The public's going to be kept behind barricades camouflaged as part of the surroundings, which should add to the realism of being in a real battle scene. In between those daily mad-minutes, everybody's going to show off the uniforms, battle-dress and weapons of the generation of the Army they're representing. We've been told to expect large numbers of visitors to the event grounds, many of which will be potential volunteers for the Army. In fact, part of our evaluation rating for this summer camp will be how many recruits we produce. Feel any better about going, now?"

"Yeah, kinda. I guess I'm more bored than anything. Here it is Monday afternoon and it seems like we've been in this bunkcar for days, instead of just leaving L.A. yesterday evening." Lee hesitated. "Where you from, Sir? How did you get assigned to this duty?"

"I live on a ranch outside of Fresno. When I graduated from Fresno State a few years back, I got a ROTC commission at the same time. I was going to go into the Regular Army, but my mother died just before graduation, so I took a reserve commission instead and went back to help my father run the ranch for awhile. I got my promotion to First Lieutenant earlier this year. When the Army discovered some ancestor's in the Revolution on my mother's side, I got picked to lead this Platoon." Erickson grinned, "When she was alive, my mother tried several times to trace our lineage back, but she wasn't very successful. I guess the Army knows more than we do."

Lee grinned back, but couldn't think of anything more to say. In the awkward silence that followed, Erickson began looking around the bunkcar at the rest of the occupants. Besides Erickson and Lee, the car held Platoon Sergeant Tom Bushnell and the rest of the 1st Squad of nine men, led by Corporal Putnam. With 18 men of the other two squads in the next bunkcars, plus the three-man Mess unit led by Corporal Dobbs, Erickson's command totaled 32. Most had never traveled east before and certainly of those that had, none had ever gone in this fashion. Where the Army had found these bunkcars would forever remain a mystery to him.

As for their selection to be included in this Platoon, most knew of some ancestral relationship, but only Sergeant Bushnell was positive. His family could be traced directly back to Carter Bushnell of the Second Maryland Battalion of the Flying Camp; a Battalion raised by the Continental Congress in 1776 as a mobile reserve unit, supplying troops to the Continental Army, wherever needed.

At 36, Bushnell had been to 15 summer camps since joining the reserves to supplement his income. He lived a quiet life in Los Angeles with his wife and two boys, looking forward each year to the summer camps as a much-needed break from the pressures of being an automotive Service Manager.

He met Erickson for the first time at Ft. MacArthur, near Los Angeles, on the previous Saturday. At first suspicious of the younger Lieutenant, Bushnell had come to like his easy manner in getting the Platoon organized into a working unit before leaving for the New Jersey. Erickson had responded to the older Sergeant's show of confidence and a rapport had developed between them. It would end up carrying them through the uncertain future.

∗　　∗　　∗

The time between Monday and Friday had been boringly long and the men had spent hours talking and daydreaming about their participation in the Bicentennial. After their train arrived in Newark, the off-loading of the trucks and gear had gone surprisingly fast and they were soon underway toward Morristown.

Erickson had bought a newspaper in the train station and was reading it as Sergeant Bushnell expertly lead the small convoy through the congested, confusing streets of Newark, then west on highway 78 to the Parkway, and then north on the Parkway itself. Erickson marveled at the Sergeant's efficiency. Putting the paper down, he leaned back in the Jeep's right-side seat to enjoy, as best he could, the three-hour ride ahead of them through heavy Friday afternoon traffic. Behind them in one of the trucks, Corporal Russell smiled to himself as he thought about the extra supplies he had added to the trailer back at Ft. MacArthur.

It was late afternoon when they finally arrived at Morristown. After a short break, they headed west again, looking for the event grounds inside Jockey Hollow. Erickson wanted to be there and set up in his assigned area before dark.

Four other Platoons of the 76th arrived at the same time with the same thought, making the assembly area totally congested. Erickson soon decided to move his little convoy onto the edge of the road and wait for the congestion to clear. The narrow road didn't permit them to clear the edge completely, but the men quickly got out anyway, stretching their legs and grumbling about the delay. Erickson let them wander for a while and then called them together.

"It may be some time, yet," he said, "but while we're waiting, I thought I might tell you why the Army picked this area for us."

The look on the men's faces showed no interest.

Ignoring the looks, Erickson continued. "Parts of Washington's Continental Army spent three winters in this area starting in late 1776. It was a strategic location, permitting Washington to control and respond to the movements of the British at New Brunswick and Amboy. Agriculture was the basic product of the area, which meant food for his men, while the iron mines and foundries at other towns nearby provided metal equipment for them. The British sent a few patrols into the area, but the natural defenses of the swamps to the east and mountains to the west precluded any great offensives. There are a number of historical sites here in Jockey Hollow, including Henry Wick's house over at the western end. It was built in 1750."

Eyeing the men as they shuffled their feet, Erickson let them return to waiting. Since they couldn't go far, they grew impatient and restless as the hours dragged on and the congestion failed to clear.

As the sun dipped lower in the western sky, Erickson saw a jeep careening down the road towards them. Forced to the center and left side of the road as it approached Erickson's trucks, the jeep's driver was angry. Skidding to a stop in front of Erickson, the driver, an MP Major, screamed at him. "Are you responsible for parking these friggin' trucks here, blocking this road?"

The vehemence of the question momentarily threw Erickson off-balance and he stammered something about waiting for his turn at the entrance. It was lost in the rage of the Major's voice: "Get them out of here! Get them out now! We've got the Governor coming down this road in a few minutes and I don't want him to have to stop or move over because your damn trucks and men are blocking the way!"

"Where in the hell do you suggest I go, Major?" Erickson's deep blue eyes glistened with anger. It wasn't his fault that the camp was congested.

"I don't give a damn, Lieutenant. Just move them. Now!"

Erickson could only glare at the Major. He had no idea where to go, and his eyes said so.

Getting angrier, the Major pointed towards the west and yelled at Erickson. "Go down this road about a mile and then turn right, near the Wick House, then drive up the hill until you get to the park! You can hole up there until this all clears!" He paused to see if Erickson understood the directions and then added emphatically, "I don't really care where you go, Lieutenant, but get your butts out of here, NOW!"

The Platoon had gathered near the jeep to watch. Erickson turned towards them with a frown, but then mindful that they had not brought on this humiliation, he quickly changed his face and flicked his arms and hands in the air, much as one would scatter chickens at the ranch. They instantly moved to the trucks. As Erickson and Bushnell got in their jeep, the Major walked towards them, hands on his hips, impatiently waiting for Erickson to get moving. As the little convoy got underway, the Major returned to his jeep and followed.

Getting down the road past the entrance to the 76th camp area was extremely difficult. Soldiers and vehicles were everywhere. Full of rage at the Major, Erickson watched in the side mirror as he forced other units to move, as well. Finally losing him in the accumulated traffic, Erickson desperately searched for the road up to the hillside park, while Bushnell sped up after finally finding open road through the wooded hollow.

"There it is!" Erickson shouted to Bushnell. "Turn right!"

Bushnell immediately complied, skidding the jeep around the corner as the trailer followed on its outside wheels. The four trucks came barreling right behind, gears gnashing as motors raced to keep the bouncing, lurching human loads up with the pace set by the jeep.

Erickson's eyes searched for the entrance to the park as they followed the bends of the climbing road through the profusion of elms and red spruce. It was a beautiful area, even at dusk, but in his anger he looked only for the side road.

"Up ahead, to the right!" he barked. This time the jeep made a more precise, but still hasty turn, leading the trucks into the empty park. Dirt and spruce needles spewed through the air as they skidded to a stop.

Once the men were off the trucks, they gathered around Erickson at one of the picnic tables. "How long do you want to stay here, Lieutenant?" asked Bushnell.

"All night," came the determined answer. "Get a camp set up. Break out what gear we need from the trailer and fire up that kitchen unit for a hot meal. We're going to spend the night here!"

FIVE

Saturday Morning

Erickson lay quietly watching the sparrows flitting about in the branches of the Spruce tree above him, tormenting a red squirrel. Mist hovered in patches around the tree trunks near the ground, sending off yellow arrows of light as the sun danced across the forest floor.

He couldn't remember that there had been this many trees last night, but then it had been a hectic time – getting run off by the Major, roaring up the hill to the park, setting up the camp area and getting the men fed.

After things had quieted down, the men had staked out areas to put up their two man tents. Forgoing his tent on such a beautiful night, Erickson had hand-raked an area of needles together as a mattress under his sleeping bag.

As the portable lanterns were extinguished for the night, he had looked around at the rustic comfort provided by the various picnic tables, water faucets and outhouses scattered around the park. It had occurred to him that it was a far cry from what they would have enjoyed had they gotten into the Jockey Hollow Bicentennial grounds.

Taking his bearings before closing his eyes, he noted that the park lay on a flat portion of the hill with its entrance facing to the west. The trucks, jeep, trailer and kitchen unit had been parked randomly, but near one another on the southwest side, between the entrance road and the jutting section of the park overlooking Jockey Hollow.

Now, dozing on and off in the morning light, he was suddenly startled wide-awake with a commotion on his left at the edge of the park.

"All right! Who's the wise-ass that's been screwing around with the outhouses? There were two of them over here last night. I'm numbed by the nervous nudges of necessity and I need one now!" Private Lewis's voice was serious. Other grumbling voices soon took up the question as well.

Before Erickson could get up to investigate, he saw Sergeant Bushnell crawling out from his tent, growling, "What the hell's going on out here?"

Erickson leaned back on his elbows to watch.

"Somebody stole the crappers, Sarge."

"Whaddaya mean, somebody stole the crappers? For Christ's sake, they're right over there." Bushnell was pointing. "They're right th . . ." But they weren't.

Erickson immediately sat up and made a quick 360-degree search with his eyes. The green outhouses on either side of the park were nowhere to be seen. He noticed the picnic tables they had eaten on the night before were gone, too.

The trucks and the jeep were where they had been parked. The kitchen unit and the trailer were between the two spruce trees where they'd been left. But, the tables and the outhouses were gone!

Not really grasping what was happening, Erickson deferred to Bushnell, who was already issuing orders.

"Putnam," he shouted, "have your people scout around and see what you can find. Porter, get your men digging a latrine in that clear area over where the outhouses used to be. We need someplace for the men to relieve themselves!"

He stopped for a moment, looking at the area where the outhouses had been.

"Wait a minute, wait a minute," he exclaimed. "The holes should still be there. Outhouses may disappear, but the holes shouldn't."

Corporal Porter ran over to the area where his men were supposed to dig. He yelled back desperately, "No holes, no outhouses – there's nothing here, Sarge."

In the distance, Putnam's men searched the rest of the park only to discover another missing essential. "They got the water pipes, too!"

That was enough. Erickson got up, and walked quickly over to Bushnell, who was muttering to himself. "I don't believe this," the Sergeant kept saying, shaking his head. "What the hell is going on here?"

Keeping a low voice, Erickson took command. "Check the guns and ammo, Sergeant. They can have the rest, but we need our gear."

Startled at the thought, Bushnell reacted immediately and called out to Corporal Russell. "Have your guys check the trailer, see if we still have all our gear."

Russell himself ran to check.

In the distance, Putnam, who was still scouting around the park, called out again. "Saaarrrge!" The usually cool Corporal sounded panicked, when he yelled, "They got the road, too!"

"Road? How can anybody take a road?" Erickson exclaimed as he started running towards Putnam. "Come on, Sergeant," he called, "let's see this."

The road they had used the night before had been two lanes wide and constructed of black top. Reaching the area, Erickson confirmed Putnam's discovery: it was now only a narrow dirt path running up and down around the knoll of the hillside.

Erickson looked at Bushnell. "Assemble the Platoon, Sergeant. Everybody up and dressed – boots and fatigues." Erickson's mind was racing. What was happening? He didn't like it, though – it wasn't natural. He had a tremendous sense of foreboding, even though the air and the morning seemed extremely tranquil . . . almost as if it were a dream.

He located his binoculars and looked east towards Jockey Hollow and the Bicentennial event grounds down the hill. Everything seemed natural enough, the paths, trails and roads within the grounds were still there but hadn't some of them been paved? And, where was the road from Jockey Hollow they had come up the night before?

He could see two buildings across from the pond located at the base of the hill. He assumed they were part of the historical monument. One was the Wick House, the other, across the road, appeared to be a tavern. To the south, beyond the buildings, Erickson could see smoke rising. It looked like campfires. He decided it was probably part of the 76th getting into the spirit of things by cooking breakfast outdoors.

"The men are ready, Sir," announced Bushnell, who had returned unheard by Erickson.

"All right, I want you to get them packed up and ready to move out when I get back. I'm going down to Jockey Hollow and find out when we can get into our assigned area."

"How do we get off this hill, Lieutenant?" Bushnell asked. "There's no road, remember."

"There's got to be a road, Sergeant. We got up here on one."

Bushnell did not reply as they walked back to the men.

"All right, men." Erickson spoke quietly as he joined them. "Something's out of order this morning, but I'm sure we can figure it out. What I do know is that we got our butts thrown out of the Hollow yesterday and drove up here in anger. Maybe we're just confused about what was really here last night. I'm sure when we get some breakfast under our belts, things will look better."

"But, Lieutenant," Corporal Porter interrupted. "I know there were outhouses here last night. I used one of them. So did the others."

"I did, too, Corporal, and I'm sure it and the rest of them are still here somewhere, right where we left them."

"Aw, come-on, Lieutenant," persisted Porter, "some of my guys looked around while we were digging the latrines; they ain't here."

"I don't know the answer, yet, Corporal, but let's get the camp organized for breakfast. Have your men finish with the latrines. Corporal Russell, take two men and locate some water. After breakfast, I'll go down the hill to find out when we can move into our assigned area. Putnam will go with me. By the time we get back, I want our gear loaded up and ready to move out."

"But, Lieutenant," Corporal Porter started to make another comment. "Don't you . . ."

"Dismissed," Erickson said, cutting him short. Then quickly added, "If the rest of the 76th isn't down at Jockey Hollow waiting for us, then I'll start worrying. Right now, let's get something to eat."

Corporal Dobbs and his men began preparing breakfast, while Russell and his men looked around for water to replenish the small supply in the kitchen unit. For the moment though, they had enough, since Dobbs had thought to top off the water supply the night before.

Erickson sat on the ground, rolling up his sleeping bag and pondering the situation. He knew there *were* picnic tables here last night; he'd eaten on one no more than 10 feet away. Now where the hell was it? The outhouse he had used had been directly in view, but it wasn't there anymore either. Damnit! What's going on? he wondered.

A while later he heard his name being called for breakfast. *If this is a dream,* he thought, *then trying to eat real food should be interesting. Maybe I'll wake up with a sock in my mouth.*

But the smell, taste and feel were of real bacon of real scrambled eggs and real coffee that no dream could duplicate – Dobbs's coffee was strong enough to wake any man.

Breakfast finished, Putnam approached Erickson, holding two-holstered .45's hooked to web belts. Erickson eyed the automatics and then Putnam.

"You expecting trouble?"

"Yep."

"Why?"

Putnam looked at Erickson warily. "Just a feeling, Lieutenant. Everything is kinda out of whack here this morning and I'd feel better having them. Besides, they won't be out of place if everyone else down there is dressed up in their period uniforms."

"I suppose you have live ammunition for them?"

"Yes, Sir. They're loaded." He didn't like what was going on. "I figure we should be prepared."

"We're only going down to get information, not fight a war." Erickson tried to be blasé, but his heart wasn't in it. Down deep, he agreed with Putnam. "We'll wear 'em, but you keep yours holstered."

"Right you are, Lieutenant. I'm no gunslinger. They're just insurance against anymore weird happenings."

"Well, let's be off," Erickson said. Turning to Bushnell, he added. "I still don't know what's going on Sergeant, so for god's sake, be careful while we're gone."

Bushnell smiled and half-chuckled. "We'll be just fine, Sir. You be careful, too." He saluted.

Erickson was a little taken back by the unexpected salute and promptly returned it.

*   *   *

Erickson and Putnam found walking down the path fairly easy as it wound in and out through the Spruce trees. Birds were chirping and in the distance, they could hear a woodpecker digging for its breakfast.

Erickson lead the way, holster flopping up and down against his leg as he walked. Putnam was a few steps behind; holding the same pace, hand on his holstered .45, ready for anything.

"What do you think is going on, Lieutenant?"

"I don't know. I'm sure we'll find out when we get down to Jockey Hollow. I'm just as concerned as you are."

Putnam wanted to say more, but he knew by now that Erickson didn't want to pursue the matter with speculation. The Corporal was a large man who had hoped in high school for a career in professional football. But, an athlete needed someplace to demonstrate his skills and Putnam's grades hadn't been good enough to go on to college. He had tried Junior College unsuccessfully, spending more time chasing girls than books.

He now worked as a furniture mover for a local van line in San Jose, where he had grown up. Like others in the Platoon, he had joined the reserves to supplement his income and then had to sweat out going to Vietnam, which he was able to avoid. Putnam liked the idea of being a soldier, liked to shoot rifles and pistols and wasn't afraid of anything, as long as he had something going for him. This time it was a .45 on his hip.

They walked on in silence, Erickson watching the trees and wildlife. Small red tree squirrels hissed and growled as they passed. A covey of grouse skittered through the forest undergrowth and then disappeared from view. He thought he saw a white-tailed deer, but it moved so quickly, he wasn't sure.

As they neared the base of the hill approaching the pond, they came upon a thick grove of black willows, some reaching 30 to 40 feet in height, blocking the view of what Erickson thought would be the road beyond. A man suddenly bolted from the nearest trees, startling both Erickson and Putnam.

"HALT!" he demanded.

Erickson and Putnam stopped, and stared. The man's coat was red, fronted by a wide, dark blue strip on either side where the buttons and buttonholes could be seen. The coat covered a white blouse and pants, tucked into knee-high black boots. A white belt covered the red coat from left shoulder to right waist. On his left side was a scabbard and saber. In his hands, right finger on the trigger, was a brown muzzleloader with bayonet. Ominously, the gun was pointed at Erickson. The man was an impressive sight. Although shorter than Erickson, the red-plumed, black helmet on his head made him look taller.

Hoping they had run into another part of the Regiment assigned to the Bicentennial celebration, Erickson asked, "Who are you with?"

"I am with the others, who are over there."

Erickson turned to his right to look at three other men, similarly garbed and similarly pointing bayonet-tipped muzzleloaders at him and Putnam.

"No, I mean, what part of the 76th do you belong to?"

"His Majesty's 76th Regiment has not arrived in the Colonies, as yet. We serve under his Majesty in the 16th Light Dragoons."

Putnam looked dumbfounded. "Serve under his Majesty in the 16th Light Dragoons? What did we do, add some British units to the affair, as well?"

"Identify yourselves." The man with the gun sounded serious.

Erickson looked at him, somewhat irritated with the demeanor of the soldier in front of him. "We're with the 4th Platoon, J Company; part of the 76th. I'd appreciate it, Private, if you would show us the way to the Officer in charge, so that we can get our Platoon set up before the celebration starts tomorrow. That's the 4th of July, you know," adding emphasis he hoped might create some urgency to the man's cooperation.

"I am not a Private. I am a Sergeant. The 4th was Thursday past. Tomorrow is July 7th. If you are trying to enlist in his Majesty's service, Captain Morgan will talk to you, but your clothing is strange. You have the look of Rebels about you."

"Yeah," responded Putnam, "that's us, rebels *with* a cause."

"Well then, since you admit to being Rebels, I believe you shall come with us."

"That's enough, Sergeant," Erickson responded disdainfully, as he and Putnam began to back away, "we'll find our way without you." Turning towards the pond, they shook their heads in disbelief at this latest incident.

"Seize them!" yelled the Sergeant. The three men standing off to the side immediately started towards Erickson and Putnam, muzzleloaders and bayonets pointed at them. The Sergeant pointed his gun directly at Erickson, touching the tip of the bayonet just at the right side of his chest.

"Hey! Watch that bayonet!" Erickson glowered at the Sergeant. "You put that thing down, or I'll shove it up your ass!"

"You are very brave for an unarmed man." The Sergeant prodded Erickson with the bayonet again, pushing him closer to Putnam, who stood facing the other three bayonets.

"Unarmed?" Putnam started to say something and then, seeing the negative cast in Erickson's eyes changed his mind. "Yeah, that's right. We're unarmed, so put down the guns and let's talk this over."

"You may speak . . . as you walk to our camp."

Erickson's jaw took on a firm set. "Knock off the kidding, Sergeant. I don't know what you're trying to prove, but you're getting me pissed-off. We don't need any trouble; we've already got more than enough. After yesterday, I'm in no mood to take any crap off of anyone, much less you. We've got three trucks, a jeep and some other equipment up there in the park, all waiting to get down into Jockey Hollow and get set up for tomorrow – which, by the way, is the 4th, not the 7th. I really haven't got the time to fool around with you anymore. So just back off, have a good laugh after we leave, and we'll try to forget we ran into you."

"You speak a strange tongue. It sounds much like English, but so many of your words do not make sense. The Captain will want to talk to you. March around the pond towards the smoke. The camp is just beyond."

"NO!" Erickson's jaw was like steel. The Sergeant pushed the bayonet at him in response.

"Ouch! Watch that bayonet, Sergeant!"

"Then march!"

Angered by what he saw happening to Erickson, Putnam reached for his .45. Reacting to the movement, the Sergeant thrust the bayonet at Erickson, just as Erickson twisted to the right to get his own automatic out. As he did, the bayonet slipped past, tearing through his fatigue blouse. With nothing to stop him, the Sergeant lost his balance and awkwardly fell forward jamming the bayonet into the ground.

Alarmed, Putnam fired the .45 as soon as it cleared the holster, the loud discharge immediately reverberating off the trees. Unaimed, the bullet hit point blank at the right ankle of the falling Sergeant, blasting black boot, bone, and blood into the ground behind. The Sergeant shuddered from the shock and immediately rolled into a ball, hands stretching for his leg. Eyes bulging, he looked at the .45 in Putnam's hand and then started a long, gut-busting scream as the pain of the vicious wound slammed into his brain.

Erickson shoved the nearest red-coated soldier into the other two, sending all three to the ground. "Let's get the hell out of here," he shouted, as he turned and started running up the trail. Putnam was already right behind him. An odd sounding click reached Erickson's ears from behind, followed immediately by a muffled retort and a zinging sound which ended as a loud thap into a tree just to his right. "They're shooting at us," he yelled back to Putnam. "The bastards are shooting at us!"

Erickson quickly sidestepped behind a tree and cut loose a three-shot volley from his .45 towards the spot where the three soldiers had been. Two zings and the resultant thaps into the tree branches beyond him were his answer, as the sounds from the muzzleloaders reached him over the echo of his own shots.

Peering out from behind the safety of the tree, Erickson watched the three red-coated soldiers standing near the downed Sergeant, loading and firing their muskets up the trail towards him. In the distance, he saw another dozen red-coated troops riding horses towards the group by the pond.

He and Putnam began to leapfrog up the trail; each firing a shot as the other ran to hide behind a new tree. The steady loading, firing and reloading by the red-coated soldiers was amazingly fast, but inaccurate, as Erickson and Putnam widened the distance between them.

The horse-mounted troops reached the others at the base of the hill, dismounted and then began shooting towards Erickson and Putnam. As he watched in fascination and then concern, Erickson saw four of the troops remount and start up the hill towards them.

Running as fast as they could, Erickson and Putnam were spurred on by the pounding of the horse's hooves on the trail in the closing distance. In desperation, Erickson yelled up towards the top of the hill, still a very long trail's length away. "Sergeant! We need help!"

"What the hell's going on down there, Lieutenant?" Bushnell had already run to the edge of the hill, looking to find Erickson. "I hear shooting!"

"Bring a couple of M-1's and some ammo! Bring some smoke grenades! We've got a problem!"

He didn't need to explain further. From his vantagepoint at the top of the hill, Bushnell could see it all. He yelled to Corporal Russell. "There's shooting going on down on the trail. Throw some smoke grenades down there to give the Lieutenant and Putnam some cover."

"Can't! It's too far. How about a mortar round, instead?"

"We weren't assigned any mortar shells," Bushnell fumed. "Besides, we need smoke, not explosives, down there."

"We got both," Russell responded, showing off what he was already dragging behind him.

"What do you mean?" Bushnell angrily yelled at him.

"I mean, I made a little addition to our stores back in L.A. I even have five or six boxes of .30 cal. ammo for the machine gun."

Bushnell was stunned. "Why did you do that?"

"I just thought we might have an opportunity to fire them someway or another, and I didn't want to be disappointed if the chance came up. Everybody gets to fire pistols, carbines and rifles, but I've never really had a chance to fire a mortar or a machine gun. I just wanted to."

"Then, let's get that mortar going, and hurry. We can settle the rest of this later!"

Russell was already hooking up the mortar's firing tube to its baseplate as Porter joined in and tore open four smoke shell canisters. "How many increment charges do you think we need?" he asked.

"Arm 'em with one each," replied Russell. "At this range and angle, that should do it."

Porter inserted the charges at the base of each shell. Designed to take up to four charges, the shells would travel varying distances depending on the number of charges inserted and the angle of the mortar tube. One charge would be sufficient for a 60mm-smoke shell to cover the distance to the trail.

Still dodging from tree to tree and running up the trail, Erickson heard the *whomp* of the first shell as it left the tube, softly whistling in its trajectory over to the far side of the pond, where it exploded into dense red smoke. "Too far," he yelled up the hill, astonished that a mortar shell had being fired from his camp. But, Russell was already correcting the angle by turning the elevation wheel located on the support leg.

Whomp. Erickson saw the second shell explode into a blue cloud of spreading smoke at the base of the hill, close to the red-coated soldiers already watching the red smoke across the pond. Frightened by the noise and the smoke, their horses broke loose and ran away.

Whomp. The next shell exploded with yellow smoke near the blue one, enveloping the soldiers at the base of the hill in a cloak of blue, yellow and green confusion.

With relief, Erickson saw the four horsemen, who were now incredibly close, suddenly wheel back towards their comrades down the hill. That act saved them, for the fourth shell exploded on the trail where they had just been. As Erickson watched, the four hastily grabbed the downed Sergeant and joined the rest of the red-coated soldiers, riding and running back to their camp.

SIX

Funston had watched Lester leave their meeting, then returned to his desk to consider what the Colonel's next move might be.

The PRA *was* responsible for the inquiries into the Erickson affair, but he hadn't been ready to tell Lester that or the reasons why. Not just then, at least.

He fully anticipated Xetrel's assigning the matter to Lester and, in fact, had counted on it. Funston smiled to himself, for he needed his old comrade and he would enjoy waiting and watching as Lester caught up – but only if it didn't take too long.

Perhaps, he had concluded, *I should do something to accelerate the matter.*

SEVEN

Saturday Morning

The sun came filtering through the yellow birch trees as it rose over the swamp and hills to the east of the British camp. The Third Troop of his Majesty's 16th (Burgoyne's Own) Light Dragoons slowly responded to the dawn and prepared to meet another day.

Sent to the Morristown area in early May 1776 by Major General Howe, their orders were to control the vital north midlands of New Jersey for the Crown. Most residents of Morristown were known to be friendly to the Rebels, but the dairy goods, meat, and other foodstuffs produced in the area were vital to the British. Without them, the 3000-mile supply line back to England would be more overburdened than ever.

The Morristown plateau and the tree covered hills and hollows to the west of it, provided a convenient area for the British to quarter themselves, being close to the major British strongholds of Amboy and New Brunswick. The iron smelters and foundries in the immediate areas also supported their requirements for arms and other implements of war, either in response to offers of hard currency, or under stern force.

Morristown had not greeted the arrival of the Dragoons with any enthusiasm. In fact, after the first few weeks of acrimonious encounters in town, the leaders if Morristown had decided the British needed their own social center closer to their camp at Jockey Hollow. The residents promptly started construction on a tavern with funds raised at two private meetings held in the Church. Completion was only slightly delayed when the British insisted upon certain changes, including the addition of three separate bedrooms for private use.

Captain Morgan, the Troop's leader, knew that Saturday, July 6, 1776, would be another day of patrolling and requisitioning for the Dragoons. He had already received messages that provisions were going to be necessary to support additional troops arriving later in the month and again the next. A long list of supplies, including food and iron products, had been sent to him.

July would be a busy month requisitioning and shipping them to Howe's Quartermasters on Staten Island.

His troop of Light Dragoons had been carefully selected for their task. Part of the full regiment of Light Dragoons, they had been sent to the Colonies to fill the need for light cavalry in helping to rout the Rebels. Major General Burgoyne had seen the need for such light cavalry at the battle of Breed's Hill and had so advised the King. Planning to return to the Colonies in June 1776 after recapturing Quebec, Burgoyne had sent the 16th on ahead to wait for his arrival. Howe had put them to use by sending them into areas where their far-ranging mobility could exert maximum pressure on the Rebels.

The Dragoons were basically infantrymen, mounted as a fast means of getting in and out of a fight. Because of the limited accuracy of their .65 cal., 37-inch long carbines, they usually dismounted to fight. They also carried pistols with a 9-inch barrel, which could be fired with some accuracy while mounted. For close fighting, they had bayonets for the carbines and stirrup-hilted swords. Morgan's Troop consisted of Lieutenant Browne, Sergeants Cilly and Ramsey, three Corporals, a blacksmith, a quartermaster, 56 privates and one trumpeter.

Because of the expected length of their stay in the Morristown area, Morgan had decided to build a permanent secured camp for his men, using the vast supplies of trees and clay available in the area. When finished there were 12 huts, eight to house eight men each, one for use by the Quartermaster as a store hut, one as a prison, one as a hospital, and one for himself and Lieutenant Browne. They soon vacated it and moved into the still unnamed tavern when it was completed. Their hut was then turned over to the Troop's blacksmith for his use.

Situated in two tiers on the slope of a hill on the southeast side of Jockey Hollow, the huts were primitive, but comfortable. Some were dug into the hillside but all had the same style, an inverted V-shaped roof reaching far down each side. Most had only a single log-framed door located at the center front. A few also had a wooden window to take advantage of cool breezes on hot summer evenings. Barrels of supplies and some wooden benches were frequently placed around the fronts and sides.

The morning cooking fires had produced the usual haze hanging over the campsite. Captain Morgan was a stern leader, but allowed his men some freedoms regarding dress and cooking in the morning, as long as they were ready for an 8 o'clock formation. He saw no need to get started too early, since they were going to be here a long time, and there was no reason to push the men too harshly.

As the morning formation was being completed, Morgan heard shouting coming from a long way away. Straining to hear, Morgan, joined by Lieutenant Browne, walked to the far western edge of the camp where they clearly heard voices coming from near the top of the hill on the other side of the pond.

The Rebels were rumored to have declared independence in Philadelphia on Thursday. Concerned the noise might be coming from some of them, Morgan ordered Browne to have some men investigate the commotion. Browne selected Sergeant Cilly to lead the group, with orders to bring back any Rebels they might find. He also took the precaution of ordering a squad of Dragoons prepared to ride, if need be, to the aid of the Sergeant.

Sergeant Cilly and three privates soon proceeded to the base of the hill on the far side of the pond, armed with carbines, bayonets and swords. They could hear the sounds of men coming down the trail. Taking up positions in the trees, Cilly and his men waited until two men came into view.

Their garb seemed strange – no hats or helmets, hair closely cut, cloth shirts colored an odd green, breeches of the same green color, and dark boots held together in an unusual manner, into which the bottoms of the legs of the breeches had been tucked. Around their waists they wore wide belts, from which hung an odd leather pouch on each man's right side. They appeared to carry no weapons.

Cilly heard them talking as they passed the tree he was hiding behind. They spoke English strangely; he was able to understand some of what they said, but not all. He quickly stepped out and ordered them to halt, which they did, but his attempt to capture them was spoiled by their resistance. Events then became unclear, but he found himself on the ground, his right leg and ankle bleeding from a severe wound. The pain was so great, he didn't know if he would live.

Through dimmed eyes, he saw the mounted squad arrive from camp, dismount and begin firing at the Rebels retreating up the trail. Loud noises of many guns, firing in fast salvos, one after another, reached his ears. There must be many more Rebels in the trees, he thought. But, he couldn't see any smoke from their muskets, to indicate where they were.

The two Rebels continued to fire as they retreated further up the trail. Cilly sensed, more than saw, some of the men from his camp remount and ride past him in pursuit. Then came the whistling noise, followed by an explosion and eruption of colored smoke. His men became totally confused as more of the colored smoke exploded near them.

Cilly dimly concluded the Rebels had a cannon on the hilltop. Dragoons, with or without horses, operating in a confined space, were no match for a cannon. Sergeant Cilly felt himself being picked up, then lost consciousness as his men hastily retreated to their camp.

*   *   *

Captain Morgan strained to see what was going on as soon as he heard the first shots. Seeing the men riding back through the yellow, green, blue and red smoke, he worried about the size and strength of the Rebel force he had encountered. And, what about the colored smoke? What a strange weapon to use. How did the Rebels come by that?

Well, soon enough he would find out. No impudent lot of Rebels was going to run his men off. He would talk to Sergeant Cilly as soon as he was back to find out what he had discovered.

But, when they came closer, Morgan drew back and gasped as he saw the blood spurting from Cilly's leg. Pointing with upraised arm, Morgan quickly directed the men to carry the Sergeant to the hospital. He stood still for a moment after they passed, looking at Lieutenant Browne at his side, but neither man said a word.

Cilly was laid out in the hospital on a table of boards. Blood had slowed from the wound, but in spite of his best efforts, the man working on him could not stop it completely. In desperation, he cut the boot away, as well as the breeches and the stocking, revealing an index finger-sized hole on the right side of the ankle. There was no left side of the ankle – only a large, jagged, blood and bone fragment-covered hole, the size of a man's fist. Cilly's foot was held to his leg only by a bit of muscle and skin; the anklebone had disappeared.

Morgan had seen many wounds from battle, but this was the worst. Turning to the three privates that had accompanied Sergeant Cilly to the pond, Morgan demanded to know what had happened. Terrified of the Captain, they were reluctant to say anything, lest they be judged guilty of allowing the terrible wound to be inflicted on the Sergeant. Finally forcing it out of them, Morgan gathered the essence of the meeting between the four of them and the two Rebels.

Since the Troopers were shaking and so obviously frightened, Morgan ignored their descriptions of the Rebels and the weapons they had used, thinking it only as pure fabrication to cover their culpability.

One told him he had seen something shiny fly out of the Rebel's weapon after it fired and picked it up. But, the used brass .45 cartridge he showed Morgan made no sense to the Captain.

As Morgan continued his questioning, Sergeant Cilly tried to get up on his elbows and speak, but, drained of much of his life's fluid, he could only expel a deep, pained moan. Morgan turned just in time to see him roll to the right and fall off the boards to the hard dirt floor, dead.

EIGHT

Saturday Morning

Erickson watched the hasty departure of the red-coated soldiers for a moment or two before Putnam's loud breaths of relief caught his attention. His own heart still pounding from having avoided death at the hands of the redcoats, he nodded to the Corporal to follow as he began to trot up the rest of the trail to the campground. No birds or animals greeted them this time; the forest was silent, save for the sounds made as their boots met the trail.

"You all right, Lieutenant?" Bushnell called out, as he ran down the trail towards him. He was armed with an M-1. "What happened?"

"I . . . don't . . . know," answered Erickson, catching his breath in between words, "Some dumb bastard . . . tried to . . . stick a bayonet . . . in me."

Bushnell waited for Erickson to catch his breath, but Putnam took over.

"Weird, really weird. Said they were his Majesty's 16th Light Dragoons. Called us Rebel's and tried to force us to go to their camp and talk to their Captain."

Erickson got his breath and continued. "They tried to capture us! They talked with a British accent and carried muskets with bayonets. That Sergeant started to push me around with his bayonet and that's when things got out of hand. Putnam shot him!"

"What? Where?" Bushnell couldn't believe his ears.

"In the leg. I shoved the others down and we started running. Then the bastards started shooting at us. Thank god, those peashooters don't have any range. Damnit, Putnam, I told you to keep that thing holstered!"

"Sir, he was sticking you with a bayonet! You shot at them, too."

"I was only being poked and you took away my options. From then on we were in a fight, and it got nasty." Softening his anger a bit, he looked at Bushnell. "And where the hell did we suddenly get mortar shells?"

"Sir, we could have used the M-1's, but the way Russell and Porter brought the mortar to bear avoided all that. They saved your lives."

Erickson relaxed his tone. "Probably. Russell, huh? We'll talk with him about that later. Let's get back to camp."

The whole Platoon was waiting for them at the top of the trail. Russell stood out in front, M-1 cradled in his left arm, right hand near the trigger.

"Sergeant," Erickson said, looking at the weapons, "get those rifles put away before someone gets hurt. Take my .45 and Putnam's, too."

"Yes, Sir." Bushnell handed his M-1 to Russell and watched Erickson and Putnam do the same with their .45's. He motioned to the Corporal to put them away in the trailer, as he turned to join Erickson and Putnam moving through the crowd of men.

"Give us some space here," Erickson said, trying to get further into the campground. "Let's move over to the clearing near the center of the camp," he said to those crowding in. "You can hear the whole story there."

The men joined him as he walked on to the clearing. Russell joined in, too, coming back from depositing the weapons in the trailer. When he got close to Erickson, he asked, "how come we put the M-1's and .45's away, Lieutenant? Maybe we'll need them."

"Good god, Corporal, this is 1976 and we're in New Jersey. I hope we don't need them again."

The men listened intently as Erickson told them what had happened. "They had an arrogance about them," he said, in conclusion. "It was an attitude of superiority. And, while their uniforms looked historically correct, they were dirty and dingy, as if they hadn't been cleaned for a long time; not what you'd expect for a Bicentennial affair. The muskets looked a lot newer than the ones I've seen in museums. The metal work was polished and the wood was smooth, not aged and cracked. The voices of the soldiers were certainly British, but the language was stilted and more formal. Yet, the words they spoke seemed to come naturally. They were confused about the day and date, yet in their minds we were the ones who were wrong. The prods that Sergeant gave me with the bayonet were real, not acting. It felt like we had stepped into the past and I didn't like it a bit."

Putnam vigorously nodded his head in agreement, but refrained from adding his own comments.

Erickson paused for a moment, then began to think outloud for all to hear. "There are a few things that don't set right in my mind. First, their statement that tomorrow is the 7th and not the 4th. Why would anyone try to confuse us as to what day it will be? Second, their eager use of force with those primitive weapons. Surely, they saw our sidearms and yet they pushed us into fighting. Moreover, they really seemed to be enjoying the part of playing

British Dragoons. Now, it may just be that they got carried away with play-acting and accidentally tore my shirt with the bayonet. Since it was Putnam who fired first, it would be understandable that they got mad and retaliated with what ever they had available."

Putnam started to stand and say something, but Erickson motioned him to sit down.

"Easy, Corporal," he said. "I'm trying to see things from both sides. We're here to celebrate our 200th birthday and it would be natural to have British-clothed soldiers around to participate. They played their part to the hilt and sucked us in. The results were disastrous. They got mad and . . . well, you know the rest. But there's got to be a logical explanation for all of this."

Eyes cast down to the ground, Putnam rolled his boot heels back and forth in the needle-covered dirt.

"Look," Erickson went on, trying to placate the Corporal. "I'm responsible for what happened. We went down there armed. No matter how I explain it, you were expecting trouble and I went along with the idea. We found trouble and reacted to it with the .45's, just as if we planned it that way. If it's anyone's fault, it's mine for agreeing to take them along."

"Lieutenant," Putnam replied, looking up at him. "I hear what you're saying and I appreciate what you're trying to do. But, I just don't agree with it. What if things aren't like you say? What if the guys down there are real? Let's take another look at the weird things that happened around here this morning. Where are the crappers, the tables and the water? That's why we took the .45's! For Christ's sake, Lieutenant, don't you see – if what happened to us wasn't play-acting, but the real thing, then . . . then we're in a hell of a fix. Where are we and how did we get here?"

Erickson looked at Putnam for a long moment. No one else said anything. Finally, he spoke. "Tell you what, Corporal, let's run a simple test. I saw some portable radios around the camp last night. If *you're* right and they are British Dragoons, then this must be sometime in the late 1700's, because that's the period when there were lots of British soldiers in the Colonies. There weren't any radios or radio stations then, so we shouldn't get anything if we turn ours on. On the other hand," he continued, "if this *is* 1976, then we ought to be blasted out of our pants with all kinds of music and news all across the dial. You willing to bet to see who's right?" Erickson asked with a deep grin.

"You're on, Lieutenant. Five bucks and I hope I lose."

"All right. Who's got those radios?" Erickson asked.

Two privates went running to retrieve their portables. Hale to the truck containing the duffel bags while Sullivan went to his backpack. Hale quickly found his large, black plastic unit with the handle on top. Jumping out of the back of the truck, he ran back to the clearing, turning it on, on the way.

Pop music filled the campground as Hale whooped and grinned!

A staccato of loud whistles and shouts greeted him as he reached the clearing. The piece ended and another started, as the men gathered around him to personally have a part in proving that the Lieutenant was right.

Behind him, Sullivan dodged the men clustered around Hale. He held his portable to his ear, turning the dial slowly. Walking directly up to Erickson, he said, "I can't get anything, Lieutenant. Nothing, but a lot of light static."

"That's all right, Sullivan," Erickson replied with a smile. "Hale's is working fine. He's got great music coming out of his!"

Abruptly, Hale's music stopped. Erickson wheeled to see what had happened and saw the incredulous looks on the faces of the men as Hale showed him the cassette in his hand. "It's a tape!" he said, dejectedly. "I had it set to play tapes, Lieutenant. We've been listening to a tape."

Erickson stood in stunned silence, staring helplessly at Hale and the portable in his hands. The group that had so eagerly surrounded Hale a moment before, now moved away, wanting to be as far away from the Private as possible.

Bushnell broke the trance. "Brown, don't you have a radio, too?"

"Yes, Sergeant, I do. It's got multi-bands – AM, FM and short-wave."

"Get it."

Brown half walked, half ran back to the truck where Hale had so quickly found his unit. Unable to decide whether he would be a savior or responsible for putting the final nail in the coffin, he climbed into the back of the truck and began digging around in his duffel bag. He finally found the radio and got down on his haunches, trying to sum up the courage to turn it on.

"Well?" Erickson demanded. He and Bushnell had come to the back of the truck and were looking at Brown through the open canvas flaps. But, Brown didn't respond; he couldn't bring himself to make the final move and turn the set on.

"Give it here." Bushnell reached in and gently removed the radio from Brown's hands. As he did, Brown said, "It runs on both batteries and AC. If you don't get anything on DC, try plugging it into the alternator-powered AC outlet under the hood of the truck." Having passed the responsibility for the set's working to Bushnell, Brown leaned back against the side of the truck and closed his eyes.

Erickson watched as Bushnell turned the radio on and twisted the volume up full. A light static came out of the speaker. The rest of the Platoon, now with them around the back of the truck, watched too, as he slowly turned the dial, pausing at the slightest noise. There was nothing. He switched to FM and repeated the slow movement of the dial. Again, he heard nothing but minor noises.

"Try the short-wave band," ordered Erickson.

Bushnell turned the selector knob to short wave and continued the slow, methodical movement of the dial. Turning to Erickson with a look of helplessness, he shook his head from side to side.

"Damn!" The one-word expletive came from Putnam, face full of dejection, standing next to Erickson.

Erickson turned to him. "You didn't cause this, Corporal. You only forced us to face up to something that's been coming all morning."

Brown moved off the bench and stuck his head through the flaps. "Why don't we try it on AC?"

Bushnell softly lobbed the radio back to him. "OK, you try it. But don't get your hopes up, 'cause mine aren't." Turning away, he walked with Erickson back to the clearing.

Erickson looked around and asked of no one in particular, "What time is it?"

Bushnell pushed his half-turned cuff away from his watch. "It's almost eleven o'clock."

"Eleven in the morning of Saturday, July 3rd, 1976, or is it 11 o'clock in the morning of July 6th, 17 something or other?" The tone of Erickson's voice made clear it was a statement of exasperation. "Well, we've got to find out," he said, settling himself on the ground, back firmly against a tall spruce tree. "Anyone here a calendar expert? I mean, is there anyone here who can figure out what year or years, July 4th fell on a Thursday? That's what the red-coated Sergeant said, so let's check it out."

"I think I can figure that out," answered Private Sullivan. "I've got a pocket-sized calendar that tells something on it about things like that." He felt his shirt pockets trying to remember where he had put it. In the distance, Brown started the truck's motor and plugged his radio into the alternator-powered AC outlet.

As he waited for Sullivan, Erickson gave some directions to the Squad Leaders. "Russell, get me a complete inventory of our supplies in the trailer. Dobbs, you do the same with the kitchen unit. Putnam, take your squad and check out the natural defenses of this park. Give me your recommendations for building any positions, if we have to. Porter, you set up some perimeter guards. Work with Putnam. Russell can issue you and your men weapons and ammunition. And, be careful, I don't want any of our people shot because of nervous trigger fingers!"

"Yes, Sir. We'll be careful," replied Porter as he and the other Squad Leaders responded to his orders.

In the distance, Erickson saw Brown turn off the truck's motor, disconnect the radio and carry it under his arm as he trudged towards the clearing.

"Nothing," he said, when he arrived. "There's absolutely nothing to hear." A tear started to roll down his face from his right eye. Reaching up to wipe it off, Brown let the radio slip from his arm and fall to the ground, breaking off part of the case.

Erickson started to move to pick it up for him, but Brown reached it first. "Forget it, Lieutenant," he said, picking it and the broken piece up, "It's no use to us now, anyway." Turning away, he walked back to the truck.

In the meantime, Sullivan had found the calendar and had been writing numbers on a scrap of paper. He looked up and pushed his horn-rimmed glasses back up on the bridge of his nose.

"There are five years from 1754 to 1800 that have July 4th on Thursday: 1754, 1776, 1782, 1793 and 1799," he said.

Erickson looked at Sullivan. "Why did you pick 1754 as a starting point?"

"It's very difficult to calculate before then," he answered. "In 1753, England and the Colonies changed over to the Gregorian calendar. Prior to that time, England and the rest of the civilized world were something like 11 days apart in their calendars. Matching historical events and British troop services in this country, I'd say our best bet is 1776, with a possibility of 1782. Dragoons of the 17th Regiment came here in 1775 and left after the peace treaty was signed in 1783. The 16th Light Dragoons came in 1776 and left in 1778."

"What are you a walking encyclopedia?" Erickson was concerned about anyone with that much knowledge.

"Not really, Lieutenant. My ancestors are English and I'm a colonial history buff. After I found out why I'd been assigned to this outfit, I did a little studying about the Dragoons. One of my ancestors served with the 16th. I also found out on the train ride here that there are others in this Platoon who think they had ancestors in the 16th, as well. The computer really knew how to pick us. We kidded among ourselves about how prolific the 16th was in creating offspring. Seems some of our ancestors stayed on here to raise the kids they fathered, while the rest of the Dragoons returned to England."

"Well, if I need any historical data, I'll certainly come to you." Erickson appreciated the kind of knowledge Sullivan displayed. If Putnam's insinuations proved to be correct, it would be handy to have Sullivan around to help him figure out what to expect. "Thanks for your help," he said to the Private.

Sullivan got up, stretched and started off to join his squad.

Erickson turned and looked at Bushnell. "*Where* are we? What the hell's going on?" There was real concern in his voice. "What kind of a weird trip are we on?" He shook his head slowly from side to side as he spoke, rejecting the situation in which he found himself.

"I don't know, Jim." Bushnell started to reach out to touch Erickson's arm, and then thought better of it. "But we've got some good soldiers here. We'll come out of it all right."

*   *   *

Dobbs completed the inventory of the kitchen unit and returned to Erickson to report. "We've got enough food to last us three days, maybe four, if everybody eats light. Most of the meals will be repeats, but nobody will go hungry until it's gone. Then, we'll have to start living off the land. Fuel for the kitchen unit will be used up about the same time."

"Four days isn't a lot of time, Corporal, when we don't know how long we have to go. I saw some deer, squirrels and grouse on our way down the trail. We'll hunt them, if we have to. How's the water?"

"A little less than 30 gallons. We topped it off last night from one of the faucets. If we can find the pipes, we won't have to worry."

"Get your people looking. There's always the pond water, but getting to it may be a problem."

"Any idea what's going on around here?" Dobbs asked. "Sullivan says he thinks that somehow we've ended up in 1776 or 1782."

"I don't want you or Sullivan spreading that around. It was 1976 last night and it should be 1976 this morning. All I asked Sullivan to do was come up with the years in which the 4th of July was on a Thursday. He did that, but it doesn't prove that this is 1776 or 1782."

In the distance behind Dobbs, Erickson could see Russell and his men return to the clearing. He decided to join them.

"How's it look, Russell?" he asked, when they met up.

"Not bad, Lieutenant. We've got two .45's, four carbines, 26 M-1's, the .30 caliber machine gun, one 60mm mortar, a box of smoke grenades and lots of ammo."

"What's the story on the mortar rounds and the ammo for the machine gun?"

"Six smoke shells and 20 live rounds for the mortar. Six boxes of 250-round belts for the machine gun."

"Anything else?" Erickson wanted a complete inventory, including whatever else Russell had pirated during their stay in Los Angeles.

"Yeah. A 48 star American flag, a bunch of steel helmets with liners and a box of live grenades." Russell told all, hoping to get it covered in one ass chewing, instead of two or more.

"Anything else?"

"No."

"Damnit, Russell!" Erickson almost shouted. "I don't know whether to be angry or happy with you. Those smoke rounds for the mortar certainly saved the morning for us. But how the hell did you get them?"

Russell stood up straight. "When we were over at Fort MacArthur picking up the stuff to go into the trailer, I saw a bunch of things in the supply room that – that I just felt we . . . I . . . wanted to have along with us. When the supply Sergeant wasn't looking, I grabbed what I could and loaded it into the trailer. Hell, Lieutenant, they'll never miss it; they don't know we have it, and besides, like you say, it did come in handy. From the looks of things around here, the rest of it is going to come in handy, too."

"What makes you think that supply Sergeant will never miss those things? He keeps an inventory, you know. He's probably got the FBI out looking for you this moment."

"You really think so, Lieutenant?"

The tone of Erickson's voice mellowed. "I hope so. I really hope someone's looking for us, Corporal; I'd even settle for that bastard Major from yesterday." Looking Russell in the eye, Erickson decided to absolve him. "OK, the damage has been done, you've got the goods and I guess we can use them. We'll have to report it, though, when we get back to California. Maybe we can justify it somehow, but the Army will probably call it grand theft."

"Grand theft?"

"Probably."

"That's great. Now what do I do?"

"Keep cool. If we're lucky, we can use it all up and then there won't be any evidence."

"But you said we'd have to report it."

"Damnit, Corporal! I changed my mind! If this is 1976, then the ground rules are played one way. If it isn't, then we'll make up our own rules as we go along."

"So, which is it, Lieutenant? 1776 or 1976?"

"Your guess is as good as anybody's right now. In the meantime, find Putnam. I want to know what he's been doing on setting up defenses."

"I think he's up on the high ground by the trees," Russell responded. "It sounds like him up there."

Erickson followed Russell's gaze up the side of the hill above them. Standing up, he motioned for Bushnell, standing a few feet away to join him. "Come on, Sergeant," he said, "we're not doing any good here, let's go see what Putnam's doing up on the hill."

The trees started to thin out as they climbed and Erickson began to think about how with a little maneuvering, the trucks and other equipment could get through if the need arose. But, what was on the other side of the hill? And, damnit, where *were* they now?

Putnam moved away from the rest of the squad to meet them. "There's not much in the way of natural defenses here, Lieutenant. The land slopes down from here through the park and then steeper down the hill towards the pond. There's a lot of different ways from the pond up to this park without taking the same path you and I used. There're lots of trees for us to hide behind, but anyone trying to get in, can hide behind them, too. The other side of this hill looks out onto some pretty open country, so we can see anybody coming from that way, but there doesn't seem to be anything worth watching over there. The real activity is down the hill and across the pond where the smoke is still rising. I guess our red-coated buddies are still there."

"OK. That's good, Corporal. Thanks. Has Porter posted his men around the perimeter?"

"Yeah, they're spread around the south and east sides of the park, facing down the hill. Most of them are standing or sitting near trees for protection. They all have generally good views of anything that might try to come up the hill."

"Sounds good, too. You station your men on this upper hill area and keep an eye out to the north and west. I don't want to belabor the point, but for God's sake, be careful with the weapons after Russell gets them issued, I don't want anybody hurt."

Erickson and Bushnell walked back down the hill to the clearing where Russell and his men were quietly waiting for them. He had the weapons neatly stacked for distribution.

Erickson was direct. "I want you to issue carbines to the Squad Leaders and M-1's to Porter's and Putnam's men. You'll find them scattered in the trees along the perimeter of the park, starting over there on the south side. The rest of the men are on the hill to the north and west of us. Give everybody a couple of clips of ammunition. Bushnell and I will take the .45's."

"You reached any conclusions, yet, Lieutenant?" Russell asked. "I mean, have you decided what's going on?"

"Not yet, Corporal. But, after this morning, I'm not going to take any chances. When you pass out the weapons, tell everyone to be careful. After all, we are overdue and the rest of the 76th may be looking for us."

Erickson motioned Bushnell to join him as he wandered away from the clearing. "We *are* overdue, Tom." he said, quietly. "But, has anyone missed us? Is anyone looking for us?"

"And, if they are looking for us," Bushnell responded, hiding a growing desperation, "will they find us?"

NINE

Treppello Gives Some Answers

The sound of the office door opening behind him startled Lester and he quickly turned in his chair to see who it was.

Carl came in, holding both copies of the report in his hands. Using his slightly rounded midriff to balance them, he pushed the door closed behind him with his foot. He took a few steps and dropped them down on the conference table.

Still festering from being lied to by Admiral Funston, Lester was brusque and to the point. "Erickson had a wet dream in which he gets attacked by Redcoats during the Bicentennial. Now Funston's people write a report that it might have really happened. How did they arrive at that incredible conclusion?"

"They researched related events from around the world and compared it to Erickson's testimony at the Board of Inquiry."

"Related events? Are they saying this type of thing has happened before?"

"Kinda, but not with the same magnitude. Their conclusion is based on two major premises. The first stems from the fact that the Earth is an energy source in its own right. We already know about magnetism and gravity. But, there seems to be a substantial body of data indicating that the earth's energy also exists in a series of worldwide paths or trails known as 'Leys'. Unusual activities occurring on or near these Leys over periods of time have been recorded by responsible people."

"*Responsible* people?"

"Yeah; those whose word is respected. Otherwise, the activities or encounters would have been treated by the general populous to be of an occult or phantom nature."

"Count me in *that* group."

Treppello ignored the comment and continued. "The other major thrust of the report pertains to some special forms of extra sensory perception involving 'retrocognition.' That's the ability of a person to see or discern events from the past, vs. 'precognition,' where an event becomes known or seen by the viewer in advance of its happening."

"I heard about both of them in my days at the PRA. Right now, I'm more interested in the Leys."

"According to the report, Colonel, around 1920 an Englishman named Watkins discovered a network of straight paths running through the countryside near his home on the Welsh border. He called them Leys, from an old Saxon word meaning a cleared strip of land. He believed the Leys were primitive trails linking various religious sites and burial mounds in the area. Apparently, they dated back as far as 2000-4000 years *before* Christ. He also noted that a great number of churches had been built along these pathways in modern times. A man named William Pidgeon had noted similar alignments of the Indian Mounds in the American Midwest around 1850. At the same time, Dr. Josef Heinsch was mapping the alignments of ancient churches in Germany, while Wilhelm Teudt was investigating what he called 'holy lines' knifing across the German countryside."

Lester kept a keen eye on Treppello as the Captain continued. "From a global standpoint," he went on, "the Ley concept extends to western Bolivia where the lines are known as 'taki'is', meaning 'straight lines of holy places'. Similar lines have also been found radiating from the Inca Temple of the Sun in Cuzco, Peru. They're not real lines, of course. It's more like an openness between places or objects; a clearway, if you will, to see what's ahead."

"Does the report say what these lines mean?"

"It concludes that the Leys represent lines of subtle force, radiating some sort of earth energy through a power grid. The areas where the Leys intersect are called Nodes. The energy there is much stronger, often producing strange manifestations. Leys apparently coincide with the geophysical power of the earth, which flows in and through the ground in definite patterns. Monuments seem to have been built more often by the ancients where the power grid was stronger. In modern times visitors to these sites have frequently claimed to have seen things from the past happening before their eyes."

"Yes, that's retrocognition. Did the PRA give any examples?"

"Yes, there are a few. The first one, on page 22 of the report, involves a country physician named Moon, and his experience while tending to a patient at the man's home on the Isle of Thanet in England. The home faced onto a semi-circular driveway that opened onto a country lane. Alongside the road was a tall hedge to provide privacy. As he prepared to leave the house one morning, Doctor Moon paused at the head of the front steps, deep in thought about his patient. While he stood there, not really mindful of what his eyes were seeing, he began to realize that there was no hedge, no driveway and, no road. Startled, he looked for other familiar landmarks and could find none. What he did see, though, was a man walking towards him across a field. The man carried a flintlock and was dressed in boots and clothing long out of date – perhaps by as much as 100 to 150 years. Moon sensed that the stranger saw him too, for the man lowered the flintlock and stopped walking while the two of them stared at each other. Feeling disoriented, Moon turned his head to make sure that his patient's house was still behind him, but when he turned back to the man, he had vanished and everything was back as it was supposed to be."

"When did that happen?"

"In 1934."

"Any examples with Americans?"

Treppello flipped through the pages of the report, looking quickly for any references he might have missed the night before. "None other than Erickson's," he responded. "I do have a few more that, even though they involve the English, should be of interest to you. Remember, the English play a big part in Erickson's story and we can't overlook the possible connection."

Lester nodded his head. "OK. Go on."

"This one starts on page 52. In August 1936, a man by the name of Jenkins was exploring in an area of the Cornish coast known as Loe Bar. It's near where King Arthur is supposed to have died in battle. Young Jenkins was stopped in his tracks as a whole group of medieval warriors, complete with chain mail and red, white and black cloaks suddenly appeared before him. Some were on horses, others were just standing, and all were positioned around one man in the center who stood, hands on his sword, apparently staring back at Jenkins. Jenkins moved towards the group to have a closer look, but in that instant, they vanished as suddenly as they had appeared. That wasn't the end of it, though. Jenkins came back in 1974 to the same spot with his wife, and the two of them saw the same vision, exactly as he had before. It even vanished just as before. It's interesting to note that Loe Bar is located on a Ley running between many churches in the area, which conjuncts with two other Leys further north near Townshend."

"Keep going."

"Yes, Sir. In 1978, a project was organized to probe the secrets of the Leys and prehistoric stone structures and megaliths dotting the English countryside. The team used modern electronic scanning equipment, Geiger counters and other measuring devices. They found unusual types and levels of energy around the sites, particularly during the period in the hour before sunrise up to two hours later. They also found ultrasounds beyond the range of human hearing, radiation levels higher than normal, high magnetic fields, and rapid fluctuations of magnetic energy. Members of the Project also reported experiencing strange occurrences in the vicinity of the site, including the sudden appearance and equally sudden disappearance of animals and vehicles, including an entire Gypsy caravan."

Lester listened intently. While not accepting all that was being offered (*a Gypsy caravan?*) he wanted to know more. "So you think there's a tie-in between these Leys and what happened to Erickson?"

"That's what the PRA thinks."

"You have any more examples?"

"Yes, Sir." Treppello picked up the report again. "Another one, on page 62, covers Cadbury Castle, located in the county of Somerset, England. In June 1934, as a local schoolteacher and a companion drove past Cadbury Hill at night, they began to see a procession of lights coming slowly down the hill. As they watched, they could see that the lights were torches, tied to the lances of armed and mounted warriors led by a huge man. They vanished as quickly as they had appeared."

Treppello took a breather as he turned the pages. "The last of the English connections is on page 80," he said. "It took place in October 1642, during the first battle of the English civil war. It was north of Oxford, in a place called Edgehill and it pitted the King's army against the forces of the third Earl of Essex, Robert Devereux. For a whole day, the forces battled, retreated and battled again, without either side gaining a clear advantage. The next morning both Armies left the field and marched away exhausted. Things stayed quiet at the site for about two months and then, late one night, the sounds of drums started to be heard. Witnesses reported seeing soldiers of the King fighting Devereux's men, *in the air,* until 2 or 3 a.m. As reported in a 1643 pamphlet, 'it was a . . . dreadful fight, the clattering of arms, noises of cannon, cries of soldiers' all heard and seen by witnesses who reported the bizarre battle to the constable. He came to the site the next night and saw a reenactment with his own eyes. Even stranger were the reports of the Officers sent to Edgehill by King Charles to investigate the matter. They told of not only seeing the ghostly armies, but *'recognized on the Royalist side several of their personal friends who had been killed.'*"

"That's bizarre," said Lester. "If you don't have any American connections, are there any non-English ones?"

"There's an interesting one."

"Let's hear it."

"It's something a little different; it involves the creation of reality."

"What?" Lester seemed incredulous at hearing the words.

"Well, Sir, a book published in 1985, describes the adventures of a Frenchwoman who was the first western female to visit Lhasha. She was a former Journalist who spent the later years of her life studying and recording the life and culture of Tibet. She was particularly intrigued with the concept of the 'Tulpa'; a magical entity that Buddhists believe is created by concentrated thought. While the Tulpa is created in the mind of one person, it can be seen by others and can have a mind of its own. Using discipline, meditation and rituals taught to her by the Buddhists, she went on to create, over a period of months, a Tulpa that turned out to be a fat, but friendly Monk, which she allowed to stay in her house."

Treppello could sense Lester's rejection of the very thought, but went on. "As time passed, however, the Monk took on an unacceptable personality and became a problem to have around. Soon after, she embarked on a reversal process to destroy the thought structure that had created him. She finally succeeded in accomplishing its destruction after six months of concentrated effort."

"I'd like to read that book sometime. Think of all the Tulpa's we could create to do things for us. Send them into battle, send them to Congress; my god," Lester exclaimed, "the possibilities are endless!" He smiled at the Captain for a moment over the idea of creating Tulpa's, then suddenly asked, "Does the report conclude there are any Leys around Jockey Hollow?"

"The PRA sent a team into that area to investigate the possibility. There were two psychics and two technicians to operate some energy measuring equipment."

"But, did they find any Leys?"

"Yes and no."

"What?"

"No, they didn't find any visible Leys of the kind found in England or Germany or South America. But, using their equipment, they did find enough residual energy in the campground above Jockey Hollow to justify further testing. Early the next morning their equipment suddenly went wild, recording all kinds of energy aberrations, and then just as suddenly, it was over. Nothing unusual happened during the rest of their stay. The techs didn't give up, though. They ventured up there a few weeks later, this time without the psychics, set up their equipment early in the morning and waited."

Lester raised his bushy eyebrows at Treppello in anticipation.

"You guessed it. The meters went wild for a short period, during which one of the techs swore the road disappeared! The other was so intent on watching the equipment and taking measurements that he didn't notice anything. There's nothing in the report about any follow-up visits being made to verify the readings or the claim about the road disappearing."

Lester frowned. "That doesn't sound like Funston. He's a very thorough person, very prone to follow-up on such matters – unless he couldn't spare anybody. Even so, I'll bet he wants to get back up there, if he hasn't already."

Standing up, he walked back to his desk and sat down in his executive chair. Hesitating for a moment, he leaned back and then said to Carl. "Let me give you my take on what's going on – since you know enough about my work at the PRA, you'll understand where I'm coming from. First, let me tell you I think the PRA's interest in Erickson is not necessarily to prove him right. It could be they hope to prove him wrong, because of its importance to their main interests."

Carl's eyes grew wider as he stared at Lester, trying to figure out where the Colonel was going.

Lester ignored the look and continued. "I think one of the PRA psychics probably came across something really different while on an intelligence mission. Most likely, it was a contact with a retrocognitive action of some sort – maybe even of historical significance. Whatever it was, after he talked about it, the whole PRA got interested and somebody began to look to see if any similar occurrences had been recorded. You've been telling me about some of the stories they found. Then, when they came up with the stuff about earth energy and Leys and Nodes, Funston really got excited. He thought he might be able to use that energy in his intelligence gathering like the Soviets used their laser beams. So, he sent some field teams around to the various parts of the world to verify the information. After they found enough evidence to support the fact that Leys and Nodes really exist, Funston decided he had a fantastic, worldwide means of transmitting his psychics wherever he wanted – without revealing their presence!

"But," Lester added, after taking a moment to organize his thoughts, "then his people came across the Erickson incident and he began to wonder if it was some type of aberration to be concerned about. Funston couldn't use the power of the Leys and Nodes if it meant his psychics might be caught somewhere on a mission with no way out. So, he decided to look into Erickson's claims to determine if they were real. He then sent his team to Jockey Hollow to put the matter to bed. But, they came up short. Oh, they recorded some intriguing squiggles on their equipment all right, and even experienced the road disappearing. But, that's not the clear-cut evidence he wanted. He had to have more."

"So he started asking questions?"

"Yes. He had to find out all he could, even if it meant surfacing his interest. Knowing Funny, he's not finished. He's developed some sort of plan to get what he wants, I daresay. He probably even had someone put the report on your chair as part of his grand scheme."

Carl didn't seem surprised at Lester's statement. "But, how do we fit in?"

"I'm not sure, yet. I sure don't believe Erickson's story, but maybe the answer to Funston's interest is in there somewhere. Start reading through his testimony to the Board and see what you can find."

TEN

Saturday Morning

"Those damned Rebels!" Morgan screamed as he turned to Lieutenant Browne, angrily shaking his fist. "They have killed my best Sergeant. Damn them. Damn them!"

Looking down at the body of Sergeant Cilly, still laying on the dirt floor of the Dragoon's hospital hut, Morgan brought his 5'9" paunchy frame to full height and continued his tirade. "They shall not go unpunished. Bring me the map, Lieutenant Browne! I want to know more about the hill they are on and how we might go about mounting an attack."

Turning to the three Privates that had accompanied Cilly to the hill, he added, "You three. As you allowed your Sergeant to be killed at the hands of the Rebels, you shall be responsible for digging his grave. Quickly now, I want him buried properly before we decamp."

With that, Morgan abruptly marched out of the hut, closely followed by the subservient Browne. That a Rebel had killed one of his troopers was not a surprise to Morgan; he had been expecting eventually to run into Rebels and engage in battle. But, the loss of Sergeant Cilly was a shock. The Sergeant had led the troopers well, expertly carrying out Morgan's orders to fill supply requirements. Sergeant Ramsey was a qualified leader of the troops, as well, but Sergeant Cilly had been a master of leading the men to achieve difficult tasks.

Morgan thought of his troops as he walked. He knew they were underpaid, led boring lives under stern discipline, and had little concept of the political ramifications of the rebellion. But, while they had not fought any major battles in the colonies, their spirit was far greater than the regular foot soldiers, and with a man such as Sergeant Cilly to guide them in battle, Morgan was certain of their performance. Now Cilly was gone and Morgan would have to rely on Ramsey.

Morgan walked across the formation grounds towards the tavern, pondering the problem. Should he send an armed group up the trail first to probe the Rebel's strength and defenses? When he mounted his attack, should he go up the trail only, or divide his forces into two or more groups, each pursuing a separate approach to the hilltop? Were the Rebels still there, or had they moved on? Should he send a mounted attack, or on foot? What about the strange smoke explosions? Was it as harmless as it seemed, or did it forebode worse? He veered into a slow arc around the camp. Browne, walking beside him, was silent, hands folded together behind his back, waiting.

"They must have set up a camp on the hill," Morgan spoke aloud at last. "They came in during the night, quietly enough to go unnoticed by us and did not discover that we were here, either. Seeking water from the pond, they sent two men down the hill. It seems odd that they were not particularly surprised or alarmed to be stopped by Sergeant Cilly. But, then again, these Rebels are an impudent lot, full of self-established importance. And, the weapons – so strange! Have you ever thought to use smoke as a weapon? And, colored, too. How did they do that?"

Browne started to answer, thinking the Captain was asking him a question, but quickly expelled his breath as Morgan went on talking, almost to himself.

"The pistol. It was certainly different given what the Privates said. And, the hole it made in Cilly's leg. Were it possible for one of our carbine balls to inflict such a wound, we would not have to rely on the bayonet as much. The garb they wore looked strange to the Privates, but we have been aware of all manner of strange garb worn by the Rebels, from homespun to animal skins. If we could examine one of them more closely, we might find nothing unusual, at all."

Looking at his pocket watch, Morgan suddenly exclaimed, "The time goes fast this morning. It is 45 minutes past the hour of ten, and we have so much to do. We must . . ."

He stopped in mid-sentence to listen to the sound coming from the hilltop. It sounded to him like music!

Music! Could it really be music? he wondered. The sound had a certain melodic quality, but was unrecognizable in its harshness as true music. It ended and then shortly thereafter started again. What did the Rebels have on that hill? A music box? But, how could he hear a music box that far away? It had to be something else, but what?

The music stopped again, this time abruptly, followed by a loud, shouted voice saying something about an Effem Band.

"Effem Band? Do those Rebels have a band up there?" Morgan shook his head in disbelief. "They must have a very large force of men to have their own band! Surely we have not heard correctly!" Turning to face Browne, he asserted his conclusion: "Lieutenant, we have to get up that hill and determine what exactly the Rebels have there and what they plan."

"We could attempt to capture one or more of them," Browne offered, hopefully. "We could question them and obtain the answers we seek."

"Yes! Capturing some of them makes good sense. That should be part of the plan we make. We shall attack only to capture, not to engage in a battle with an uncertain outcome. Yes, Lieutenant, we will make that a part of our plan, indeed."

Morgan strode back to the center of the campground where Sergeant Ramsey and the troop's three corporals stood talking. On the far, east side of the campground he could see the three Privates digging the grave for Sergeant Cilly.

"Where is Sergeant Cilly's body?" Morgan asked Ramsey.

"The Quartermaster is still in the hospital hut preparing it. They found a good uniform in his hut and have dressed him in it." Ramsey wondered if the Captain would speak to him now about assuming the leadership void created by Cilly's death. He was eager to prove to the Captain that he was as capable as the senior Sergeant had been.

"How much longer will it be?"

"Very shortly, Captain."

A few moments later, the Quartermaster exited from the hospital hut and signaled for some of the Dragoons nearby to move the casket. Six of them entered the hut and soon emerged, awkwardly manhandling the simple casket through the narrow door. Once outside, they assumed better positions around it and proceeded down the path towards the center of the campground, where Captain Morgan and the group stood watching.

"Lieutenant," said Morgan, "Have some supports brought over here for the casket, then have the troops mount and assemble here to observe the burial ceremony for our fallen friend."

Lieutenant Browne ordered one of the Corporals to get supports, then turned to Ramsey. "Assemble the Troop to observe the burial ceremony; two lines, from here to the gravesite. Sabers to be held at the salute as the casket passes."

Turning to Morgan, Browne asked, "Will you be reading from the New Testament or the Military Manual?"

"Sergeant Cilly was a religious man, and I believe he would have preferred that we pass him into the hands of the Lord with readings from the New Testament."

Men and horses assembled along a loose line from the center of the campground to the grave, as the supports from the hospital table were hurriedly set in front of Browne to receive the casket.

Once in place, Morgan's eyes stared directly at the casket, seeing nothing else. "Are the troops ready, Lieutenant?"

"Yes, Sir."

"Then, let us proceed."

Browne stood at his side as Morgan began. The Lieutenant's mind was neither on the Captain nor the ceremony, though, as he wondered how Sergeant Cilly came to be in such high favor with Morgan. Browne was better educated than Cilly, was an Officer, had fought in battles on the continent, and had been assigned in England to Morgan with excellent references. Still, the Captain had remained close to the Sergeant and had not allowed any significant amount of command authority to pass to Browne. Someday he would seek the answer – but not today.

The readings from the Bible finished, Morgan nodded to the Quartermaster and the six Privates gently picked the casket off the supports and carried it through the ranks of Dragoons to the grave site as sunlight danced off the saber blades held in salute.

Morgan again read from the Bible as they lowered the casket into the grave. Standing for a brief moment of final respect, Morgan bent down and grabbed a handful of dirt, which he threw on the casket before walking away. Neither he nor Browne looked back as the Privates started to shovel the rest of the dirt into the hole.

"Those damned Rebels," Morgan raged under his breath. "I will show them. I *will!*" He was determined to avenge the death of Cilly. "Bring Sergeant Ramsey, I want to speak to you both of my plans."

When they joined Morgan by a tree at the edge of the campground, he had already cleared the weeds and grass to expose the dirt. In it, he had drawn a rough outline of the hill, the pond and their campground.

"We shall all go, except the Quartermaster and the Blacksmith," Morgan stated as he drew more lines in the dirt. "The troop will be divided into three parts, one will go up the path, one will go up the east side of the hill through the trees, and the other will go up from the south and west side of the hill, beyond the trail. The map I have of this vicinity is of little use in planning this attack, but my eyes see what appears to be enough open space in the trees for mounted Dragoons to move with swiftness from each side. We will take the carbines, bayonets and pistols, but I expect that the saber may prove to be the superior weapon in amongst the trees. Pistols may also be effective. I want to embark with the half-hour. Lieutenant, get the men ready for battle and inform them that the main purpose of the attack is to capture prisoners for questioning. Kill Rebels if they must to get in or out, but come back with prisoners for questioning!"

Browne promptly did as ordered. Informed of Morgan's decision, the men eagerly awaited the order to charge up the hill into the Rebel camp to avenge the loss of the popular Sergeant. In spite of the enthusiasm, Browne cautioned them all to remember Morgan's orders. "This time," he said sternly, "bringing back prisoners is more important than killing Rebels."

At 50 minutes after the hour of eleven, on the morning of Saturday, July 6, 1776, the Third Troop of his Majesty's 16th Light Dragoons was prepared for battle. Mounted, fully armed and battle dressed, the three columns responded to the trumpeter's call and, with Captain Morgan in the lead, moved out smartly towards the base of the Rebel-held hill.

ELEVEN

Saturday Afternoon

Erickson and Bushnell finished their inspection of the guards posted around the perimeter of the campground and returned to a point near where the trail met the edge of the hill. Here they could get a good view of Jockey Hollow. Erickson immediately noticed that the smoke from beyond the Wick House had disappeared and he assumed that the morning breakfast fires had been put out by whoever was down there.

He and Bushnell wore their .45's; silently hoping there would no need for their use. Standing at the edge of the hill, they shared a pair of binoculars, peering at the terrain that spread out before them. Bushnell had just handed the binoculars back to Erickson when they heard the sounds of a trumpet.

"That sounds like a bugler," exclaimed Bushnell. "Do you see anything?"

"No," he replied, adjusting the binoculars to his eyes. "It sounded to me like it came from beyond the Wick House, maybe even beyond the tavern." Then, "Wait a minute! I think I see something moving on the far side of the trees near the pond."

"What is it?"

"It's a lot more of those guys I saw this morning. They're mounted in three columns. There's one fancy-dressed guy in front leading, the bugler's beside him, then two more fancy-dressed guys, followed by the three columns of horsemen. Here," said Erickson, handing the binoculars back to Bushnell, "take a look at the bugler, it looks like he's carrying a hunting horn."

As Bushnell looked at the bugler, Erickson turned towards the campground and shouted for Sullivan to join them. Turning back, he said to Bushnell, "I want him to look at what's going on down there and tell us what he thinks it is."

Taking the binoculars once more, Erickson focused them to watch as the three columns moved at a steady pace, passing the west side of the Wick House. It seemed they were heading directly for the pond.

Minutes later they stopped at its far side. The man on the lead horse backed up a few paces to talk with the two men behind him. When he finished, he rode back to the head of the troop, while one of the other two men turned and rode the short distance back to the main body of troops. There he signaled for the head of each column to come forward. Erickson could see him saying something to them while pointing to the base of the hill upon which Erickson stood.

Sullivan arrived. "You wanted me, Sir?"

Erickson handed him the binoculars. "Take a look down there. What do you make of it?"

Sullivan removed his glasses and adjusted the binoculars to get a better focus. He let out a long, soft whistle. "Right out of the history books, Lieutenant, including the trumpeter. Those guys are dressed just like a troop of Dragoons would be, complete with carbines, pistols and sabers. The helmets with the red plumes, and the blue center stripe on their red coats indicate to me they're supposed to be Light Dragoons of the 16th Regiment. God, they look authentic from here."

"Any idea what they're going to do?"

"Hard to tell, Lieutenant. They *are* dressed for battle though, with their carbines hooked to their saddles. My guess is that if this were for real, they'd be getting ready to charge up this hill and attack us."

Sullivan handed the binoculars back to Erickson just as the trumpet blew again. All three quickly turned their attention back to the pond. They could see the three columns were splitting up.

Taking a closer look with the binoculars, Erickson saw one column head around the pond for the trail, while the other two columns split wide to the right and left at the base of the hill. Riders from the left column urged their horses up the hill through the trees.

Erickson lost sight of all three units, then momentarily regained contact with the one on his left as its men passed through open spaces in the trees. Losing them again, he searched in deliberate patterns, but could not find them or the others.

Concerned, he immediately issued an order to Bushnell. "Let's not get caught with our pants down, Sergeant. Tell the perimeter guards to keep their eyes open and report any horsemen they see coming up the hill. Tell everyone to be prepared to fall back to the clearing in the center of the camp. No shooting unless attacked. And, I mean attacked, not someone just being funny with them. I want everyone to exercise restraint."

Turning to Sullivan, Erickson gave another order. "Find Russell and tell him to bring the smoke grenades to the clearing. Also, tell him I want the battery-powered megaphone. After you find him, come back here and start watching for those horsemen again. If you see anything, let me know."

"Yes, Sir." Sullivan took off to find Russell, while Bushnell left to pass on Erickson's instructions to Putnam and Porter. Erickson, himself, moved to the center clearing.

Bushnell came up to him a few minutes later. "I've talked to the perimeter guards, Jim, but there's nothing to report. Nobody's seen the horsemen since they went into the trees."

"Do the guards understand that restraint is mandatory?"

"Yes, they're just as concerned as you are that we might end up shooting someone from the 76th. But, word's also gotten around about this being 1776 or 1782. Putnam and Porter have gotten a lot of questions. It's obvious that more than one of the men think that we've somehow gone back in time two centuries."

"Tom, if we don't watch out, our worst enemy is going to be hysteria. We need proof, not assumptions! That unit down there has to be the 76th out looking for us. No matter what happened this morning, there is no other rational explanation."

"Then why don't we just go down and meet them? We know where they are – at least where they were a few minutes ago. If that's the 76th, then our problems are over – well, except for answering to somebody about the guy that got shot."

"Part of me agrees with that. But, something stronger inside says not to. I said we should be cautious, and cautious we'll be." Catching a glimpse of movement beyond Bushnell's shoulder, Erickson looked and saw Russell coming into the clearing.

Laying the megaphone and the box of smoke grenades on the ground near Erickson, he tore open the canisters and pointed to the round, can-like grenades. "Color's marked on each can, Lieutenant, if it makes any difference."

"Not really, they're more for confusion and disruption. Did you check the megaphone's battery?"

"I didn't speak through it, but the charge indicator shows its up to full power."

"OK, let's try it out." Erickson placed it to his mouth and pressed the button. "Dobbs, you and Russell will be responsible for the security of the vehicles over there. I don't want anything to happen to them." His voice boomed across the clearing.

Bringing the device down as he turned back to Russell, he said, "Better get back over there and get yours and Dobbs's people into a defensive mode. I'll stay here and call signals with the megaphone."

"What do you expect to happen, Lieutenant?"

"Don't know, Corporal. But whatever it is, I've got a feeling it's going to happen soon."

Russell trotted back to the trucks and trailer where Dobbs had already started to place the men in defensive positions. He was about five yards from him when he heard the blast of a trumpet from above him on the west hill of the camp. Shouts and the sounds of horses racing through the trees immediately followed it.

Erickson looked in the direction of the sound but could see nothing. Then, to his left and from behind he heard the movement of other horses. Beyond the edge of the campground Porter's men began shouting, "Here they come!"

Putnam heard the shouts and looked around his own area for intruders. Finding none, he saw that his own men had gravitated to the lower side of the campground, trying to help find the red-coated horsemen that had disappeared from view into the trees.

"Damn it! Get back up here!" he yelled at them. "I hear them over here, too!"

Erickson moved to get a better view of what was happening on the west hill. A shouted, "There they are!" from Putnam, focused his attention on the hilltop where he saw a column of red-coated horsemen charging down towards the campground. Bushnell tugged at his sleeve and pointed to his left, to the top of the trail where another column of charging horsemen were heading into the campground from below.

From behind him, Erickson sensed, then turned to see the charge of the third group as it crested the eastern slope of the camp, chasing five or six of Porter's riflemen before them. The horsemen were brandishing sabers and yelling as they came.

Throughout the camp, the scene was the same as the three groups of Redcoats came together in the campground to chase Erickson's men. Their greater numbers gave them a hunting superiority, but Erickson's men took full advantage of the trees to confuse and avoid them.

At first, Erickson's men held back in spite of swinging sabers being used so wildly and menacingly. But, when Erickson saw one of his men get cut by a slashing saber, he decided it was for real and felt perversely satisfied when that soldier turned his M-1 on his attacker and fired a couple of quick rounds in the direction of the passing horseman.

Dobbs heard the shots and looked over to see who had fired them. He saw the soldier standing there, M-1 butt resting on his right hip, obviously exasperated over missing his target.

Dobbs started to yell something to him, when he heard "LOOK OUT!" being shouted at himself from behind. He spun around just in time to see a Dragoon swinging his saber at him for a deadly blow. Reacting instantly, Dobbs ducked, turned and started running at the same time. Watching the charging Dragoon over his shoulder, he failed to see the exposed tree roots in front of him. Stumbling, he lost his balance and fell headfirst into the trunk of the enormous spruce, severely scraping his cheek and knocking him out. Thinking him dead, the Dragoon sought other prey.

Hale was next to feel the sharp blade of a saber. He dodged behind a tree to escape one blow, only to emerge from the other side into the path of another Dragoon who had just swung and missed another soldier. The carry-through of his blade caught Hale in the right shoulder. Screaming in pain, he saw the Dragoon raise the saber for another strike, but could not find the strength to raise his rifle and shoot his attacker.

Others weren't so reserved. Erickson could hear sporadic shooting around the campground, with distinctive sounds obviously coming from weapons on both sides. As the shooting increased, Brown got hit in the heel of his right foot without ever seeing the Dragoon that did it. The pain was so fierce, it dropped him to the ground where he tried to untie the heavy combat boot to apply first aid. He started to call for a medic, then remembered they didn't have one.

Erickson had seen enough and yelled into the megaphone, "PULL BACK TO THE CLEARING!" But, the order had little effect as his men continued to dodge and run from the horsemen, constantly using the trees for protection. Erickson could hear muskets being fired amid angry shouts on all sides of him and drew his own .45 in response. Unable to find a target without risk of hitting his own men, he soon reholstered it.

Across the campground, he saw a redcoat fire at one of his men and miss. The Dragoon then chased the soldier with his saber, swinging it in slashing arcs through the air. Ducking behind a spruce, the soldier missed getting hit as the saber slammed into the trunk. The sound of more shots, followed by the staccato of a rapidly fired M-1, drew Erickson's attention away from the scene, as the whine of ricocheting bullets provided an echo.

As if spurred on by the shooting, the red-coated horsemen moved more quickly to isolate small groups of Erickson's men, trying to complete their main task of capture.

On the north side of the camp, Putnam had reassembled his squad and ordered them to fire at the horses. If they missed and hit a redcoat, well, that was tough. The din of the battle increased as his men began shooting, but with little effect – they simply were not battle-hardened killers of men and horses.

Porter and some of the Privates in his squad had been by-passed by the Dragoons and began to work their way to the clearing to join Erickson and Bushnell. Erickson shouted his command, "PULL BACK!" once more into the megaphone then put it down and started grabbing smoke grenades from the open canisters. He pulled the pin on the first one and threw it as hard as he could towards the trucks, where Dobbs, Russell and their men were fighting off Dragoons. The explosion and cloud of smoke drew the horsemen's attention away, allowing Private Hale to free himself from the grasp of the horseman still attacking him. Running for cover under one of the trucks, Hale now did what he hadn't done before and pulled his rifle into position. Taking aim at the pursuing redcoat, he squeezed the trigger. His former captor jerked back in the saddle and fell off, hitting the ground hard. The horse climbed the air with his front hooves and then ran off down the trail towards the pond.

As if to punctuate that act, Russell cut loose with a burst from the .30 cal. machine gun he had set up near the kitchen unit. Purposefully aimed high, the bullets sprayed the area, zinging through open space or thudding into high tree branches.

On the north side of the camp, Putnam stood up and took careful aim on a red-coated horseman heading hell-bent towards him. He fired three quick shots and the horseman twisted violently in his saddle, then slid to the ground as the horse pulled him along. "How do you like that, you bastard!" he yelled at the dead body.

Back in the clearing, Bushnell joined Erickson in throwing grenades and hurled two in rapid succession towards a large group of horsemen coming back into the camp from the edge of the hill. Erickson again drew his .45 and waited for a target. None came close enough. Frustrated, he kept the automatic in his hand this time, watching the action continue around the campground.

Porter and Private Lewis had just reached the edge of the clearing, when a Dragoon grabbed Lewis by the scruff of the neck. Jerking in pain as he twisted to face his adversary, Lewis yelled, "Lemme go, you sonofabitch. Lemme go!" Off balance and unable to bring his rifle up to fire, Lewis could only struggle as the horseman tightened his grip and dragged him away, heading towards the edge of the campground and down the hill.

Desperately trying to get free, Lewis felt the grip on his neck suddenly turn loose at the same time he heard the rifle shot close behind. The Dragoon's hand dropped completely away as he fell forward over the head of his horse to the ground. Lewis ran up to the figure and pointed his rifle at the downed man's head.

"Forget him. He's dead," yelled Porter, who had fired the shot. "Get your butt back here!"

As another burst from Russell's machine gun cut through the high branches of the campground, a trumpet sounded from the hill to the west. Looking toward the sound, Erickson saw three horsemen and the trumpeter. Within a moment, all four turned and disappeared over the hill.

In the campground, red-coated horsemen everywhere pushed their steeds to the gallop as they hastily retreated from the battle scene. In a few moments they were all gone, save for the three dead they left behind. No one bothered to shoot after them.

It had taken less than five minutes. Now quiet returned to the campground as the sounds of the fleeing horsemen disappeared in the distance.

Bushnell turned and looked at Erickson and stated matter-of-factly, "I'm ready to believe it."

Erickson slowly turned around, taking in the whole scene of battle. "There aren't a lot of choices, are there?" he replied. His voice was low, a combination of dejection and acceptance as comprehension set in. "We're either up against a bunch of kooks, or . . . or, and I hate to say this out loud, Sergeant, or we're in a time other than 1976."

"How about the beginning of the Revolutionary War?"

"Maybe." Erickson stared at Bushnell and then again at the scene in the campground. "But, how did we get here?"

Bushnell didn't concern himself with responding, since the four Squad Leaders were fast approaching.

"How do we stand?" Erickson asked.

"One dead redcoat in our area," said Putnam.

Porter chimed in, as well. "I killed the one trying to take Lewis. Brown's wounded in his right heel and one of my guys got banged on the head with a saber."

"Dobbs?" Erickson turned to the Mess Corporal, and seeing his deeply scrapped cheek, asked, "How's the face?"

"It's gonna hurt some, but I'll make it. One of my guys has a small wound in the shoulder and another got a small saber cut on the ear. Both are being taken care of. I can't seem to find Hale, though. Last time I saw him, he was under one of the trucks shooting at a redcoat. Got him too, the body's laying on the ground, near the truck."

"Where have you looked for him?" Erickson asked.

"All around the area there. I'll take some more men and try again. I'm sure he's over there somewhere."

"You get your face fixed. Have your guys look for Hale. It looked to me like those guys were trying to take prisoners – I hope they didn't get him."

As Dobbs left, Erickson turned to Russell. "How about your squad?"

"Everybody and everything is fine. Nobody came near us after I opened up with the machine gun."

"Where were you aiming that thing, anyway?"

"High, in the tree branches. You said not to shoot anybody unless it was necessary, so I shot high to scare 'em off. Seemed to work."

"Sure did. Good thinking."

"Sergeant," Erickson said, turning to Bushnell, "Post some guards around the perimeter. Tell them to shoot to kill if they see anymore of those Redcoats up here." Turning back to the three remaining Corporals, Erickson added, "Keep your men on their toes. I don't want any repeats. This situation is too real and I'm afraid we've found ourselves somewhere other than in a Bicentennial celebration. Until we find out differently, treat this situation as if we *are* in the Revolutionary War. God knows how I can explain *that* to you, but that's the way things are. Worse yet, I don't have any idea on how to get back to where we're supposed to be."

Those standing within earshot stopped what they were doing, but said nothing, keeping their thoughts to themselves. The enormity of Erickson's statement was so great that many just shook their heads, not daring to say a word for fear of proving it right.

Dobbs came running back to the clearing, calling out to Erickson as he came. "He's gone, Lieutenant. My men can't find him anywhere. He must have been captured."

"You're absolutely sure he's gone? You've looked everywhere?"

"Absolutely, Lieutenant. They searched the whole camp for him. Hale's gone!"

TWELVE

Another Copy – Xetrel Lights a Fire

Colonel Lester sat deep in his chair, phone pressed tightly to his ear, trying desperately and diplomatically to respond to General Xetrel's anger.

"Yes, Sir, I *know* about the report, we got a copy, too . . . No, Sir, I don't know who else has a copy . . . Yes, I *do* understand the importance of keeping the Erickson incident under control . . . Yes, Sir, Captain Treppello understands the matter the same way . . . Yes, we *are* doing everything we can."

Xetrel was upset after finding a copy of the PRA report on his chair, too, when he opened his office that morning. Infuriated by the implications about lax office security and the obvious compromise of the Army's cover-up, he'd called Lester. Ignoring their long-time friendship, he belligerently voiced his rage, then hung up.

Lester took a moment to calm himself, for it wouldn't do to have both of them running around in a panic, especially one that was being orchestrated for some ulterior purpose.

Obviously, the appearance of the PRA report had pressed the right buttons on the General. It clearly signaled that if someone could enter his locked office unnoticed and leave a copy of the report, then other copies could be sent elsewhere – to the media, or, even worse, to Erickson.

It seemed clear to Lester that Funston had struck again. But, to what end? To goad Xetrel? If so, into what? The immediate result was to create more pressure on Lester. Was that what this was all about? More pressure on him? If so, to do what?

As he churned the thoughts over in his mind, he knew he had to contain the situation. But, how? It wasn't possible to simply tell the Admiral to stop digging into the Erickson matter; Lester would be laughed out of his office. In addition, there weren't any physical restrictions he could exercise over Funston; his people could keep on distributing copies at will.

No, this was going to come down to finding out what Funston's real goals were. At the same time, though, he had to be prepared to mock any public disclosure of the affair. What news media editor in his right mind would believe Erickson, after Lester got the public laughing at his outrageous testimony? What Congressmen would dare take on the Army over something so bizarre as the Erickson matter? No, he and Treppello would make sure of that.

Yet, one could never tell for sure what a politician might do in any given situation, or what angle an editor might take in pursuing a sensational story, especially if Erickson were to gain center stage.

Clearly, he was not in a position to directly control or contain the entire situation. But, if forced, he could make Funston and the PRA out to be idiots to the public, especially with all their delving into the supernatural at Government expense. That alone could slow 'Funny' down considerably. Yes, that would be the way he could contain it for now.

He picked up the phone and called Carl, but no one answered. As the day wore on, he tried again several times, without success.

The late afternoon sun had moved well behind the main buildings at Fort McNair when Treppello strode into the office. "I finished reading Erickson's testimony. Got some time to talk about it?"

"Sure. Where have you been? I called you several times."

"In the small conference room down the hall. Too much noise around my desk, so I went there and closed the door. You irritated?"

"No. I just wanted to let you know Xetrel got a copy of the PRA report. Now he's panicky, but I think we can keep things under control. Let me share my plans with you, before we start talking about Erickson's testimony at the Inquiry."

A few moments later, as he concluded telling him about his plans, Lester realized that Treppello seemed to be only listening and nodding half-heartedly.

"What is it?" he demanded, "something about Erickson's testimony get your attention?"

"It's very absorbing, Sir. 18th Century Dragoons vs. 20th Century Soldiers. Horsemen and old weapons vs. infantry and machine guns. Man against man in the unknown. Real drama and excitement!"

"So? Do you believe it?"

Treppello eyed his Colonel with a certain trepidation. He knew what he was going to say would place him squarely in opposition to Lester's opinion of Erickson, yet he also knew the Colonel expected him to be honest.

"Sir, not only is it fascinating, but I can see how it might have happened, especially with the energy they found at the campground in Jockey Hollow. I suspect there are Leys and Nodes there."

"Hang on a second, Carl. There's no proof of any Leys or Nodes at Jockey Hollow. Even if there were, none of the historical events in the PRA report involved people getting shot at, while looking at or being in a past time. Don't you think that's a big difference? Don't you think that puts the entire Erickson situation into direct conflict with its being a retrocognition? I agree that Erickson's testimony and the PRA report both make fascinating reading, but that's not the issue that faces us. Our job is *not* to prove it happened, our job is to make the report and the testimony totally unbelievable to anyone who might find out about it."

"Yes, Sir. That's right, as far as our job goes," Treppello responded. "But, what happens to our position, if it actually happened? Times have changed considerably since 1976; situations that couldn't be accepted then, might be now. We've been to the moon, sent probes to Venus, Mars, the outer planets, even beyond our solar system. We've launched Space Shuttles and huge telescopes and taken all kinds of pictures of the universe and the earth. Man is redefining his relationship with the world and himself, and attitudes *are* changing. People may now be ready for the Erickson matter, when they weren't before!"

"It's not important if they, or even you, are ready for it! Our job is to make them reject it! That's what we have to do, to comply with our orders!"

Stung by the rebuke, Treppello could only stare back at his Colonel.

"Oh, don't look at me like that, Carl. What I'm trying to get across is that there are two distinct sides to this matter. There's Erickson's side, as reported to the Board of Inquiry, which is being supported by the fascinating, but incomplete work of the PRA. The other is the side of reason and logic. There's a large credibility gap between the two and that's what we have to count on in keeping this matter contained! It's one thing for the report to bring in all the various benign examples of retrocognition and precognition, but it's another matter entirely for anybody to fully connect those instances to Erickson's dilemma. From the standpoint of our orders, that's good!"

Softening, as a smile flowed to his face and voice, he added, "Look, Carl. You've got to admit that Erickson's testimony goes far beyond anything described in the PRA report about benign events involving humans and apparitions. In those cases, one's mind can identify with the events for the fun it. But, Erickson's situation is far too real. In Erickson's case, there are real guns and real bullets and real deaths."

"Then you're banking on the public feeling safe with the fantasy," responded Treppello, "but rejecting the main show because it's too real?"

"I'm not saying it's *too* real, I'm saying that it's *unreal.*"

"But Colonel, is it unreal only because *you* have no basis for acceptance; because there's no record of any prior events of a similar nature *you* could turn to?"

"I don't think that's it, at all," Lester replied. "I can't accept it because it's *not logical.* What's past is past. It's one thing for some people to get a glimpse of it somehow and quite another matter for a whole damn platoon of soldiers to actually find themselves in the middle of the past, shooting soldiers of that time and being shot at in return."

"Do you agree that reality is what we make of it?"

"It may surprise you, Carl, but I do understand a lot about that concept. Its genesis is in the Far East, but its well known in those parts of Europe where I was stationed. I know of studies by respected universities that have concluded that we are each responsible for our own physical and emotional make up – that we are what we eat and what we think. Hell, Carl, a lot of people use that concept all the time, whether to get psyched up to win a game, or to get mentally and physically prepared to succeed at some other goal."

"Yes, Sir, that's right. And what you said about getting psyched up can be expanded to include visualization and creating one's own reality."

"Yes, Carl, both of those concepts are in wide use in many fields. The field of medicine has enjoyed some successes where people have created a different reality for themselves, curing cancers and other major illnesses. So?"

"What I mean is, whether a person recognizes it or not, they have always created their own realities, moment by moment, day by day, through their conscious or subconscious thoughts and actions."

"And?"

"Would that idea have been acceptable in the world of 1976?"

"No."

"That's my point. Since that time we've gained tremendous insight into the parts each of us play in how our lives are lived."

"What has that got to do with Erickson and our problem, Carl?"

"Well, for instance – and this may not be so far-fetched as it first sounds – what if the public can be led to believe that the Erickson experience was something he and the others created for themselves – something akin to that Tulpa that got out of hand with the French woman. What if they all had a lot of fun with their experience and played it to the hilt, until it got too real and they became

desperate to get out. When they reached that point, they quickly came back
to where they started."

"Are you telling me Erickson and his men purposefully created that
'reality' for themselves?"

"Not on a conscious level, Colonel. More like a subconscious agreement
among people thinking the same thing. Remember, they were on the train
together for what, almost a week? And what happened to them during that
time, with nothing to do but daydream about what they were going to do
when they got to the Bicentennial event? I'm young, they were young, we've
all had our daydreams about saving the world, or at least our portion of it.
Don't you think they were all daydreaming about what fun it would have
been to be heroes, fighting the British, changing the course of history?"

"We've all had those types of daydreams," Lester replied. "They're harmless
and a lot of fun to enjoy. But, what you're saying is they all collaborated on
the same daydream to become the ultimate heroes of 1776. I think it would
have taken a monumental leap of joint faith to bring that to reality!"

"What if that leap was assisted by a bunch of powerful Leys?"

The thought caught Lester off guard and he tried to organize his thoughts
to respond, but Treppello didn't give him any time.

"I read an article not too long ago," he continued, "where some Professor
wrote about a type of group response to certain situations which he called
the Synergistic Coupling Effect. Under this Professor's thesis – I think his
name was Whitcombe Halledyne – synergistic coupling takes effect when
each member of a group subconsciously agrees to participate in a larger group
event. Each contributes mentally to expand the experience by introducing
their own variants, moving the event along to a choice of logical conclusions,
subject to the total subconscious will of the entire group. What I'm saying,
Colonel, is this: Erickson's platoon, without talking about it on the conscious
level, decided on a collective subconscious level to play soldier during the
Revolutionary War. And, that's as far as it would have gone, except the MP
Major banished them to a campground where that kind of thinking could,
in fact, become reality because of the Leys and Nodes. Once it got started,
everyone began to play out their fantasies until the horror of it all caused the
group to decide it was over."

Lester shook his head. "Look, Carl, it took six months of concentrated
energy to dissolve the Tulpa. Erickson's people must have been really good to
merely take days to create and then dissolve their Tulpa's" He was tired, feeling
sarcastic and wished he hadn't allowed Carl to get started. "It stretches the
imagination to conclude the energy measurements taken by the PRA at Jockey

Hollow represented a major road of energy, capable of literally slamming the super daydream of Erickson and his men into reality."

"Sure, Colonel, I agree. The energy levels they found were not what you and I, as non-experts, would envision as necessary for the results Erickson encountered. But, *they did find* levels of energy higher than the ordinary amount. Therefore, it seems reasonable to me to assume that even greater levels of energy may have been there on Erickson's first day in the campground, and that those levels were great enough to drive the synergistically coupled super daydream they were all having, into a new dimension of reality."

"That's a lot of conjecture," Lester responded disdainfully.

"Yes, Sir. But, its very interesting conjecture. I took the time to get some detailed topographical and landmark maps of the Jockey Hollow area. You know what I found?"

Lester looked up. "Religious grounds and structures?"

"All kinds, small and large, including outdoor revival campsites, baptismal ponds, graveyards, and old Indian sacred grounds. Look at this," he said, pulling a map from his back pocket and opening it on Lester's desk. "Look at these straight lines I drew connecting the markers for all the various structures and places. The campground where Erickson stayed is right in the middle of all of it. There's so many lines crisscrossing the area, they form a huge triangle."

Lester took the map and looked at the lines and penciled descriptions. The black lines created a perfect triangle around the Jockey Hollow campground.

"I wonder why Funston's team didn't get readings verifying such a concentration of Leys and Nodes?" Lester asked.

"I don't know, Colonel. But I believe we ought to go up to New Jersey and verify the levels of energy for ourselves."

"You want us to go up there and take readings?"

"Yes, Sir."

It suddenly dawned on Lester that this was exactly what Funston wanted done. Surely Funston knew that General Xetrel would get panicky; knew that such panic would turn into more pressure on Lester; and, knew that Lester would try to get as much information as he could about the situation to gain some space to maneuver. *What you've overlooked, Funny,* he thought, *is that I don't need a lot of room to maneuver. All I need is a little space for my plan to work and the world will end up laughing at you.*

Then, Lester had a second, more devious thought. Since he was being manipulated, why not treat it as a game? Since games always had a purpose, why not learn the rules of this one and get on with winning?

Nodding his head in agreement with himself, he looked at Treppello. "Well, Captain, you can't plan a battle without knowing the terrain. I guess we've got to know what we're dealing with up there so we can deal with it down here."

Encouraged, Treppello asked, "When do you want to go?"

"May as well be tomorrow. There's still time enough today for me to line up the measurement gear and a pickup truck."

"Do we need anybody to help operate the equipment?"

"I'll get instructions. I don't want anybody else up there with us."

Treppello nodded his head in understanding. What they were going to do *should* be kept to themselves.

*   *   *

Three time zones to the west, Erickson watched the mail truck leave as he stood holding a large envelope.

THIRTEEN

Saturday Afternoon

Captain Morgan had seen enough. His plan to capture some of the Rebels for questioning had seemed at first as though it would succeed, but the Rebels had made excellent use of the trees, hiding, running and dodging around and through them. Then, worst of all, they had started shooting at his men, killing at least two, if not three of them.

The smoke explosions had been used again by the Rebels and then hundreds of Rebel reinforcements had fired from their hiding places. He couldn't see where they were hiding, but he could see that their rapidly fired shots were wild, mostly into the tree branches. The fact that perhaps as many as a hundred or more Rebels were there was cause for immediate despair. The Rebels had quickly reloaded, for he heard them begin firing again in the same peculiar, measured, staccato manner. He wondered at their poor aim for they continued to miss his troops. Nevertheless, he could not gamble that they would miss the next time and ordered the trumpeter to sound the retreat.

Satisfied that his troopers had responded to the trumpeter's signal and spurred their horses away from the Rebel camp, Morgan rode down the west side of the hill, followed by Browne and Ramsey. No one said anything as Morgan set a fast pace through the trees, bringing them to clear running room at the base of the hill. From there, they galloped their horses towards the pond.

Ahead, Morgan could see his troops coming together in groups as they galloped towards their campground. "Sergeant Ramsey," he shouted, "prepare the troops for a counter-attack. With that many Rebels on the hill," he said, "it should come soon."

Browne did not agree and found himself saying so to Morgan. "In my judgment, Captain, those Rebels are only a small band of disciplined marauders. They choose not to fight, despite having weapons to protect themselves." Pausing for a moment, Browne decided to go on. "Their weapons are unusual, Captain. I saw not one of them stop to reload; yet, they continued to fire. Corporal Hale charged some of them and was shot three times by one Rebel who did not stop to reload!"

Morgan stiffened in his saddle and looked with suspicion at his Lieutenant.

Browne confidently continued. "During the battle, I watched one man sit on the ground behind a strange looking weapon. He fired many shots at the tree branches – without reloading! I believe that had he chosen to do so, he could have aimed that weapon to kill many of our troops."

The look on Morgan's face changed to disbelief. "What manner of madness are you expounding this noontime, Lieutenant? Weapons that do not require reloading to be fired again? A Rebel sitting on the ground shooting a weapon – an amazing weapon as you describe it – without trying to kill troopers attacking him? Come, come, Lieutenant. I clearly saw what was happening. You must have had the noon sun blinding your vision!"

Browne knew differently, but it would do him no good to pursue the matter any further for now. Morgan was one of those Officers, so prevalent in the British Army that had won his rank by his social position in life. As such, his grasp of military matters was severely limited. Browne, on the other hand, was proud that his family had supplied Officers to the Crown for many generations and knew that when necessary, he could influence the politically appointed Captain.

With discretion in mind, Browne responded. "Perhaps so, Sir. The Captain *did* enjoy a better position to see the events than I."

They rode back to the campground silently, each deep in their own thoughts. Morgan ignored Browne's presence, keeping his eyes instead on Ramsey who was closing towards them.

"There is much concern and confusion amongst the troops, Sir," he said, as he came up to Morgan. "Many of them report seeing strange weapons and peculiar carriages, unlike anything they have seen before. Some even insist that the Rebels did not reload their weapons before firing them a second and third time. Many think the Rebels were disciplined, experienced soldiers, who could have killed all of us if they had chosen. Sir, the men are afraid."

Morgan was stunned. Cilly would never have permitted such thinking. Now, his command was collapsing. Cilly was dead, Lieutenant Browne was seeing apparitions, and Ramsey was unable to keep the troops from voicing fear about battling the Rebels. Fear! The 16th Light Dragoons feared no one! They fought like men and died like men, without questioning, *and without FEAR!*

Deep in his own thoughts about what to do, Morgan didn't see Browne quietly dismount and tell Ramsey, "We will need a list of the dead and wounded. Bring it to me at the tavern." Then, taking his and Morgan's reins, he lead the two horses across the camp to the rear of the tavern, where he tied them to the rail and patiently waited for Morgan to dismount. Together, they walked in silence around to the front of the building.

While the primary purpose of the tavern had been to keep the Dragoons out of Morristown, the residents had also recognized that more inns and taverns would be needed to accommodate increased travel between New York and the British strongholds to the south. Taking advantage of the location and potential for profit, they constructed a two-story building consisting of a first floor with taproom, kitchen and social area at one end and the three bedrooms the Dragoons had demanded, at the other. Another four bedrooms and a large community sleeping room were on the second floor. The upstairs bedrooms were reserved for ladies, while traveling men would sleep two or three to a bed in the community sleeping room.

Browne and Morgan walked up the two steps leading to the front door of the tavern and pushed it open. The tavern keeper stood behind the serving bar and nodded to them, but both Officers ignored him and turned right and walked directly towards the small door at the end of the bar, leading to the three downstairs bedrooms beyond. Browne removed his riding gloves as he continued straight ahead past the door towards his room, while Morgan turned left into his own.

At the door he stopped briefly and without looking at Browne, stated, "There is much to ponder. I will take some time, now." He quietly entered and then closed his door behind him.

"*Odd,*" thought Browne, "*he orders preparation for a counter-attack, then broods. Perhaps he will change his mind.*"

Browne walked over to his desk and sat down, looking out the window. Though his view was slightly obscured by the trees, he could still discern Wick's farmhouse and its brick chimney protruding from the center of the roof peak. Wick's wife and daughter lived there with him, but Browne had seen them only once. The Troopers used his well from time to time, but Browne suspected it was really Wick's daughter that kept them coming back.

Browne turned from the window, and engrossed in thought, walked slowly out of the bedroom, through the tavern and then out the front door. He couldn't help thinking that the Americans were constantly full of surprises. Their roads were bad, their means of communication were worse, and yet, they succeeded in making 1776 a bad year so far for the English. The King's armies had been beaten at Moores Creek in the Colony of North Carolina. Then, Boston was abandoned by General Howe, losing 250 cannons! Then, the Rebel Navy successfully attacked Nassau. And, the Crown was again defeated when they attacked Charleston harbor. If the rumor were true that the rebellion has turned into a fight for independence, July could just as well be another disastrous month.

The sound of a door opening and shoes scrapping on the porch behind him made him turn around.

Upon seeing Ramsey, he asked, "What do you have you to report, Sergeant?"

"There are three dead, Sir. Corporal Hale, shot while charging a group of Rebels, Private Henrauther, shot as he tried to drag a prisoner away, and Private Barrow, killed while chasing a Rebel he had captured and then lost in a smoke explosion. Some of the troops have scratches and small wounds that are being ministered to. I have taken the liberty of placing Private Thacker in charge of Corporal Hale's men. I hope you will see fit to recognize him with the Corporal's rank."

"I will consider it. You best wait in the taproom whilst I roust the Captain and tell him of your report. He may have questions for you."

Browne walked back through the tavern to Morgan's room. As he started to knock, the sound of a female giggling stopped him. Quickly concluding that if the Captain had time for that, he had obviously changed his mind about the Rebel counterattack. Browne softly retreated from the door and walked to the taproom.

The tap occupied the area inside the building just to the right of the entrance. Beyond was the social area, dominated by the fireplace and the wall separating it from the kitchen that spread across most of the back of the building.

It was only mid afternoon, but the cooking fire had already been lit for the evening meal. The smoke and heat of the fireplace, mixed with the still air and heat of the July day, made Browne thirsty. Since the tavern was not noted for either good tasting coffee or tea, he decided upon cider and asked the keeper to bring two mugs to the table where Ramsey was already seated.

As he sat down, he told the Sergeant, "The Captain is preoccupied at the moment, I do not know how long it will be, but you may pass the time with me here." Looking up as the keeper approached, he said, "Here, I ordered us some cider."

The keeper unceremoniously placed the pewter mugs on the table between them, spilling some cider on the table. Ignoring the spill, he walked away without a word.

"He becomes more insolent each day," Ramsey commented, loudly enough for the keeper to hear.

"Yes," replied Browne, "someday, we may have to do something about it." Raising the mug, Browne downed half the cider in two swallows.

Ramsey raised his own mug and drank his fill. Putting the mug down, he wiped his mouth on his sleeve and said, "I should return to the troops, Sir. They are still positioned for a Rebel counter-attack, but feeling is strong that it will not come."

"You have your orders, Sergeant. We shall remain prepared, until the orders are changed. Return to the troops, if you wish. I will summon you when the Captain is ready."

Upon Ramsey's departure, Browne approached the keeper and demanded, "Which one is with him?"

The unsmiling keeper narrowed his eyes and looked straight at the Lieutenant. "Beth. Molly refuses his advances. She does not like either of you. Why do you both keep after her so? Send her back to Morristown and find some new wenches to chase. Use your rank and connections to get more wenches from the entire countryside, so your men are taken care of, too!"

Browne glared back at the keeper, then stalked out of the tavern.

FOURTEEN

Saturday Afternoon/Evening

Erickson and Bushnell stood in the clearing as Putnam and Russell walked up. "Hey, Lieutenant, take a look at what we found on that redcoat I shot. It's a letter addressed to Corporal D. Hale, 16th Dragoons."

Erickson looked at the folded paper. "A dead Hale for a missing Hale? I don't like the trade, Corporal."

"Come on Lieutenant! That guy was armed and charging us. I *had* to shoot him."

Startled, Erickson stared at Putnam. "I didn't mean it *that* way, Corporal. You did fine. Don't worry about it, I shouldn't have made the comment."

The platoon had eaten a light lunch after cleaning up the campground from the raid. The men relaxed and cleaned their weapons, while guards still stood at posts around the perimeter of the grounds. Putnam and his men had searched the dead Dragoons before burying them.

"Did you find anything out about the other two?" asked Erickson.

"Not much. One's name was Henrauther and the other was Barrow, but that's all we could find. Henrauther is the one Porter stopped from taking Lewis and Barrow must have been the one that Hale shot from under the truck . . ." Putnam started to add . . . *before he disappeared,* but stopped quickly enough.

"Sergeant," exclaimed Erickson, "I want to take a patrol down there tonight and scout around. I need to see what they've got and what we're up against. And, I want to find out what year it really is! I want two groups, one to go with me while we try to get inside the tavern. Part of the other group can act as guards for us and what's left can scout around the edge of the Dragoon camp."

"Right, Lieutenant," Bushnell responded. Turning to Russell and Putnam, he gave the orders. "Russell, you take Butler and Sullivan and go with the Lieutenant tonight. Putnam, you go too. Post Lee and Durkee as guards down at the tavern when you get there, then take Arnold and check out the

Dragoon camp. All right, take the rest of the afternoon to get your bearings. Know your destinations so you won't get lost in the dark."

The hours passed quickly for Erickson as he continued to think through his plans. Bushnell spent much of his time checking the camp and talking to the guards, periodically interrupting Erickson's thoughts to report they had seen no Dragoon activity. As evening approached, Erickson checked his watch, stretched and then called to Dobbs. "About time to start chow, isn't it?" he said. "We've got a patrol to get out of here."

Rubbing the bandaged wound on his cheek, Dobbs whistled for his men to join him. Soon his squad was at the kitchen unit, hustling to get out an evening meal.

Bushnell returned from his last circuit of the camp and walked over to Erickson, half-laughing. "You know, Jim, I've been thinking. If this *is* 1776, why the hell shouldn't I try and look up my ancestor, Carter Bushnell? I told you about him. He's in Maryland."

Erickson stared at him and started to laugh, but quickly suppressed it when he realized that Bushnell was serious.

Seeing the look on his face, Bushnell started to laugh, himself. "Maybe it *is* silly, thinking I could meet him – but what the hell, if we're actually here, why not? It's exciting just to think that *I could*. Probably scare the piss out of him, though, if I were to convince him who I was. God, what an adventure this is! If we live through it, who will ever believe us when we tell them what's happened?"

Erickson shook his head. "I'll be happy just to get through it, without having to worry about telling anyone afterwards." Looking at the kitchen unit as he spoke, Erickson added, "I see Dobbs waving at us for chow; let's go over."

*　　*　　*

After supper, Dobbs approached Russell with an empty canteen. "Bring me some of that water from the pond, will ya? I need to check it out to see if we can use it for cooking and drinking. We're going to run out of ours pretty soon."

Russell nodded and took the canteen as he and Putnam moved their men to the clearing near Erickson and Bushnell.

Erickson was waiting. "Well guys," he said, "here's what we're going to do: we'll ease ourselves down the trail to the pond, then go around it using the trees on the east side for cover. From there, we'll stay on the edge of the trail past the Wick house, homing in on the lights of the tavern. Stay in pairs and spread yourselves out a bit, but not too far apart. Butler, get me a small flashlight, something like a penlight. I can use it to signal Sergeant Bushnell that's everything's all right, without worrying that the Dragoons will see its light."

Bushnell looked at Erickson. "What if everything isn't all right?"

Russell answered instead. "Hell, Sergeant, you'll hear us shooting and running. That's when you should start pumping H.E. out of the mortar."

Erickson jerked his head towards Russell, instantly concerned. "High Explosives in the dark, when our guys can't see where we are? That's a hell of a risk, Corporal. A hell of a risk!"

"Not if they fired a star shell first."

"Now we've got star shells, too?"

"I forgot to tell you. So help me god, Lieutenant, I forgot they were in there, until this afternoon when Putnam and I got to talking about the patrol."

"Russell, what do you do in real life?"

"I run an auto parts store; wholesale and retail. Run the junkyard next door, too. We're up in San Luis Obispo, if you ever need any parts you can't find."

"Would it be that I can't find any, anywhere else, because you've scrounged them all?"

"Lieutenant, that's not kind." Russell was enjoying the banter.

"When we get to the Tavern," Erickson continued, "you, Sullivan and Butler will go in with me while Lee and Durkee stand guard outside. We'll find out what we can and then get the hell out of there. In the meantime, Arnold and Putnam will move over to the edge of the Dragoon camp. You guys keep to the trees as much as possible, but see if you can find any trace of Hale. Take no more than ten minutes from the time you leave us at the tavern. Then rejoin us and we'll all come back here together.

"If you get into trouble, head back to the tavern. If you hear us in trouble, come running to help." Looking at his wristwatch, Erickson motioned for them to start. "Let's move out."

Erickson and Putnam led the way, setting a slow pace to minimize the noise in the extreme quiet of the 18th Century night. Moving steadily, they soon reached the bottom of the trail and the pond, where Erickson aimed the penlight up the hill towards the campground and pushed the button twice.

"Let's move on," he said.

They began moving around the edge of the pond. The trees were thicker now, with the branches of the willows reaching down to brush their shoulders as they walked by. The pond was about 35 to 40 feet across at its middle and about 60 feet long.

Russell found the source of its water as he slipped on the wet clay at the edge of the small stream feeding it. Catching himself in time to keep from falling in, he swore under his breath as he hung onto the low hanging tree branch that had saved him. Putnam, a few steps behind, saw what happened in time to keep himself from repeating the same dance in the mud.

Erickson, helping Russell regain his balance, tried to pull him across, but he held back.

"Hey Lieutenant," he whispered, "hold up a couple of seconds, will ya? Dobbs wants me to bring back some water so he can test it." Stooping over, Russell eased himself through the tree branches to a convenient spot where he could fill the canteen without falling in.

"Watch yourself, ol' buddy," Putnam cautioned under his breath. "Don't want the bog turtles or the milk snakes to get ya."

"Hey Putnam," Russell replied caustically, "you want to do this? I'll let ya."

"No. Looks like you're doing just fine," Putnam answered, holding the same soft voice. "Just fine. But, tell me, where did you ever learn to get in that kind of position? I don't think I've ever seen anybody do it better!"

"For Christ's sake, Putnam," Russell retorted in a loud whisper, "if you're so damn smart, get over here and show me how to do it better."

Erickson quickly cut in, in an even louder whisper. "All right! Knock it off, you guys! The whole damn British Army will hear you."

Russell finished filling the canteen and screwed the lid back on as he gingerly moved away from the stream and ducked through the branches. "Pass this back for Lee to carry, will ya?" he said, handing the full canteen to Arnold. "And tell him not to drink it!"

Erickson took up the lead again and continued to move the patrol around the north side of the pond. The going got a little harder and slower as the men took care not to fall in or get a tree branch in the face. Coming up on the east side of the pond, Erickson set a faster pace through the tall grass and flowery shrubs just outside the edge of the trees. The noise they made, while small, seemed to Arnold to sound like an Army on the move. He was sure the Dragoons were listening, had heard them coming and were waiting in the darkness up ahead. Arnold was not alone in his concern.

Reaching the far side of the pond without challenge, a relieved Erickson signaled the campsite again. Twenty feet further on, the trees abruptly ended and Erickson was able to see clearly the lights coming from the Wick house.

While it was at least 50 yards away on the north side of the trail, Erickson could still make out a three-tier fence of sapling trunks, which surrounded the property.

Tensed in anticipation of meeting hidden Dragoons, the men cautiously moved steadily and quietly towards the house. Suddenly, they saw movement in the shadows and slowed as they anxiously watched a figure moving about. Creeping closer, Erickson was able to discern a young girl, out near the well beside the house, twirling and dancing by herself in the dim moonlight.

"Now what?" Putnam asked, as Erickson stopped the patrol.

"We'll wait for a few minutes," he said in a soft whisper. "If nothing happens by then, we'll move out in pairs. As soon as one pair gets safely by, the next one will start out. She looks harmless enough, but anyone can scream if they're frightened, and we're getting too close to the Dragoons' camp for that."

"OK, Lieutenant. I'll pass the word."

"While you're doing that, Corporal, ask Sullivan to come up here and share what he knows about that house and the girl."

Moments later Sullivan was by his side. "I think the girl's name is Tempe, Lieutenant," he said. "Should be about 14 years old now. She's a scrappy kid, hid her horse in the dining room to keep the American troops from stealing it when they mutinied in 1781."

As Erickson marveled at Sullivan's memory for history, the back door of the house opened and a woman stepped into the yard. "Tempe. Come in now, Tempe. It's getting late and there is a chill to the night air." The girl ceased her dancing and walked quickly to her mother.

As soon as the door closed, Erickson motioned the patrol to start moving again. At the trail's intersection with the road that led to the tavern, Erickson again signaled Bushnell with the flashlight.

"So far, so good," he cautioned. "Everybody keep sharp, now; we're getting close."

The tavern was lit up as expected, but seemed much larger than Erickson had thought it would be. Holding up his hand, he stopped them all again just short of the clearing at the west edge of the building itself.

"I hear people talking," Putnam whispered into Erickson's ear.

"So do I," he answered. He could see lights in most of the downstairs and upstairs windows, from the middle to the far left end of the Tavern. No light came from the window at the narrow end of the building nearest him, or from the first three windows along the front. *Probably bedrooms,* he thought. Just then, someone upstairs walked past the window directly above the front door.

Turning to the two men next to him, Erickson said, "Lee, you and Durkee take a look around the backside."

The two men moved off into the dark and, after more than a few tense minutes, quietly returned. "Nothing there but a couple of horses," reported Durkee. "The backside is lit up the same as the front."

Erickson made a quick count outloud. "Two horses in back and five in front. There's at least seven people in there, plus the tavern keeper and the help." Turning back to Putnam, he said, "Send up Sullivan again, will you? Let's see what he has to say about this place."

Sullivan, hearing his name, took a few steps forward. "Somebody want me?" he whispered.

"Yeah," said Erickson. "Want to try for two out of two? What are we going to find when we go in this tavern?"

"I'm not sure about this one in particular, Lieutenant, but generally speaking, taverns and inns weren't the greatest of places. And, in order to understand them you have to know that travel in colonial America was – maybe I should say *is* – completely different from what we know in the 20th Century. The countryside was very sparsely populated and most people didn't travel very far from where they lived, either because they didn't have the means or because it was so dangerous. There were highwaymen everywhere and if they didn't get you, the wolves, Indians or rattlesnakes probably would. That road out there is excellent compared to what I've read they had."

"But, what about the tavern, Sullivan," Erickson reiterated in terse terms. "What I need to know is about this tavern."

"OK, sorry Lieutenant. There's probably a large table in the kitchen or dining area around which as many as 25 people can be seated. Generally, the travelers sit around a table, eating family style. The food could run from great to god-awful, depending on the location and what was available. Drinks included tea and coffee, wine or cider, rum – Americans of this time love their rum – whiskey, and beer. You may see them heating their drinks with a red-hot iron called a loggerhead. As far as sleeping, you wouldn't get much if you were to stay there; drinking and carousing by the male travelers usually goes on to all hours of the morning. This place looks rather large, but seems to have been hastily put together: rough wood exterior, no paint, and windows of really poor quality. The tavern looks fairly new – the area out front here doesn't have that trampled look from a lot of use. I'd say the place is probably here just for the Dragoons and a few hell raisers from Morristown."

Erickson was mulling what Sullivan said, when he added more.

"One last thing, Lieutenant. Don't be surprised if we get asked a lot of questions. Our fatigues may not stand out, since almost any kind of clothing was worn then, but the people in there will want the news you bring with you. You gotta remember, out here in the boonies, word of mouth was the major source of communication. We may have to give as much information as we expect to get."

"Thanks, professor." Erickson said, terminating the lesson by shaking Sullivan's hand. Turning back to Russell, he said, "OK. What do you think? Ready to go in?"

"May as well, Sir, that's what we came for."

Putnam looked at Erickson and seeing the nod in return, knew it was time for assignments. "Durkee," he ordered, "you stay here and keep an eye peeled for Dragoons. Lee, go to the backside and find a place where you can watch the road, the tavern and the Dragoon camp. Don't screw up, if you see anything funny that the Lieutenant needs to know, you come a runnin' into the tavern and tell him!"

Nodding his head in acknowledgement, Lee kept his hurt feelings to himself. He could and would do his job; Putnam didn't have to be climbing on him all the time.

Putnam threw a highball salute to Erickson and Russell as he left with Arnold for the Dragoon camp via the backside of the Tavern, soon disappearing into the darkness of the trees.

After his final signal to the hilltop, Erickson led Russell, Butler and Sullivan to the front door of the tavern.

"We all going in at once?" asked Russell.

"Yes. But let me take a peek, first."

Erickson pushed the door open a bit and cautiously looked around. He saw two men seated at the table in the social area, the coals of the fireplace casting a warm, yellow-orange glow over them. A third man stood near their table, back to the wall, smoking a long-stemmed pipe. To the right a man stood at the bar top, leaning forward, talking to a girl that looked to be in her early twenties. Two people were just disappearing from view up the steps to the second floor.

As his eyes followed them, the man behind the bar spied Erickson and called out, "Come in, traveler! Where ya from and where ya going?"

Seeing no Dragoons, Erickson pushed the door open wider and motioned the others to follow him in. Russell carried his carbine easily, ready to fire if the need arose. Behind him, Sullivan had his M-1 cradled in the crook of his left arm, right hand around the trigger housing. A step further behind, Butler pointed his M-1 in an angle towards to the floor, also ready to bring it into action.

Erickson's eyes moved quickly around the room, taking in the whole scene. The kitchen seemed to be empty, while overhead, the sounds of people walking around and talking could be heard.

"Hullo. Set a spell. Tell us the news you carry." The girl who spoke smiled at them and pointed to the chairs near the front window, across from the serving bar.

"We'll stand," Erickson replied, curtly. "We haven't much time."

"What's your hurry?" asked the keeper. "There is nowhere else to go. You should spend the night."

"Yes." The man with the long pipe walked towards Erickson. "Tell us your name and where you come from."

Ignoring him, Erickson looked at Russell. "Watch the stairs, Corporal," he ordered. "Cover anybody that comes down."

"Right, Lieutenant." Russell's response was given coolly, his eyes already on the move.

"Corporal? Lieutenant? Are you fighting men?" asked the keeper as he moved down the bar, closer to Erickson.

Erickson held up his hand, stopping the questions. "I don't mean to be rude, Sir, but if you can give us the answers to a few of our questions, we'll be on our way. This may sound odd, but what is the date?"

"Why today is Saturday, the 6th. Have you been out that long, that time has escaped you?"

"Something like that. What month and year?"

"You *have* been away, lad. This is July, '76."

Hearing the answer as he looked at the girl, Russell interjected, "17 or 19?"

"She is twenty-two."

"Not the girl, damnit! 1776 or 1976?" Russell exploded.

"Why 1776, of course. It's two hundred years to 1976. You can be sure of that."

"Damn!"

"Sir?"

"I said damn!" Russell shifted the carbine and rubbed the right side of his neck with the barrel and stock.

"That is a most unusual weapon you carry, Corporal. What is it?"

Erickson interceded before Russell could answer. "Are there any Dragoons in here?"

"Are you mercenaries?" The keeper wouldn't give up.

"No. We're soldiers of the United States Army. Now, please answer me. Are there any Dragoons in this building?"

"There are two quartered here. Captain Morgan and Lieutenant Browne. The rest of them have less favorable lodgings out back across the clearing."

"What Regiment are they with?"

"They are Light Dragoons of the 16th. A fierce lot, they are; came over here in early May. Sent by Burgoyne himself, to help rout the Rebels. But, Howe's got them under his command now, running them around hereabouts gathering up supplies for some upcoming battle. Rumor has it that it's for New York."

"New York? Why New York? Sullivan? What's he talking about?"

As soon as Sullivan started to reply, Erickson remembered the history lesson he had given his troops before the Major ran them off. Embarrassed, he didn't feel now he could cut him off.

"Howe attacked New York from Staten Island in late August," Sullivan intoned. "Washington had most of his Army there and Howe decided to get them while he could. Didn't work out though. Washington got away and ended up here."

"You speak as if it has already happened." The keeper said with a quizzical look on his face. August is next month, and General Washington has certainly not been here."

"Yes, we know that," Erickson replied, still perturbed with himself. "You say there are Dragoons quartered here. Are they here now?"

"Their rooms are beyond that door." The keeper pointed to the small door at the end of the bar, leading to the three downstairs bedrooms. "Molly, go get them."

"No!" Erickson almost shouted it. Then in a much lower voice, "Butler, get over to that door. Watch her and be careful."

The sound of running outside diverted their attention to the front door. Lee bounded up the steps through the opened door and promptly bumped into Erickson. Regaining his balance, the Private blurted out his message.

"Three Dragoons are heading for the back door. Be here in seconds!"

"Where's Durkee?" Erickson didn't see him behind Lee.

"Catching his breath from running," Lee wheezed back, "he's at the edge of the Tavern, in the trees."

Erickson's eyes darted around the room, trying to decide whether to hide or run. The girl made his mind up for him.

"Quickly," she commanded, "up the stairs. There are only friends up there. No one here is loyal to the Crown or the Dragoons."

Erickson led the way, followed by Sullivan, Russell and Lee. Butler eyed the girl as if to say 'you better be right,' and quickly followed the others up the stairs. No sooner had they all reached the second level, than the kitchen door burst open and the three Dragoons entered and walked straight through to the bar in the front of the tavern. Erickson had a clear view of them from his hiding place at the top of the stairs.

"Beer, three mugs, and no water cutting," the tallest of the three Dragoons told the keeper, sternly.

"You have never been cheated here, Corporal MacKenzie." The keeper looked right back at him as he placed three mugs out for the beer.

"And I never will, while puss is here!" The Corporal pulled his flintlock pistol from his belt and laid it on the bar pointed at the keeper. Fondling the pistol where it laid on the bar, the Corporal went on, "Puss here keeps you honest."

The keeper ignored him, turning instead to face the other two while he drew the beer. He recognized one but not the other and asked the first, "Who is this with you, Corporal McDougall, a new man?"

"No. 'Tis a new Corporal, Thacker."

"What happened to Corporal Hale?" The keeper was curious about all the shooting he had heard just after noon. He had seen the Dragoons riding hard back to their camp, but no one had said anything to him about the details.

"Corporal Hale is dead. Killed by the Rebels you are so much in sympathy with. Corporal Thacker has taken his place."

"You must have killed many in return." The keeper continued to dig for information, hoping some would be worthy of sale.

"Yes, many, many – of those that came out to fight. The rest hid like the scared rabbits they are." McDougall would exaggerate the success of the 16th to this man, no matter what.

"How many did you capture?"

"None. We took no prisoners."

Molly let out a screech as McDougall pinched her and then tried to pull her over to him. "Come here, me lass, I want to put me arms around you."

"Get away, you overgrown lobster! I want no part of you."

"Ah, you would change your tune, if you would but give me a fling. I could make you purr like a kitten."

"I'll not purr with the likes of you. Get away!"

McDougall grabbed her closer and aimed a kiss at her mouth. Dodging, Molly bit him on the chin instead. McDougall only laughed. "Do not be difficult, wench. You know you want me."

"I do not!" Wiggling and squirming, she pulled away from McDougall only to be caught by Corporal MacKenzie at her breasts.

"Let go of me," she screamed, and turning in his grasp, aimed a pointed-toed shoe at his ankle. Missing, she screamed again, "Let me go!"

The three men in the social area began to move further away, huddling together in the doorway between the social area and the kitchen. There, they eyed what McDougall, MacKenzie and Thacker did not see: Erickson and Russell coming slowly, cautiously down the stairs behind them.

"Let her go! Now!" Erickson commanded at full voice, as he stood midway down the stairs, pointing his .45 directly at Corporal MacKenzie. Russell continued down the stairs, easing past Erickson, and reached the tavern floor. Moving to the edge of the social area where he could see both the front and rear entrances, he pointed his carbine at the other two Dragoons. Lee remained crouched at the top of the stairs, shoulder to shoulder with Butler and Sullivan, nervously ready to act if needed.

Startled, Corporal MacKenzie stood there, mouth hanging open as if he was trying to say something.

"I said, let her go!" Erickson repeated his command.

"Rebels!" the Corporal yelled back, and in one move threw Molly into the table next to the front window and grabbed his pistol from the bar, aiming it at Erickson. He never fired it. Four quick blasts from the muzzle of Russell's carbine slammed the Corporal around and into the door leading to the bedrooms behind him. His body hung there for a second or two and then slumped to the floor.

As Russell turned to check for other Dragoons, Butler fired his M-l from the top of the stairs and splintered a pewter mug on the bar. "Hold it!" he yelled at McDougall, trying to sneak his pistol out for a shot. "Leave that pistol in your belt."

McDougall dropped his hand away and stood frozen at the bar, looking helplessly at his fellow Dragoon, Thacker.

Erickson, still pointing his .45, jerked around to cover the back door as it flew open. Putnam and Arnold crashed into the three men standing in the way, sending the one man's pipe skittering across the floor.

Reaching Erickson's side, Putnam swung his carbine around the room, looking for a target. He instantly found one as Lieutenant Browne opened the door and stood there, gaping at the body of Corporal MacKenzie. Putnam sprayed the doorjamb over Browne's head with .30 caliber slugs from the semi-automatic. Browne ducked and slammed the door as he ran back to his bedroom.

"Let's get out of here!" Erickson yelled, leading the others towards the door as Putnam ran to the bar to pull the pistols from the two Dragoons.

"Be right with you," he called to Erickson. Smirking at the Dragoons as he stuck their pistols in his belt, he ran to catch up.

Outside, Durkee ran out of the trees and joined them in the mad dash to the intersection. In his haste, he stumbled and fell on a soft body. Picking himself up, he reached over to help his comrade get up, only to discover a girl's small hand in his. Not bothering to ask questions, he pulled her up and they both ran to catch up with the rest of the group. They all stopped on the far side of the road and hid behind the trees while they caught their breath.

"What the hell happened?" asked Putnam. "We were over in the Dragoon camp when we heard shooting. Took off running as fast as we could."

"Sons of bitches tried to molest a girl in there," replied Russell. "We stopped 'em."

Across the trail, the lights had gone out in the Wick house. Vaguely visible in the quarter moon, Erickson could see a man's form near the back door, musket in hand. "We got everybody?" he whispered.

"Don't know," said Russell,

"OK. Let's take a quick roll call, then. Arnold?"

"Right here."

"Durkee?"

"Over here."

"Butler?"

"Yo," answered Butler.

"Lee's gasping for breath, so I know he's here. I can see Sullivan right there, Putnam's here and so am I. That takes care of all of us."

"This isn't Sullivan," Durkee exclaimed as he moved the girl so Erickson could see her better. "She says her name is Molly."

"Then where's Sullivan?" Erickson asked, not wanting to lose anyone. "He was with me when we left the tavern."

"Right here, Lieutenant. I'm in the trees to your right."

"That's a tally, then. We're all here." Looking at the girl, Erickson added, "including Molly."

"Here comes the cavalry!" Putnam pointed towards the British camp where the Dragoons could be seen and heard, mounting up and riding hard out of their camp.

Erickson leaned to get a better view. "Hang on. Let's stay where we are for a bit. Bushnell is sure to have heard the shooting, too. They'll be firing the mortar soon and I don't want to be dodging exploding shells!"

Almost instantly, a star shell burst high overhead and the half-million candlepower flare drifted slowly down under its small parachute. A few moments later, the first H.E. shell exploded in the trees, well beyond the intersection. Three more followed it, spread in front of the mounted Dragoons.

When the shelling stopped, Erickson quickly led his group away from the intersection, running hard and fast around the pond to the start of the trail at the bottom of the hill. There they stopped to catch their breath.

"It looks like we're going to be OK," he said. "I think the Dragoons are turning back."

He was right. Lieutenant Browne, in the lead, had reined in his horse at the first explosion. The bright fireball, followed by huge clouds of dust and falling debris visible in the eerie light of the flare, told him these were not just Rebel smoke shells again. The next three shells, while exploding well in front of him, showered more dirt and debris, this time over him and the troopers behind.

Browne rode swiftly back to his men. "Let them go. They have the advantage. We shall stay alive, to fight another day."

FIFTEEN

As Erickson reached the campground, Bushnell came running to meet him. "This is getting to be a habit, Lieutenant," he said humorously as he grabbed Erickson by the elbow to steady his stance. "You and Putnam go down the hill. There's shooting. Then you and Putnam come running back up the hill, while we cover you with the mortar. The best part, of course, is where I get to ask, 'what happened'?"

Erickson tried to laugh and catch his breath at the same time, but ended up in a fit of coughing. "Ask Russell," he said, then sat down on the ground next to Putnam, still coughing.

"Ask me what?" Russell said, as he and the rest of the patrol reached the top of the path.

But, Bushnell ignored him and went on with Erickson. "I heard the shooting and got a flare up as soon as I could. Saw the Dragoons coming out of their camp towards the road, but couldn't see you guys, so Porter lobbed a few across their front. They turned and high-tailed it back to their camp. So – what happened down there, Lieutenant?"

Not to be ignored, Russell chimed in, "Here's part of the answer," as he guided Molly to the front.

Before Bushnell could respond, Erickson finally recovered from his coughing spat. "I was asking some questions of the tavern keeper, when three Dragoon Corporals showed up. Molly here told us to hide up the stairs. One of the Corporals started to force his attentions on her and things got a little rough, so I came down and told him to let her go. Instead, he tried to shoot me. Russell took him out with three or four slugs from the carbine. Butler shot up some beer mugs to keep another Corporal from pulling his pistol, and then Putnam and Arnold came busting in through the rear door and scared hell out of some Officer that rooms there. Putnam shot some holes in his doorjamb after he started to come out to see what was happening. We got the hell out of there as quick as we could." Erickson smiled his thanks at

Bushnell and shrugged his shoulders. "Not much else to say. You guys covered our return as usual and here we are."

Erickson turned to Molly. "Hello. I'm Lieutenant Erickson. This is Sergeant Bushnell. Have you been introduced to these other characters yet?"

"No. It all happened so fast; we just ran. Oh! I did get the name of that one," pointing at Durkee, "He fell over me on the road and told me his name after we hid in the trees." Durkee nodded his head in agreement. "How do you make the light in the sky?" she asked of Erickson.

"It's called a flare. We shot it up there," Durkee said, putting his arm around her shoulder. He guided her the rest of the way into the camp and the clearing. "I'll tell you all about it. Just stay close to me."

As the entire group moved around the campfire, Erickson called over to Corporal Porter, "Fire another flare. See what those bastards are doing down there." He felt vulnerable to a sneak attack in the dark.

Turning to Putnam, he asked: "Did you find Hale down there?"

"No. Arnold and I were only able to scout around the edges of the Dragoon camp. They've got a pretty big set-up there, with permanent wood huts and a lot of gear. Overheard a few conversations that had to do with their attack on us this morning. They were ordered to capture some of us for questioning, but got the hell scared out of them, instead, when Russell opened up with the machine gun. They thought there were hundreds of us hidden in the trees."

"Did they say anything about capturing Hale?"

"No, Sir. In fact, I heard some dude named Ramsey berating the hell out of them for not capturing anybody and for losing their man Hale and two others. He was also all over them for being so fearful of our weapons and us. But, the Dragoons couldn't stop talking about our weapons and the fact that they didn't have to be reloaded. Ramsey said the Captain, a guy named Morgan, was very upset with them as soldiers. I don't think they'll be back up here for awhile."

"You know these people he's talking about, Molly?" Erickson asked.

"Yes. Captain Morgan is the troop leader. He lives at the tavern. So does Lieutenant Browne. The Ramsey he speaks of is Sergeant Ramsey. There used to be another Sergeant named Cilly, but they buried him this morning before they left camp."

"What happened to him?"

"Why, you should know that! One of you Rebels shot him."

Erickson counted on his fingers. "That makes five by my count. Corporal Hale, and Henrauther and Barrow here this morning, Corporal, what's his name, MacKenzie, at the tavern, and apparently the Sergeant at the pond. Two Corporals and a Sergeant – how many non-coms do they have, Molly?"

"Non-coms?"

"Yes, non-commissioned officers. Uh, Corporals and Sergeants."

"Oh, I know what you ask. There's Sergeant Ramsey, Corporal McDougall, Corporal MacKenzie – no, he's dead – and Corporal Thacker, who took Corporal Hale's place. That is all."

"Did you hear any talk about them capturing one of our men? His name is Hale."

"The only Hale I knew was Corporal Hale. I heard no mention of capturing any of your men."

"That's right, Lieutenant," said Russell. "Remember, the keeper down at the tavern asked Corporal MacKenzie the same thing about how many they captured this morning. MacKenzie told him there were none."

Erickson shook his head. "If *they* haven't got Hale, where the hell is he? He must be down there someplace; he's sure not up here. By the way, Sullivan, what was your impression when you got down there?" Erickson wanted his history expert's opinion on the situation.

"A classic text-book scene. Everything was just as you would expect it, if this were the second half of the 18th Century. And that seems to be the Century we're in, since the keeper told us it was 1776."

Sullivan's pronouncement set off an immediate buzz around the campfire, but Erickson quickly noted that the men were surprisingly subdued at the revelation – more relieved it seemed at finally knowing what year it really was, than concerned over the fact that they were in another century. Obviously, the encounters with the Dragoons had changed their perceptions of reality, he noted wryly. In that instant, he realized his had, too. *Maybe, just maybe,* he thought, *that's going to save us in the end.*

"Well, that's about all there is, for now," he said, cutting off the inevitable questions and concerns over the date. Time now to let it sink in for a bit, let them absorb it. He knew now they could be trusted not to panic. Options could be pursued after they'd had time to mull the reality over in their minds. Purposefully turning his attention to Molly, he asked, "Well, young lady, have you had any supper?"

"I have, sir. But, please, tell me. Who are you? Where do you come from? How are you able to see into the future?"

"That's a lot of questions."

"I have more, when you answer those."

Erickson smiled amid subdued laughter around the fire. "I'll start then, with a question of my own. What you mean by 'see into the future'?"

"That man there," she said, pointing at Sullivan, "said things at the tavern that were all about the future. The way he talked, they had already happened."

"Well, Sullivan is an expert in history," replied Erickson. "What he tells you will be true."

"But how does he do it?" she pressed for an answer. At that moment, Durkee shifted position on the ground and Molly, who had been leaning on him, fell sideways into his arms. Hoots, whistles and a lot of 'atta-boy, Durkee' comments came flooding across the fire at him. Molly only smiled. Durkee, with complete aplomb, merely adjusted his position to make the two of them more comfortable – while still holding her closely. Turning his face to hers, he preempted Erickson. "We're all from another time and place; 1976, in fact. We're not sure how we got here and I guess most of us still don't quite believe it. But, now that you're here, I think it's going to be a lot easier."

More hoots and whistles greeted that remark.

"We live in a time," he went on, "when this country is called the United States of America and is the most powerful country in the world. Our population is over 250 million and we're spread out from the Atlantic to the Pacific oceans; about 3,000 miles from coast to coast."

"I know of the Atlantic Ocean, but have only heard about the other one."

"The Pacific? It's even bigger than the Atlantic, by many times. It's way off to the west of us. And, everywhere in-between, there are big, big cities all connected by six and eight-lane highways. New York – you know about New York, don't you? Well, in our time it's a huge metropolitan city of about 13 million people. In other words, there are about four times as many people in the New York of our time as there are in all the colonies of your time."

Molly looked at him and didn't know whether to believe him or not. But, Durkee went on.

"Where the people of your time have horses and wagons to carry them around, we have self-powered cars, trucks and ships." He decided not to mention trains and planes, or how fast each of the vehicles could go. That would come later.

Molly poked him and tried to get away. "You're not telling me the truth! You make fun of me."

Erickson leaned over. "No, Molly, it's true. I can imagine how hard it is for you to understand and believe him; but believe me, he's telling you the truth. When it's daylight, Durkee will show you some of the special vehicles we have that are parked over there in the trees. That may help convince you. But please believe him, he's describing the kind of things that exist where we live, two hundred years from now."

Molly resettled herself next to Durkee. He reached out without the others noticing and quietly took her hand in his. "It's a wonderful world we live in," he went on. "We have bright lights that don't require candles. There are large numbers of huge shops called stores that are built together in groups called shopping malls. And, we have small machines called telephones that let us talk with others over long distances."

Durkee could see from the look on Molly's face that she didn't believe him, but was trying. "You said you had more questions. Would you like me to answer some more?"

Saying nothing, she stood up, looking around the fire at the faces of the men seated on the ground. The crackling fire, while small, danced a glow of warmth off the men and the rifles many of them held between their legs.

"You are soldiers," she said. "Do you come to help us win our independence? Is that why you're here?"

Durkee looked at her. "We don't know why we're here. If we can help, we may. That's up to the Lieutenant. Come, sit down again."

"All this excitement has made me tired."

"Durkee," said Erickson, "find Molly a comfortable place to sleep. And remember, the night has a thousand eyes!"

Durkee blushed. He started to stammer a response, but thought better of it, then got up and held out his hand to guide Molly. She smiled at him as they walked away from the firelight to find her a sleeping bag and a tent for the night.

Far above her, the flare ordered by Erickson burst over the night sky.

As they all watched it slowly descend, Private Lewis edged over to Bushnell and Erickson. "Lieutenant," he said in a voice sure to be heard by all, "why do we have to be in such a hurry to get back to 1976? I mean, *why can't* we take advantage of our mobility and firepower and help the revolution?" He'd thought about it long enough and couldn't hold it back any longer. In those two simple sentences, Lewis succeeded in electrifying the consciousness of the entire platoon.

If it *was* July 1776, why couldn't they join the revolution? he wondered. "Why fool around with those guys down there," he demanded aloud. "We can wipe them out in short order. We could use a few mortar rounds, or go down in force with the machine gun – hell, Lieutenant, we could even mount it on the jeep and get them all before they knew what was happening!"

Erickson shook his head. He knew it had been bound to come, but had hoped it would be later. "You've seen too many war movies, Lewis," he responded. "For one thing, we haven't got that many shells for the mortar. And, how do you figure to get the jeep off this hill? Certainly not down that trail over there. Be realistic. After you shoot your wad with what we have here – and it's damn little – we'll be left with nothing more than a platoon of very frustrated fighting men."

"What do you mean, Lieutenant?" Lewis's pride was hurt.

"Well, you've been trained to fight with modern weapons. All the tactics you know are based on the use of those weapons. So, what happens when you run out of ammunition for those weapons? What are you going to do then? Beat 'em to death with the rifle butts? You'll never make it out there fighting their kind of war. You'll end up frustrated as hell, trying to do something to change history and instead, have to devote all your time to surviving in a strange environment."

"But, isn't it worth it, to change history for the better?" Butler asked from across the fire.

"What happens then?" Erickson replied. "Does life in the 20th Century turn out better, like we all hope, or does it change in other ways too, for the worse? We've already killed five Redcoats. What chain of history is broken because of that? What happens to other chains, if we kill more?"

"Good god," Sullivan gasped. "If we're all here because our ancestors were either British soldiers, or lived in the Colonies, who's to say we won't be knocking off our own ancestor's? And, if our ancestors get killed, what happens to us?"

Bushnell didn't like that thought. "I guess that all depends on whether the guy had any kids or not before he got killed. If the chain is broken, then maybe the whole future is broken too. But, if the guy already had kids, then that's something else. There's a bunch of guys here who have at least one British soldier as an ancestor, and didn't I heard talk that maybe some of them were with the 16th Dragoons? All of a sudden it bothers me, when you guys start talk about killing those Dragoons down there to help your country!"

"And rightfully so, Sergeant," added Sullivan. "I'll bet McDougall and Thacker here are more than a little concerned ever since Molly mentioned similarly named Corporals with the Dragoons."

Putnam suddenly slapped his hands to his forehead. "Ooohhh noooo!"

Bushnell reached over and grabbed him. "What's the matter? What is it?"

"Hale. I shot a Hale and our Hale's missing. I must have shot Hale's ancestor!" Putnam's face reflected total horror.

Erickson moved quickly to control the situation. "Don't get carried away, Putnam! Or, any of the rest of you, for that matter! Killing off one guy named Hale in the 18th Century doesn't mean you've killed off all the other Hales in the 20th Century! Besides, you don't even know if they were related."

"I'm not so sure about that, Lieutenant," interjected Sullivan. "Seems to me Hale was one of the ones who had an ancestor that served in the 16th."

"You're a big help, Sullivan," Erickson replied disdainfully. "Even if Hale did have a relative in the 16th, how do we know he's the one Putnam shot? Didn't you tell me that the 16th was a Regiment? That's no Regiment down there. There are not enough men. Hale's ancestor could be – hell, probably is – far from here enjoying a romp in the hay at the moment."

Porter came into the firelight from the edge of the campground where he had been watching the falling flare burn itself out. "Couldn't see anything moving down there anywhere, Lieutenant. There is still light coming from the tavern, but I couldn't see anybody go in or out. The Wick house is dark. No sign of the Dragoons, other than fires back at their camp."

"Good. How many men do you have on guard?"

"I've got five. They've been out there since the patrol went down the hill. Not much going on, but they should be relieved anyway."

"You're right. Sergeant Bushnell, set up a rotation; cut it to four guards at a time, two-hour shifts each. Once that's in place, we better get this platoon bedded down. We may need all the sleep we can get."

"So what are we going to do about fighting the Dragoons, Lieutenant?" Russell asked.

Erickson didn't hesitate. "Avoid battle, if we can. Protect ourselves if we have to. But, I think our main concern should be getting back to 1976. There's got to be some way we can do that. If it turns out that we're stuck here, then I'll consider the alternates, including suggestions from you guys. But, we don't know that we *are* stuck here. Hell, we've only been here a day!"

"Excuse me, Lieutenant," Brown interrupted from the other side of the campfire. "But, do you *really think* we can get out of here and back to 1976?" His voice covered the pain in his heel, but as one who had been wounded by the Redcoats, he felt he had a special right to ask the question.

Erickson paused for a moment. "I, none of us for that matter, know enough at the moment about getting back to 1976, to make any decisions whether we can, or can't. Something brought us here, and it seems reasonable to me that that something can take us back. One thing I do know, I don't want us to get attached to this place. Right now, some of you are kinda excited about it. People everywhere dream about going back in time, about seeing things the way they were. But, god, now that it's happened to us, I don't like it that much."

"You mean because of the Dragoons and the fighting?" Brown asked.

"Yes, mostly. But we also face a greater, more terrible foe – the urge to play God."

"Play God? What you mean, Sir?"

"Take medicine, for example. You've been wounded, but you're going to be all right because we know how to treat your foot with the medicine and knowledge of our time. And, that's the point. Anyone of you knows more about basic preventative medicine and cleanliness than most all of the doctors of this time put together. Naturally, if we're forced to stay here, sooner or later you'd be putting your knowledge to use. If they didn't hang you as a charlatan or a witch, then the result would certainly be increasingly healthier people, living longer lives. Right?"

"Right. That's good, isn't it, Lieutenant?" Brown was confused.

"Is it? The increased population growth that would surely go along with such improved health would probably outstrip the capacity of the land to support that many more people. In our time, we can support hundreds of millions of people because of a fully integrated society in which a relatively small number of agri-businesses produce enough food for most everyone to eat well. But, how would *this* 1776 society support large numbers of additional people? Along with the advances in medicine you've given them, you'd have to give them equal advances in machinery, communications, transportation, and all the other basic essentials to match. How you gonna do that? Even if you could; even if you were able to provide a quantum leap to this new nation – the economics of the situation would require that the rest of the world keep up, just so our people would be able to maintain the new standard of living you've given them."

Erickson took a deep breath for emphasis, then continued. "Look, in spite of everything you'd like to believe to the contrary, the whole world we live in *is, and has been,* tied together for a long time. An advance one place has allowed or forced advances to be made elsewhere. All in good order, all in good time, with plenty of time for people to get adjusted and accept it. It's mind-boggling to think of the awesome problems that we could cause playing God. Everything we do has to be questioned in the light of what affect it will have on the world as we know it in 1976."

"What the hell can we do then?" asked Brown.

"Play it cool and take it as it comes. Mind you, our friends in the Dragoon camp don't have the problems we do. They see things differently – we're here, we're Rebels, and it's their job to get us, one way or another. They may yet force us to do things that I don't want to do – and end up changing history in the process. Quite frankly, it scares the hell out of me, and it should you, too."

His comments were met only with the shuffling of feet of those sitting around the fire.

Suddenly Putnam jumped up. Embarrassed over his comments about killing Hale and looking for a way to redeem himself, he called out, "Hey, Lieutenant, I just remembered! I took a couple of flintlock pistols away from the Dragoons at the tavern. Want to see them?"

"Yes," Erickson quickly replied, thankful for the interruption. "Where are they?"

"Right here." Putnam thrust them towards Erickson. "Aren't they beauties?"

Erickson grasped them. Handing one to Sullivan, he moved closer to the fire for more light.

"Careful," cautioned Sullivan, "they're probably loaded."

"Thanks. They're heavier than I expected. Let me see the other for a second."

Getting it back from Sullivan, Erickson compared the two and then handed it back, saying, "I thought so. They look similar, but they're different in length and their fittings on the side. This one has a triangular side plate, while that one has a curved 'S'. This one is longer and that one has a fancier butt cap. Hey, I think I see a name on the lock here. Let's see . . . yeah, looks like 'Tower'!"

Sullivan came over to Erickson's side. "The names usually told where or by whom the weapon was made. Tower probably means the Tower of London. There should be a capital letter up there with the name, you know, A, B, C, etc. that indicates the year the pistol was made."

"I see one. But I can't make it out, looks like it's got some sort of a funny shaped line around it."

"That's the heraldic shield. Different shield designs indicate different periods of time, usually twenty-year periods. The combination of the shield and the letter gives the date."

"Can you figure out this one?"

"No. I'd need a reference book. These pistols look like they've been around for a while, though."

"How long?"

"Not sure. The only thing I can tell you is that they're not officer's pistols. They're not ornate enough. I'd also say that the longer of the two came from the new Corporal, while the shorter is a true Dragoon-type pistol and probably was taken off Corporal McDougall. Seniority and rank have always had their privileges."

Passing the pistols back to Putnam, Erickson told him, "You ought to keep these and take 'em back with you."

"Yes Sir." He said, softly; Putnam wasn't sure they were going to get back.

A few of the men began to move away from the fire and find their tents for the night. "Good idea," said Erickson, taking advantage of their move. "Let's get some sleep."

"Lieutenant, can I see you for a minute?" Sergeant Bushnell was back from posting the guards.

"Sure, what is it?"

"Over here, Sir." Bushnell motioned for Erickson to join him.

"Something up?"

"Yes."

"What?"

"MacKenzie's gone. He may have left the camp."

Erickson stopped walking. "My god! When?"

"Two of the guards said they saw him at his post, even talked to him before the shooting at the tavern got everyone's attention. After it was over, they heard something going down the hill in the trees. They assumed it was MacKenzie going down to help the patrol, but they're not sure – could have been a deer. Anyway, when he didn't show up with the others coming up the trail, they went looking for him. Not good guard practice, but they did it anyway. Couldn't find him anywhere."

"That's two for two, Tom. Wait 'til that gets around the camp. Tell me, is it possible he got captured?"

"That's hard to say, Lieutenant. All I can tell you for sure is that he's not in camp!"

SIXTEEN

Off to Jockey Hollow

Colonel Lester was ready to leave the motor pool by the time Carl arrived at 7 a.m. Treppello walked over and opened the door of the brown pickup in which Lester sat waiting, pulled himself up into the cab and settled onto the partially ripped passenger seat.

"I see you've got the measurement gear in the back already," he said, as a greeting. "That was quick."

"I called some friends last night after you left. Told them what I needed. It was ready when I arrived this morning."

"I'm impressed. They get this unmarked pickup for you, too?"

"Of course."

"Thought so." Treppello wasn't being sarcastic; he said in recognition of the power Lester had demonstrated. "What's back there, anyway?"

"Oh, some sensors and meters. There are also some poles, some rolls of copper screen, some copper wire, a roll of coaxial cable and a multi-channel recorder. I'll tell you about it when we set it up. Did you have a big breakfast?"

"Yes, Sir."

"Good. So did I. We can get some miles behind us before we have to eat again."

"What route are we taking to get there?"

"First to Baltimore, then up to Philadelphia. From there, we'll go over to Trenton and New Brunswick. I plan to avoid Newark by taking the back roads from there to Morristown. Jockey Hollow's not far after that."

"Sounds like a long drive."

"It's about 230 miles. It'll take the better part of the day to get there, but there's no rush. If we get the equipment set up tonight, we can start measuring and recording in the morning."

"In the morning? Are we going to spend the night up there in that campground?" Carl had assumed there was a soft bed in a motel in his future.

"Sure. But, once the equipment is in place, it will run on its own. If anything happens while we're asleep, the recorder will catch it for us."

"I hope we have sleeping bags and a tent with us?"

"Yep. In with all the other stuff – along with some packaged food and a flashlight or two. Getting approvals for meals and lodging would have not only delayed our trip, but also revealed what we're going to do to prying eyes. Relax. Look at it as a Government-paid outing."

Treppello wasn't keen on camping, but what the hell, since it would only be for one night – why not?

*　　*　　*

Five hours later, they arrived at their destination.

Carl marveled at the lush greenery and huge trees which dominated the rural area west of Morristown. Jockey Hollow itself was even more magnificent, and he eagerly looked for the place where Erickson's platoon had been run off by the MP Major and then for the campground where they sought refuge.

Lester had said little during the entire trip, concentrating instead on driving on one road and then another in the long drive.

Now, after reaching the campground, he got out, stretched and asked Carl if he was hungry.

"The Mess Sergeant gave me some sandwiches and a couple of Cokes for the drive," he said. "Since we've been doing nothing but sitting on our asses for the last five hours, I think that ought to be enough until dinner." Carl was used to eating more than that for lunch, but didn't say anything.

They sat at a table across from each other, but said little as they ate. After they finished, Lester said, "You take care of the tent, sleeping bags and other stuff. I'll get the measurement gear out and placed where it goes. By the time you get done setting up camp, I'll be ready for your help with the other."

Carl nodded and headed for the green outhouse first. Coming back through the campground he recognized some features mentioned in Erickson's testimony, but couldn't place others. It was a pleasant campground and he felt comfortable in its surroundings. As he removed the tent and other items from the back of the truck, he couldn't help trying to put himself in Erickson's shoes, wondering what it must have been like then.

Lester had already moved the sensors and meters into position and was returning for the poles and wire by the time Carl finished setting up the tent. When he finished, he walked over to join Lester.

"What do you want me to do?" he asked. "I'm ready to help."

"We've got to drill some holes in the ground. Take the gas-powered auger from under the tarp in the back of the truck and drill a hole wherever I've placed a sensor. You don't have to worry about being too precise. Just fire it up and drill a hole for each of the three sensors. By the time you're done, I'll have the poles where I want them and you can drill holes for them, too."

Treppello hadn't used a gas-powered auger since he was a kid helping his father plant trees at their home near Chicago. Back then, he remembered, the auger had easily dug a four-foot deep hole in a matter of minutes.

Lester had placed a sensor unit in each corner of a large triangular pattern around the camp, generally coinciding with the lines Treppello had drawn on the map back at Fort McNair. Each unit consisted of a sensor, enclosed in a pointed copper tube about three inches in diameter and twelve inches long, which was connected by a thin, black, six foot coaxial cable to a rectangular olive drab box containing the measurement meter.

Picking up one of the hefty sensors, Treppello called out, "What are these things, Colonel?"

"The original models were developed to measure energy created by underground nuclear tests, but later they were modified to measure the energy unleashed during a earthquake."

"Why would the Army be interested in measuring earthquakes?"

"They weren't. Tried to use them in 'Nam to see who was digging tunnels below. Great idea; wrong conclusion. They didn't work, so they were sent from one post to another until they ended up at McNair. They've been there since the days when I worked at the PRA. I think they're the only ones of their kind around. I knew they were there and when we decided to come up here, I knew exactly how I would use them."

"How do they work?"

"We shove the pointed tube in the hole you're going to dig and then pack it tight with dirt. Each unit is designed to sense telluric energy, which is measured by the meter."

"Telluric energy?"

"It's a natural electric current that Geologists discovered flowing near the earth's surface – they measure the amount and strength of it by using volt and amp meters.

"What are the poles and the screen for?"

"We'll plant the poles near the sensors and suspend sections of the copper screen between them, about six feet off the ground. That way there'll be a sensor at each of the three Node corners of your triangle, with sections of screen running between. We'll measure the telluric energy in the ground at the corners with the buried sensors. At the same time, we'll measure any energy flowing through the screens above the ground by hooking them up to separate meters. All of the measurements from each meter will be fed to the recorder. There's nothing really complicated about it. When we get it all set up, it's going to be like a giant lie detector with cables snaking around on the ground and in the air. It really shouldn't take us very long to get it all assembled and operating, maybe only a couple of hours."

Treppello fired up the gas-powered auger and began digging the holes for the sensors and poles. As he finished with each sensor hole, Lester inserted a tube, carefully packing the dirt to avoid crimping the thin cable leading to the meter. When he was finished burying all the sensors, he straightened the cables to the meters before connecting the meters to the multi-channel recorder.

Treppello helped him bury the poles, one at each corner from which they draped the copper screen. If it drooped too much, they added another pole in the middle. Each of the long sections of screen was connected by a length of copper wire to a separate meter. Each meter was then attached to the multi-channel recorder.

"Now, we've got it," said Lester when they finished. "Six meters hooked up to six channels ready to record any energy flowing at and between those three points above and below the ground. If there's anything going on around here, we're going to see it there," he said, pointing at the recorder with its pens ready to record the energy flow.

He started to press the switch to turn the recorder on when Treppello tapped his shoulder and asked, "Don't you have to plug it in first?"

"Nope. Doesn't need to be plugged in, Captain. This baby is powered by an internal, eighteen hour, rechargeable, lithium battery pack. That's why it's so heavy and you grunted so much moving it from the truck to this picnic table. Eighteen hours should be more than enough for what we want to do here."

Treppello nodded and watched as Lester turned the machine on and the pens began to gently scribble their marks on the moving paper. The Telluric energy was very low, with little energy to be recorded. Everything was normal.

They watched the machine doing its job for a while, Treppello expecting something to happen at any moment, while Lester remained confident that nothing would happen at all. As the late afternoon turned into the cool of the evening, they ate and began to settle in for the night. Treppello felt that one or both should try to stay awake to observe anything unusual, but Lester ruled it out as foolish and tiresome. Eventually they both got into the tent and, finding the sleeping bags and air mattresses comfortable, fell off to sleep.

*   *   *

The morning air felt cool as Treppello peered through the opening of the tent. He decided that it must be time to get up. The sun was already working its way over the hill to the east of the camp and his bladder was full. Yes, it was time to move his body, and do it now.

Orienting himself to his surroundings as he stood up outside the tent, he looked around to find the nearest outhouse, but was stopped by the sound of the squirrels squabbling in the branches of the tree above his head. Hissing and grunting at each other, the two quickly vanished into the foliage as one chased the other.

Movement behind him caught his attention as Lester, now awake too, crawled from the tent.

"Good morning, Sir. Sleep well?" Treppello said cheerily.

"Absolutely. It must have been the fresh air. You?"

"Just fine, Sir. Was getting ready to head to the latrine when I heard some squirrels up the tree."

"The latrines are still here, then?" Lester asked, humorously.

"Yes Sir. Right over there." He pointed at the green outhouses near the edge of the camp. "Excuse me, Colonel, I've gotta go." Treppello trotted off to relieve himself.

Lester soon followed.

Having taken care of their immediate needs, they both headed to the table where the recorder was set up. They watched in passive fascination as the pens continued their rather benign oscillations, recording the innocent energy moving through the meters. Lester lifted the cover from the tray at the end of the recorder and began to unroll the paper containing the pen markings of the recorded energy flow.

"What do you see, Colonel?"

"The energy levels look pretty low from what I see so far. When I get it all unrolled we'll see if they've been higher."

Lester didn't really expect to see any significant differences in the levels. As he continued to unroll the paper on the top of the concrete picnic table, though, he was jolted to see that the meters attached to the screen sections had gone wild about an hour ago, at 6 a.m.!

"My god," he exclaimed. "Look at that! What happened there? Did something run through the camp and vibrate the screens?"

Carl looked at the lines. "If something ran across this campground with that much force, we'd have heard it. It had to be something else! Unroll the paper some more and let's see what happened during the night."

"OK," replied Lester, somewhat dejectedly, concerned at what they might find.

What they found was that energy levels for all meters been stable up to midnight, when telluric energy began increasing at a steady but significant rate each hour until just before 4 a.m. Then it suddenly reversed itself and a negative flow was recorded. About ten minutes later, the energy turned positive again, returning to a normal, low-level flow.

Then, a spectacular burst of telluric energy occurred just before 6 a.m.! The meters attached to the buried sensors had sent the pens careening violently from side to side.

Moments later the telluric energy ceased and the pens for the screen sections had begun recording a violent pace of energy flowing around the edge of the campground. The screen meters were pegged at maximum levels for long minutes until it abruptly stopped.

Lester looked intently at the recording, then walked over to the nearest screen section to inspect it for damage.

Treppello quickly followed. "What do you see?" he asked.

"Nothing. It's amazing, there's no damage at all! That level of energy should have melted this screen into a big blob of copper. I don't understand it. I don't understand this at all." Lester shook his head as he spoke, fingering the screen and noting how cool it was to the touch.

They inspected each of the other screens, as well, but found nothing. Nor did they find any damage to any of the meters or their connecting wires or cables.

Lester was perplexed. "It just doesn't fit. The levels of energy were so high and so abrupt in their actions, that we should have seen a catastrophic failure of the entire system – sensors, meters and wire. Yet, it worked perfectly. It's absolutely amazing."

"Maybe we're not dealing with normal kinds of energy."

"What do you mean?"

"I mean, we've been measuring volts and amps, but does that tell the whole story about the energy itself? We've proved some kind of powerful energy exists here and it seems to be a pretty unusual type of energy. Maybe it's time to take the other circumstances into consideration."

Lester started to reply, but Carl went on. "I know you don't want to hear this, Colonel, but maybe this unusual energy is just the kind it takes to let people see or be part of the past. An energy that we can't begin to understand or explain at this time."

"Come on, Carl, let's not get started on that again," Lester responded, caustically. "Those types of occurrences are interesting to contemplate, but I don't believe it happened here to Erickson."

"What do those recorded squiggles mean, then?"

"It means that there were some very high levels of energy in this campground this morning. Levels of energy that somehow didn't burn up our equipment."

"Damnit, Colonel!"

"What!?"

"Sorry. But, you know we came here to find out if what the PRA said about the energy here was true. I think we've done that!"

"It doesn't prove the energy we recorded was responsible in any way for Erickson going AWOL with his men, or that Erickson went back in time from here. No sirée. It doesn't prove that one bit!" Lester thumped the top of the picnic table with his index finger as he spoke.

Treppello felt defeated. There was no sense in trying to convert his boss. He gave Lester a half smile and slowly walked to the tent, where he started letting the air out of the mattress and breaking camp.

Neither spoke much as they disassembled the sensing and recording system and repacked it with the rest of their gear in the back of the truck. They forgot about breakfast until they were well on their way back to Washington, and by then it was time for lunch. They had a hamburger and fries at a roadside fast-food outlet.

It was still early in the afternoon when they reached the entrance to the motor pool and Lester dropped Treppello off to go his own way for the rest of the day. As they started to part, Lester held the Captain by the arm for a moment.

"I want you to think about our job here, Carl. It's important to the Army and General Xetrel, and it's important to me, that we do it right. I want you *with* me, but if your personal beliefs about this situation are going to get in our way, then I want you to drop out – on your own. Don't force me to take you out; that would only hurt me and your career."

Treppello had been expecting it, no mater how brief and blunt it was presented.

"Thanks, Colonel," he replied. "A lot of Officers would have just canned me this morning. I've thought about it all the way back. I'll be in your office first thing tomorrow, ready and willing to support you fully."

Lester nodded, then drove the truck into the motor pool area. There he gave a high sign to the two soldiers waiting nearby. They promptly came over and began unloading the gear. He remained behind the steering wheel and mulled over the question that had been nagging him since yesterday – why had he been manipulated into going to Jockey Hollow? He certainly hadn't personally seen or found anything up there that would have warranted the trip, in spite of the fact that he now had some spectacular recordings.

No, someone had wanted him to be there for another reason and he was determined to find out why.

*   *   *

Late that evening, Admiral Funston leaned back in the green leather easy chair in his den and opened the envelope just delivered to him by a messenger.

A half-hour later, he put the contents down, pleased with the person he had assigned to watch Lester and his activities.

The readings that Lester had recorded certainly verified what he had anticipated. Now, he knew he could move forward with the next step in his plan.

By god, he *was* going to pull it off!

SEVENTEEN

Sunday Morning

Private Lee tossed and turned in his sleeping bag, dreaming of rivers, streams and rain. His lower abdomen ached, sending intermittent jabs of pain down his leg from time to time. Dully, slowly, he awakened and sat up, cold sweat over most of his body. He rubbed the cotton-taste off his teeth with the tip of his tongue, smacked his lips several times and finally decided that he couldn't hold it any longer. Crawling out of the sleeping bag, he eased himself out of the end of the tent and looked around for a convenient spot to relieve himself.

Stumbling over a tree root as he started to move, he tried to catch his balance and instead banged his left knee on the edge of a concrete-topped picnic table.

"Damn!" he muttered to himself as he instinctively stopped and rubbed the knee. Looking up, he saw the distinctive shape of an outhouse in the distance. The pain of a full bladder being greater than the pain in his knee, he hobbled across the park to the hinged door, flung it open and stepped inside. A wave of relief passed over his body as he emptied his bladder into the smelly pit.

Zipping up his pants as he returned to his tent, Lee stopped only long enough to take a short drink of water from one of the faucets. Somewhere high overhead a jet passed in the darkness.

Wiggling back into his tent and the sleeping bag, he curled up in the pre-natal position and was soon dreaming.

*   *   *

Dawn broke early over the campground and Dobbs soon had his men up, making breakfast. Concerned there could be more fighting today, he ordered up a hearty meal that could sustain the men past lunch, if need be.

The smell of coffee wafted through the camp and like a finger beckoning, drew men towards the kitchen unit. Russell sauntered up, pushing his fatigue blouse into his yet-to-be zipped, pants. Yawning loudly, he reached out for a coffee cup. Dobbs looked at him questioningly. "Did you get some water for me?"

"Huh?"

"Last night, at the pond; you were gonna get some water so I could check it out to see if we could use it."

"Oh, yeah. Gimme some coffee, let me wake up." Russell held out his cup. Dobbs poured from the large aluminum pot. Russell smelled, then sipped. "Yeeck! Is this the best you can do?"

"With what I have to work with – yes. You remember the old camping story; if you think you can do better, be my guest!"

"No thanks. I remember that story – everybody ended up eating cow shit."

"Right – you got the message. You awake now?"

"Yeah. Let's see . . . I filled a canteen with water and then gave it to somebody to bring back with us. Uh, told 'em not to drink from it. Lee! Lee's the one who has it unless he drank it all last night."

"Drank what last night?" Bushnell wondered aloud as he walked up to the kitchen unit.

"Water, Sarge. Russell was telling me about the canteen of water he got from the pond last night. Lee carried it back."

"Oh, I get the picture. Lee may or may not have the canteen, and if he does have it, it may be empty by now. Right?"

"Right!" Russell and Dobbs chorused the answer.

"Why don't we ask him?" Bushnell nodded towards the direction of the tents. Lee was walking towards them.

"Hey, Lee!" shouted Russell. "You still got that canteen we gave you last night?"

Lee rubbed his eyes, then his left knee as he screwed his still sleepy eyes into a quizzical look. "Yeah, its back at the tent. But why do you need it?"

"To check the water, of course, dummy!" Russell answered disdainfully. "Dobbs is running low and we gotta find out if the pond water is good enough to drink and cook with."

"Why? Can't we just use the faucets?"

"What faucets? We ain't got any faucets, remember?"

"Sure we do, I got a drink from one last night."

Russell and the others immediately twisted around, frantically looking for the faucet. They didn't see it.

Russell turned angrily back to Lee. "Smart-ass kid! Whatcha doin', playing kid games, again?"

"No! I did use one! I had to piss, got up, and used the outhouse. On the way back, I got a drink from one of the faucets."

"Bullshit, little man." Russell reached out to grab him. "Show me an outhouse; show me a water faucet; any water faucet!"

Breaking Russell's grasp, Lee squealed as he twisted his knee. "Wait a minute! Wait a minute!" he cried, throwing up his hands in defense. "I ran into one of the picnic tables with my knee. Still hurts like crazy. Look!" Dropping his pants, Lee pointed to and held the injured knee for them to see. "See. See. I told you so!"

Russell bent over to take a closer look at the leg, then quickly backed away. "For Christ's sake, Lee, don't you bathe? You stink like you've been living in those shorts for a week!"

"I have been! So, have you. I bet you stink too, Corporal!"

Russell cocked his arm and fist, but Bushnell caught him. "OK, you two. Knock it off, here comes the Lieutenant."

Erickson was obviously in a good mood. "Good morning all. This is going to be a great day!"

Looking at the scowling Russell, Erickson exclaimed, "A great day, Corporal. A great day!"

"Not easy, with the likes of him around." Russell pointed at Lee, who was pulling up his pants.

Still jovial, Erickson turned to Lee, looked and then quizzically raised an eyebrow.

"I was showing them the bruises on my knee, Lieutenant. I ran into one of the picnic tables last night."

"Picnic table? – Where? – When? – Show me!"

Lee started to drop his pants again, but Erickson stopped him. "Not the bruises, Lee. The table!"

"It's not there now, Sir."

Erickson quickly scanned the park, searching for a table. "How do you know it was a table you ran into?"

"I felt it with my hand. I ran into it and when I stopped to rub my knee, I put my hand on to it, to hold myself up."

"What time was that?"

"Don't know, Lieutenant. It was dark. I had to pee, so I got up. Ran into the table when I stumbled over a tree root or something right outside my tent."

Erickson looked at Lee, wondering.

"Tell him the rest of it, Lee," Bushnell ordered.

"There's more?" asked Erickson.

"Yep. Tell him, Lee."

"I used one of the outhouses and took a drink from one of the faucets on my way back to the tent. You've *gotta* believe me, Lieutenant, I really did!"

"I *want* to believe you, Lee. If what you say is true, we may have a way out of here!"

Putnam had joined them, at first listening without comment. No longer able to contain himself, though, he burst forth. "Damnit, Lieutenant, he's the biggest exaggerator in the platoon! In my book, he's nothing but a goddamn liar."

Looking at the crowd of men now gathered around them, Erickson nodded to Dobbs. "Feed 'em, will you Corporal? Sergeant Bushnell and I can talk to Lee over in the clearing. When it's ready, send some chow over to us."

With his hand on Lee's shoulder, Erickson guided him away from the kitchen unit. Bushnell followed as they walked towards the clearing.

"Where, exactly, did you run into the table?" asked Erickson.

"Right over there, next to my tent," Lee replied, pointing and leading the way. All three inspected the ground.

"Nothing here but seedlings, and damn few of them, Lieutenant," said Bushnell. "I sure as hell don't see any big tree roots, or anything else that Lee could have fallen over." Bushnell was as skeptical of Lee as were Russell and Putnam.

Erickson got down on his haunches and put his hand to the ground. Feeling around in the dirt, he asked, "You sure you were here when you fell into the table?"

"Yes, Sir. Right around here."

"Look, Lieutenant," said Bushnell, "this is a wild goose chase. There's nothing here; no roots, no table, nothing."

"That's true, Sergeant," said Erickson, still looking at the ground for some sort of evidence. "But, if it were 1976, wouldn't these little seedlings have grown into huge trees with huge roots above the ground? Two hundred years would do that to trees, wouldn't it?"

"Yes, but I don't get the point."

"The point is, Sergeant, if what Lee says is true, sometime before light this morning, he walked across this campground in 1976! Lee may have literally stumbled onto our way out of here!"

Lee grinned at the Lieutenant. Someone believed him.

"Come on, Lee," urged Erickson. "You've got to figure out the time you got up. It may be very important."

"I'm don't know, Lieutenant. I didn't look at my watch. I just don't know."

"Well, was the moon still up?"

"I don't remember seeing the moon."

"How about any stars. Did you see any of the constellations?"

Lee was getting exasperated. "Sir, there were tree branches over my head and all around me. I couldn't have seen any stars, without moving over to a clearing."

"OK, Lee, relax. Don't get up tight. Dobbs is bringing over some chow right now. Take yours and go find a quiet place to sit down. Try to remember everything you can and how it happened. We'll talk later."

"OK, Lieutenant."

Dobbs arrived and passed out the metal food trays. Lee took his and looked for a place to sit away from them, leaving Erickson with Dobbs and Bushnell.

Russell and Putnam, seeing Lee leave, started over to join the group. Erickson saw them and shouted to them, "Get Porter, we may as well have morning staff while we're at it."

Russell gave a high sign, turned and went to find Porter.

"You don't believe Lee, do you Lieutenant?" Putnam asked.

"I don't know yet. But, I'm not going to dismiss it out of hand. There may be something to it, and if so, it may hold the key to our getting out of here. Let's wait for the others. We can discuss it when we're all here."

Erickson and Bushnell eased themselves into sitting positions on the ground and began to eat. Having already eaten, Dobbs and Putnam watched in a silence interrupted only by the sound of forks clinking and scrapping on the metal trays. As Erickson finished and was downing the last of Dobbs's coffee, Russell appeared with Porter.

"Morning, Porter, good to see you," said Erickson.

"Morning, Lieutenant. We all getting together?"

"Right. Have you all eaten?" he asked, looking around the group. Everybody nodded their heads.

"Good. All right, here's the deal. Lee may have actually been in 1976 at one time during the night while the rest of us were sleeping. He doesn't know how it happened, but he's certain he hurt his knee on one of the picnic tables when he got up to use an outhouse. He also says he took a drink from a faucet."

Holding up his hand to silence Putnam before he could interrupt, Erickson went on. "I don't know what happened, but if it happened once, it can happen again. And, if it does, I want to be ready. So, we're going to take some time and do some planning this morning around two issues. How do we get ourselves organized to leave on a moments notice and, if that opportunity comes, what do we do about Hale and MacKenzie?"

"MacKenzie?" Porter screwed his face into a question mark. "What the hell happened to MacKenzie?"

Bushnell answered for Erickson. "We think MacKenzie left the camp last night, maybe to go see what the shooting was about. A couple of the guards think they heard him going down the hill, but they're not sure. Looked for him last night, still can't find him this morning."

"My god," exclaimed Putnam, "That's two for two, now," then said no more as the stern-faced Erickson stared at him.

"Don't get carried away, Corporal." Erickson stated softly. "It may be easy to conclude we're killing off our ancestor's, but I find that hard to accept. I know the platoon has talked about that subject a lot, but from my standpoint, it's going to have to be put into the context of the rest of our problems, and we've got a pot full of *them* already!"

"Hey!" Dobbs exclaimed, pointing. "Would you look at that? There's Durkee and Molly, coming out of the same tent." Everyone looked in the direction Dobbs was pointing. "Ah, youth," he added, "what a sly fox he is."

Putnam didn't think it was so sly and said so in his own jealous way, "I think I'll kill him!"

Dobbs looked at him. "For sleeping with the girl?"

"No. For letting us see that he did."

Everyone laughed.

The tension broken, Erickson waited for the laughter to subside before getting back to the business at hand.

"It just occurred to me," he said, "we rotated guards all night. Did any of them see anything unusual, use an outhouse, or run into a picnic table?"

"Nobody reported anything of that sort when I made my rounds this morning," Bushnell replied.

"How many guards have you posted?"

"Still four. I can put more out if you want."

"Not right now. Maybe later. Right now, let's continue to look at our options. Give me your ideas."

Across the campground at the kitchen unit, Durkee looked at Erickson and the non-coms as they huddled together, seated on the ground.

"What's going on over there?" he asked Sullivan, standing close by. Sullivan repeated the story about Lee running into the picnic table. Knowing Lee as they did, they both laughed, while Molly stood by, puzzled.

Looking at her, Durkee couldn't help himself from leaning over and kissing her on the neck, as he handed her a tray for breakfast. "I'm going to take you back with me. You know that, don't you?"

Molly looked as warm and appealing in the morning light as she had the night before. "Part of me would like that," she said, "but another part of me would be terribly afraid. How would I learn to live in your world?"

"You'd do just fine, honey. You'd do just fine." Durkee put his arm around her and squeezed her to his side. Seeing the others at the kitchen unit smiling at them, the two separated and sat down on the ground to eat their breakfast.

*　　*　　*

Lee finished his breakfast, got up and walked over to where Erickson and the others were carrying on their discussions. "I'm sorry, Lieutenant," he said, interrupting them. "I've tried and tried, but I can't remember what time it was when I got up." He looked as if he might cry any moment.

"OK, Lee," said Erickson, "if you come up with anything later, holler. In the meantime, go on back to your tent and relax."

As Lee started to walk off, Bushnell called after him. "If you still have the canteen that Russell gave you last night, take it over to Dobbs's place. He'll check the water when he's done here."

Lee waved an acknowledgement and set off to bring the canteen to the kitchen unit.

Bushnell, Erickson and the four Corporals silently watched Lee depart. "It's nice to know he still has it," sneered Putnam. "Wouldn't want Russell to have to go and get some more on his own."

"Your turn, next time, buddy," Russell responded.

"OK. Let's get back to it," said Erickson, determined to get a consensus going. "So far we've decided to rotate duty during the night so that one of the six of us will always be watching for signs that 1976 has returned. Secondly, nobody wants to leave unless Hale and MacKenzie are with us, if they're still alive." Looking at Putnam, Erickson continued. "Of course, that brings us to the ultimate question: are they Morgan's captives who we might get back – or are they gone forever, because we're fought and killed their ancestors, breaking some descendant trail between the past and the future?"

"There's a related question that hasn't been answered," Bushnell added.

"Yes," agreed Erickson. "How much risk does the rest of the platoon face, if we're forced to stay? Where's Sullivan? Maybe he can help us with that one." Even as he asked, Erickson spied him near the kitchen unit. He called to him across the campground. "Join us, I need your help."

Sullivan ran over. "Yes, Sir?"

"You told me yesterday that Hale had an ancestor in the 16th. Are there any others you know of?"

"Yes."

"Who are they?"

"There's Thacker, MacKenzie and me. Maybe McDougall. I'll have to check him out, though."

"How do *you feel* about our fighting the Dragoons?"

"Creepy."

"Succinct answer. OK, thanks." Sullivan left and Erickson went on.

"Now I know what it's like to be between a rock and a hard spot. We've got to prepare ourselves against the attack the Dragoon's are no doubt planning against us right now. At the same time, we've got to be concerned with those of us who have ancestors down there and what might happen in the process of protecting ourselves. It may be the best solution, for both reasons, is to leave. Sergeant Bushnell, I want you to take the jeep and go scout the area to the north of us. The trees are thinner there and it looks like we could probably get the trucks through if we were forced to. Putnam, I want you to get a few men and organize a search for Hale and MacKenzie."

"How far are you willing to let us look?" he asked.

"Everywhere they might logically be. That includes the Dragoon camp, as long as you don't get yourself captured in the process. The sooner Hale and MacKenzie are back with us, the sooner we can take advantage of what happened to Lee, if it happens again."

"Then you believe him?" Bushnell asked.

Erickson looked at each man in the group, then back at Bushnell. "I've got to, Sergeant. We've all got to!"

Durkee and Molly had finished their breakfast. Looking at the trucks parked nearby, Molly asked, "Are those the vehicles you talked about last night?"

"Yes. The four large ones are called trucks, and the little one is called a jeep. The trucks are used for moving people and equipment and the jeep is used more for personal transportation. It carries four or five people at once. Would you like me to show them to you?"

"Yes. But, they look so odd. Where do the horses or mules go?"

"They don't use any. Let me show you." Durkee lifted the hood of the jeep. "That funny looking metal thing in there is called a motor. Depending on its size, it performs the work of 80 to 200 horses."

"How does it do that?" she asked in awe.

"The motor is powered by exploding gasoline, making parts called pistons go up and down. This thing here – it's called a spark plug – ignites the gasoline and the explosion forces the piston down, turning a flywheel. It causes the wheels in back to turn, making the jeep move."

"Oh." Molly didn't understand a word he'd said.

"Would you like to sit in it?"

"Can I?"

"Sure, let me help you." Durkee helped her into the driver's seat of the jeep, then reached past her to set the hand brake. She looked at everything, but kept her hands folded in her lap.

"Push the clutch in. That's it right there. Put your left foot on that pedal and push it to the floor." Molly did as she was told. "Now, take that stick there – it's called a gear shift, and move it slightly forward. That's it. Now move it back and forth from side to side. Easy, isn't it? The jeep is now in neutral and we can start it."

"Start it?"

"Yes. There's the key. Turn it all the way to the right and hold it for a second or two."

Again, Molly did as she was told. The jeep's motor tried to start, caught, coughed, and then, fighting against the starter motor, died. Molly eyes were wide open, looking for a way out of the jeep, but Durkee blocked the only easy escape route.

"Try it again, this time let go of the key right away."

Game for anything he told her, Molly turned the key again and this time the engine caught and started, very roughly. Not having been run for a while, the engine coughed and sputtered, but eventually settled down and ran smoothly.

"Ready to go?" asked Bushnell, coming up unseen. He was ready to leave on the scouting trip. Swinging into the front passenger seat, he looked at Molly and said, "Well? Let's do it."

Molly's answer was to jump out of the jeep, pushing Durkee aside in the process. Blushing, she just stood there, staring at the Sergeant.

"Sorry. Thought you were my WAC driver," he said, laughing. "Tell you what. I'll make it up to you by taking you for a ride. We're gonna head north and see what's up there. Come on, get in."

Molly hesitated, then with the gentle prodding of Durkee, walked around and climbed into the front seat, while Bushnell moved over to the driver's side. Holding on dearly to Durkee's hand, Molly pulled him into the jeep, too. Durkee wiggled past her and seated himself in back.

"Chaperone?" asked Bushnell.

"Why Sergeant," exclaimed Durkee, "I'm sure you offered the ride to both of us."

Bushnell put the jeep in gear and headed across the clearing. As they crested the north side of the park and started to disappear from view, those left in camp could hear Molly shrieking.

EIGHTEEN

Sunday Morning

Browne dressed quickly and went to Morgan's door to see if he was awake. The night before had bestowed more disaster upon the 16th Light Dragoons and Browne was disturbed that Morgan had slept through it all.

He felt no closeness to Morgan. He did not understand nor like the man. Yet, he knew he must try, for Morgan would not be the only erratic Officer he would encounter during his military career. Perhaps the loss of Cilly and the failure of his arrogant attempt to punish the rebels had caused him to seek refuge in solitude? A professional Officer would not, but Morgan was another sort.

Browne knocked at the door. He heard footsteps inside, followed by "A moment, please." Then, "Come in."

It was a different man that grinned at Browne as he entered. Morgan was his old self. Standing fully erect and proud in his uniform, wig combed back in a tight pigtail, he was just putting on his helmet. His uniform looked freshly cleaned-up and pressed. Perhaps by Beth?

"Ah, good morning, Lieutenant Browne. Did you rest well?" There was no mention of the afternoon and the night before.

"Not well at all, Sir. Not well at all. The Rebels . . ."

"Ah, we shall take care of the Rebels, Lieutenant, for I have decided to obtain help for our cause. I shall send riders this morning to Howe and the Commandants to the south, with news of the large force we face. With the arrival of troops and cannon, we will destroy them!"

Closing the door behind him as they left his room, Morgan guided Browne into the main tavern and then through the kitchen to the back door. "Where are the horses?" he asked, as they stepped outside.

"They were taken back to camp last night. I used mine in the chase of the Rebels. Yours was curried and fed."

"Chased the Rebels? When did you do that?"

"After they killed Corporal MacKenzie."

Morgan looked at him quizzically. "What!?" he demanded.

"Four or so Rebels came down to the tavern last night. MacKenzie, Thacker and McDougall caught them inside. There was a fight and the Rebels shot MacKenzie. Corporals Thacker and McDougall tell me they fought back valiantly, but were outnumbered. I believe them, for I also heard the shooting and came out of my bedroom and was shot at many times. MacKenzie's body was at my boot tips when I opened the door. I jumped out of the way and closed the door. When I reopened it, they were gone. McDougall and Thacker had been disarmed and the Rebels had kidnapped the girl, Molly."

"Molly! Kidnapped? Did you chase them?"

"Yes! I mounted the troop and rode after them."

"Well?"

"The Rebels fired their cannon at us. We were stopped and they got away in the dark."

"Why didn't you wake me?"

"I knocked on your door before I left to chase the Rebels, but received no answer."

"And after your return? Did you try again?"

"Yes. After we came back, I knocked again."

Morgan looked away, not wanting to have Browne see his face. Clearly embarrassed, he whispered the next words. "There may be times, when . . . when it may be necessary to enter the room and shake me." He said nothing further in way of explanation.

Morgan began walking towards the camp and Browne fell in beside him, gauging the man as they went. He quickly concluded that the Captain was the type of Officer that must never appear to be wrong, and that his shortcomings must be overlooked, if not hidden from the rest of the troop.

With that in mind, Browne decided to tell Morgan about chasing the Rebels. "I know you will think me daft, Sir, but last night as we chased the Rebels, a strange thing occurred. A bright light exploded in the night sky and illuminated everything around us. I am sure the Rebels saw us because of it. I believe the Rebels fired it from their cannon."

"What an unusual imagination you have, Lieutenant. You must tell me about these . . . these hallucinations. I would be most interested to hear more, in private."

Encouraged by the exchange, Browne smiled to himself and added a little briskness to his step. "Would the Captain prefer to do that this morning, or later, at a time, more to his convenience?" he asked, hopefully.

"All in good time, Lieutenant; all in good time. We shall eat first and I must send out the riders. After that, we shall talk of your . . . hallucinations."

As they reached the edge of the camp, Sergeant Ramsey, followed by Corporals McDougall and Thacker, came towards the two officers. Browne dropped back a step or two and with a slight motion of his finger across his lips, signaled their silence. After passing morning pleasantries, Morgan gave instructions.

"Sergeant Ramsey, pick three good riders and horses. I have messages to send. Corporal Thacker, I saw no breakfast prepared for us at the tavern. Fetch us some will you?"

Morgan and Browne walked over to the benches outside the Quartermaster's hut and sat down. Corporal Thacker soon returned bringing food. They ate in silence, constantly brushing away the buzzing flies so prevalent in the camp.

The bench they sat on was not well built and each brushing wave of an arm only served to rock it back and forth. Still, neither officer said anything and soon finished their food. Seeing them finish, Thacker quickly picked up the plates and utensils, whisking them away to some unseen Private to return to the tavern. Around the rest of the camp, troopers of the 16th were busying themselves, eating and preparing for formation.

"Lieutenant, call Sergeant Ramsey here." Morgan belched quietly under his breath and waited.

Browne saw Ramsey standing nearby, trying to look unobtrusive. He called to him and Ramsey immediately assumed a military posture and advanced. He stood at attention in front of them, waiting.

"Sergeant," Morgan ordered, "I want some paper, and a quill and ink. I have some messages to write. When they are written, the riders you have selected shall deliver them for me."

Ramsey saluted, turned and walked a discreet distance and, when hidden from view, ran towards the tavern to find the items. He hesitated in mid-run, suddenly remembering the Quartermaster had such materials in his hut, but quickly decided it would never do to go back. Reaching the back door, he stopped briefly to regain his military bearing before entering the kitchen, only to find it empty. Moving into the other room, he found the keeper bent over behind the bar, putting something away on the shelf.

"Where are your morning patrons?" Ramsey asked. "There were many here last night. Are you not serving them breakfast?"

"It's your doing they all left without breakfast. It's a bad day when a decent person cannot spend the night in peace, without fear of losing life or limb to the likes of you!"

"The Rebels were responsible for last night! We were attacked whilst we sought refreshment at your bar! Someday keeper, I will give you some lessons in manners, so you are less insolent! But, now, my Captain needs paper, and quill and ink. Bring them to me now. I have no more time for you."

The keeper left the bar and went upstairs, returning with the materials. No further words were spoken as Ramsey left through the back door and hurried to Morgan.

Receiving the items, Morgan retired to the interior of the Quartermaster's hut. To Howe, Morgan wrote of the encounter with the large force of Rebels. He expressed fear that such a force could distract Howe from his intended battle for New York, by attacking his flanks. He also told Howe that the Rebels, by their presence, would inhibit the Dragoons from securing the supplies they had been ordered to obtain. Under these conditions, Morgan requested Howe to dispatch 400 troops and six cannon to Jockey Hollow.

To the Commandants of the British strongholds at Amboy and New Brunswick, Morgan wrote of the threat posed by the Rebel force and the possibility of loosing Morristown to them. To the Commandant at New Brunswick, Morgan specifically took note of how the great supply base and the paymaster's gold maintained there could be at risk. Morgan requested as many troops as they could spare, but not less than 150 from each, with two or more cannons each.

The distance to New York was approximately thirty miles, to Amboy and New Brunswick, slightly farther. Morgan knew that with fast horses and good riders, the distance could be covered in less than a half-day. Return messages could be brought to him that night, or early next morning. He did not really expect Howe to respond with troops or cannon, but it was politically proper to have advised the General.

The real help would come from the Commandants to the south. They each had much to protect, as well as the troops to spare for such an encounter with the Rebels. It bothered him slightly though, that he knew neither of them by name nor reputation. However, that was of little consequence, since a Captain in the 16th Light Dragoons commanded respect – the Dragoons *were* the eyes and ears of the Army. Morgan would get the help he wanted!

Morgan gave the messages to Browne to give to Ramsey for dispatch. He silently prayed for answers back yet tonight.

He waited to hear the riders leave the campground and then motioned Browne to come near. Whispering in his ear, Morgan asked discreetly, "Was MacKenzie given the burial rites?"

Equally discreetly, Browne replied. "Yes, Captain. I thought it best to bury him last night after we returned from chasing the Rebels."

"Excellent, Lieutenant. The time has passed for morning formation. Did Sergeant Ramsey conduct it for us?"

"It would appear so, Sir."

"Then, Lieutenant, let us return to the tavern and talk." Morgan got up from the table, capped the ink well and neatly piled the paper in the center of the uncovered wood top. He walked out into the bright morning sun. "We have not had any rain for days now, Lieutenant. I would enjoy some. It cleans the air and settles the dust."

"I would hope for some tomorrow or Tuesday, Sir. As you know, the troopers do not like it, for it interferes with their riding when they are securing supplies. Still, they may like an excuse to stay in camp. At least the flies would not be here."

Morgan laughed. He envisioned the men, sitting in their huts, watching the rain and being thankful for the lack of flies – while cursing the leaking roofs! He laughed louder. Browne had no courage to ask why.

They walked slowly through the camp, Morgan stopping frequently to inspect a man's equipment or horse, or just to say a word or two. Browne watched in fascination as the man attempted to rectify his lack of leadership the night before.

As for Morgan, he felt in a rare mood and sought to give the men an opportunity to see him as an interested leader concerned with their welfare, something every leader should do occasionally.

Browne pointed to MacKenzie's grave, next to Cilly's, but Morgan did not stop as they kept on towards the tavern. Holding the back door open, Browne followed him in and saw that no one was about. The fire was dead in the fireplace and the tavern walls echoed to their footsteps as they walked around the bar to their bedrooms. If Morgan saw the bullet holes over the doorway, he said nothing. Quietly closing the door from the bar behind them, Morgan gestured that they would use Browne's room.

Inside, he removed his helmet and sword and dropped them on the bed. His pistol remained in place. Seating themselves in the two straight back chairs on either side of Browne's table, they made themselves as comfortable as possible. Morgan smiled and waited.

Browne reached into the desk drawer and removed some dull, yellow-colored tubes with odd-looking ends. There were two long and nine short ones. "We found these on the tavern floor after the Rebels ran away. They are similar to the one found on the trail after the encounter between Sergeant Cilly and the Rebels."

He handed the brass cartridges to Morgan who fingered them lightly as Browne continued.

"Corporals McDougall and Thacker swear that they saw these tubes fly through the air from the Rebels' guns each time they were fired. They also swear they did not see the Rebels stop to reload before the guns were fired again. They say MacKenzie was killed by four shots from the same gun fired by one Rebel. The gun was much shorter than our carbines."

"Go on, Lieutenant."

"The Rebel at the top of the stairs shot a longer gun. It was aimed at the mugs, which were destroyed. He could have killed McDougall and Thacker, but did not. Another Rebel took their pistols when they left. The longer tubes came from the longer gun. All the tubes have flat ends with the little silver centers. Each of them has the center pushed in and they all smell of gunpowder."

Morgan picked up one of each size and held them to his nostrils. Nodding his head about the smell, he turned them around in his hands and looked into the open ends. Placing the two open ends together, he observed the size of the openings. "The holes are the same size, yet one cylinder is longer than the other. And, notice the shapes. Each has a flat end and round sides that taper near the open end. Strange. You say the Corporals insist they saw these fly from the rebel guns? And that the rebels did not reload between firings of the guns?"

"That is true, Captain."

Morgan placed the brass tubes on the desk, started to pick one up again, then thought better of it and moved his head to look out the window. Staring at nothing, Morgan drummed the fingers of his left hand on the table. After a short period he lifted his hand, stroked his nose, mouth and chin several times and looked back at Browne. "I would like to hear more about what you saw yesterday at the rebel camp. You spoke of a strange weapon being shot at the tree branches."

Browne hesitated before he answered. How best to describe what he had seen from the hill top the previous morning? He felt he had gained some of the Captain's confidence and must not exaggerate what he had seen.

"Two men assembled it on the ground. One man carried a three-legged base and the other man placed the weapon on it. The first man brought over a metal box, opened it and pulled out a flat ribbon of shiny objects to hand to the other man. The second man lifted up the top of the weapon and laid the flat ribbon inside before pushing the top down again. He pulled something on the right side of the weapon – twice, back and forth, like this . . ." Browne indicated with his right hand how Russell had pulled the bolt handle back and released it twice to arm the machine gun.

"Then the Rebel sat down on the ground behind the weapon, pushed down on the back of it, pointing the front up towards the tree branches. He had his right hand on something protruding from the back of the weapon when it fired." Proceeding more cautiously, Browne continued. "When the weapon was fired . . . it did not fire just once. It . . . fired many times . . . as long as the Rebel held the handle in the rear." Watching the Captain's eyes for a reaction, Browne saw none. "The ribbon entered the weapon from the left and appeared to be pulled from the box through the weapon as it was fired. Objects that looked like those on the table, came from the weapon as it was fired; they stopped when the Rebel took his hand away from the back."

Browne could see every detail of the Rebel's movements in his mind's eye as he relived that morning's events. His eyes were searching his memory for more when Morgan spoke, bringing him back to the present.

"Very strange, Lieutenant; very strange. What else did you see?"

"The Rebel moved the weapon from side to side while he fired it. It fired very rapidly . . . and, Captain, the Rebel did not stop to reload it each time." There, he said it. Browne waited for the Captain's reaction, but it did not immediately come. Morgan just stared at Browne, then at the metal cartridges on the table, and then back at Browne again. Browne became uncomfortable and squirmed around in his chair a little before the Captain finally spoke.

"Is it your contention that there were not a hundred or so Rebels hidden in the trees? That one Rebel, firing the weapon you described, caused as much noise as the shooting of a hundred muskets?" Morgan paused and looked at Browne and the cartridges again. Then he added. "Did you see strange looking carriages, as well?"

God, yes, he had seen them, but had been afraid to mention the fact. "Yes, Captain. Some small, some large, but I saw no horses or mules to pull them."

"Did you see any musical instruments? I am still curious about the yelling we heard yesterday concerning the Effem Band. I could see no band or instruments as I looked over the Rebel camp."

"Nor could I, Captain. But I did see and hear an unusual thing: a man in the center of their camp, placed a red and gray horn to his mouth and shouted to the Rebels to retreat to the clearing. His voice boomed across the camp like the sound of a cannon!"

"I heard that too, Lieutenant." Morgan's facial features had softened considerably since the start of the conversation. "I fear we have run into a hornet's nest. These Rebels are not the usual lot we have encountered before. They are dressed alike and appear to have considerable military discipline. While they ran from our horsemen, I think they did so not from fear, but to gain an advantage. But, when they had the advantage, they did not use it! Only three of our men were killed in the battle, yet with the rapid firing weapons they possessed, many more should have been killed or wounded. If I were their leader and possessed such weapons, I would know how to use them! If such weapons exist, why are we all not dead?"

Morgan looked out the window again, before continuing. "It would seem that the hallucination affecting you and the others . . . has . . . also affected me. I too, have seen and heard the same things you have described here this morning. I know what we have seen cannot exist, so it must be Rebel witchcraft or trickery to deceive and overwhelm us! We cannot be intimidated. We must ignore their deceptions and defeat them!"

*   *   *

Sunday Noon

The sound of the jeep returning loudly and raucously preceded its arrival on the north side of the campground. It soon popped its nose over the hill and came down towards the clearing where Erickson was sitting.

He could see Molly in the back seat with Durkee, her hair blowing as the jeep sped along, while he held her steady with his arm around her shoulder. As Bushnell skidded to a stop near Erickson, Durkee smiled at Molly. "Wasn't that great?" he asked. "When you get back with us to our time, I'll take you for a lot of rides like this, only better!"

Erickson got up. "See anything worthwhile?" he asked Bushnell.

"Yeah. We can get out of here if we have to. The trees are thinner to the north. In fact, there are some pretty wide-open spaces up there. It will be rough going up and down the hills, but our biggest problem may be getting the trucks and trailer through the trees right here in camp."

"How far did you go?"

"Two, maybe three miles. We could see a big valley off in the distance to the northwest. It's probably ten miles further. Everything looked the same, though, plenty of running room; I don't know where it will get us, but we *can* get out of here."

"Good. How did Molly do? It must have been quite an experience for her."

"You should have seen her! Squealing like a little kid. Happy, scared; eyes open, then closed; hands on the seat, holding on for dear life, then clenched in prayer. On the way back she climbed over to be with Durkee and held onto him like she thought the end was in sight."

"The way you drive, I can see why."

"Thanks a lot. How do you know Durkee didn't pay me?"

Erickson laughed. "You're nothing but a mother hen, you old softy."

As they started to walk across the campground, Putnam approached them from the side.

"Hey, Lieutenant," he said. "Got a minute? I've been working out the assignment you gave me. Sullivan, Arnold and I will go back down to the tavern after it's dark. We'll snoop around it and the Dragoon camp to see what we can find out about Hale and MacKenzie. We'll spend the night down there, if necessary." Then, dropping his voice so as not to set Erickson off on him again, he added, "if they're not down there and they don't show up around here, then . . . well then . . . maybe we've got something else on our hands."

Erickson nodded. "You find them if they're there. If they're not, then we'll consider the alternatives. Be sure you're well armed; I don't want anymore missing soldiers. If you get into trouble, we'll try to follow the same procedure with the flare and the mortar shells. You might think about leaving earlier, before it's too dark. That might make it a little easier getting down; then stay hidden in the trees until dark, before entering the tavern. You could see all the comings and goings and get your bearings."

"Sounds all right to me, Lieutenant. We'll get an early supper and then start." Putnam trotted off to tell Sullivan and Arnold.

Bushnell and Erickson continued across the camp towards the kitchen unit. As they walked, Erickson asked, "Did they check the water out?"

"Huh?" Bushnell's mind was on Putnam and the patrol. "Oh. Yeah. Canteen was half-empty, but Dobbs checked it out and told me it's good. When we run short on water, I'll have some of my guys go down and get some."

The camp was generally quiet. Men sat in the shade away from the hot, noontime sun, checking their weapons, or talking in low tones about Lee and his 'nightmare'. Dobbs's crew was starting to prepare a light lunch. The woods were full of animal and bird noises, interrupted occasionally by noises made by the soldiers.

The atmosphere stayed calm and relaxed throughout the rest of the day. No one thought to mention or celebrate the fact that it was the 4th of July.

* * *

Dobbs served an early supper so Putnam, Sullivan and Arnold could leave in the evening light. They were all armed and carried a bit of food in case they decided to spend the night.

On the way down the trail, Sullivan and Arnold were hopeful they would find Hale and MacKenzie, but Putnam was pessimistic. "They're gone for good," he said, "we've killed their ancestors and they won't be back."

Reaching the bottom of the trail, they moved into the thick willows near the pond where they could watch the tavern and the Dragoon camp. When it was fully dark, they would move on.

NINETEEN

Monday Morning

Monday, July 8, 1776 scudded into the Dragoon camp on a gusting wave of high dark clouds. The wind blew briskly and the smell of rain was in the air. Morgan awakened early, but quickly became irritated when he found no sunlight beaming through his curtains. The riders had not returned before he went to bed and now, if it rained, they could be delayed further. The portent of foul weather was putting him in a foul mood.

His thoughts regressed to the conversation yesterday with Lieutenant Browne. It had gone well but, now, his mood was spawning second thoughts about the propriety of having confided his own fears and feelings to the Lieutenant. Cilly could have been trusted with such knowledge without fear of recourse. But, Browne was another matter. He was ambitious and might use any real or apparent weakness against him. Time would only tell. Still, Browne seemed to be trying to accommodate him and, perhaps, all would be well, after all.

He had retired later than usual the night before, waiting in vain for the return of any of the messengers. When they didn't come, he went looking for Beth, needing the comfort and tenderness she provided during his moods of anxiety. But, she was nowhere to be found either. Since the tavern had remained void of travelers and customers after the incident with the Rebels on Saturday night, there was nothing else to do. Morgan spent a fitful night, finally reaching the morning without having received much rest.

He pulled his uniform on in haste and adjusted his wig without the benefit of a mirror, resulting in a disheveled appearance. Ignoring his saber and pistol, he decided to awaken Browne to accompany him to breakfast in the tavern. He walked to Browne's door, stomping his right foot as he went, trying to get his heel to settle into the tight-fitting boot.

The stomping noise brought Browne fully awake. He had first awakened a half-hour earlier, but then had drifted off again. Not knowing what was outside his door making that awful pounding noise, and fearing the worst from a possible Rebel attack, Browne reached for his pistol and was aiming it at the door when Morgan knocked.

"Who is it?" he demanded.

Morgan turned the handle and slowly pushed the door open. Browne took closer aim at the widening gap between door and jamb. Abruptly, he put the pistol down and hid it under the covers as he recognized the black boot and white breeched leg growing into the full body of his Captain.

"'Tis me," Morgan said. "Get dressed. It is time for us to breakfast."

Browne looked at Morgan, trying to gauge the temper of his mood. This act had no precedence in their relationship and Browne did not know what to make of it.

"Yes, Sir. I'll be but a moment." Browne slid across the bed and got up. Morgan looked at his Lieutenant briefly before finally sitting down in the chair by the desk. Morgan said nothing further, looking alternatively about the room and out the window. His eyes soon settled again on Browne.

"Come, Lieutenant. We have many things to do today."

Browne continued to dress quickly, but precisely. He hoped his appearance would encourage the Captain to take some time to adjust his own dress, as well.

"Do you know the time, Sir?" asked Browne.

"Approximately 30 minutes after the hour of six, Lieutenant. We shall have to raise the tavern keeper for breakfast, but I shan't mind doing that."

Morgan led the way to the tavern. Seeing no one about, he pounded his fist on the bar top and called loudly for the tavern keeper.

A few moments later, the man appeared from around the corner of the kitchen, yawning and scratching his stomach, his nightcap twisted about his head. Seeing the two Dragoon Officers in their uniforms, he stopped and glared at him. "What is it you want at this hour of the morning?"

"Breakfast, keeper. Breakfast, *now*." Morgan glared back at him.

"But Captain, we are not ready for breakfast, we . . ."

Morgan slammed his fist down on the bar top again, cutting him off. "Now, keeper. We want breakfast, now!"

The keeper looked at him for a moment, then sensing the danger in not complying with the demand promptly started the morning fire and then hurried off to dress.

As Morgan and Browne walked through the kitchen towards the back door, they caught sight of the keeper scurrying up the narrow back steps to the second floor. Ignoring him, they stepped outside. "You predicted rain, Lieutenant. It smells of it in the air. We may yet have some today."

"That would be fine, Sir."

"Not if troops are coming to our aid, Lieutenant. The rain would slow them and I have plans for the Rebels when the troops arrive."

"Have you received answers to your messages?" The way Morgan had spoken led Browne to believe that good news had been received from Howe and the Commandants to the south.

"No. But, the answers will be here this morning. Of that you can be sure."

The two of them walked around the outside near the rear of the tavern for a while, venturing towards the Dragoon camp and then back to the tavern again, waiting for the keeper to serve up breakfast. They had reached the back door when Morgan heard, then saw a rider galloping from the direction of Morristown. He quickly headed around the side of the building to be in front when the horseman arrived.

The Dragoon began dismounting before his horse stopped, handing the message to his Captain just as his foot reached the ground.

"The reply from General Howe, Sir. The delay was caused by his temporary absence from his headquarters on Staten Island."

Morgan snatched the message from the Dragoon's hand and hurried into the tavern to read it. Browne dismissed the man and went to join Morgan. He found the Captain seated at the table near the fireplace. Ignoring the heat from the blaze, Morgan was frowning, shaking his head, left fist clenching the message.

"He implies that we must be new and inexperienced in fighting Rebels for them to cause us so much concern. He is occupied readying for the attack on New York and considers this to be a simple matter that Burgoyne's best Dragoons should quickly dispose of." Morgan hesitated. "Howe is willing to send a new Troop Leader, if I am indisposed to attack the Rebels." He crumpled the message and threw it into the fireplace. "Damn him!" he said under his breath as he slammed his fist onto the table. "Damn him!"

Upstairs, Putnam, Arnold and Sullivan heard everything. Warned by the keeper that the two Dragoon Officers were up, they had watched the rider deliver the message to Morgan from their hiding place near an upstairs window. When Morgan came inside, they had moved their position to the top of the stairs, to better observe and hear what took place below.

The three had hidden in the tavern the night before, after reconnoitering the Dragoon camp in a vain attempt to find Hale and MacKenzie. They had watched a few Dragoons come and go, but it was soon empty except for the keeper, and Morgan and Browne. After discovering them skulking near the back door, the keeper had guided them up the narrow back stairs to one of the rear bedrooms reserved for lady travelers. When Morgan finally retired, they, too, were able to retire, getting a good night's sleep.

Below them, Browne spoke measuredly, trying to keep Morgan from exploding with further anger. "You did not expect troops from Howe, no matter how the message reads, Captain. The troops you need to assist us against the Rebels will come from the Commandants to the South. They have much to protect. They will respond to your request."

Morgan slammed his fist onto the table again with such force that it lifted it off the floor. "Keeper! Where is our breakfast? I want our breakfast, now!"

"Coming, Captain Morgan. I have it right here. It will be on your table in a moment." A few minutes later the keeper set before them two plates of pork slab and eggs and two mugs of hot tea. He hastily retreated to the kitchen without asking if there was anymore that they wanted. From there, he quickly climbed the backstairs and walked over to join the Americans.

Morgan and Browne ate in silence, each avoiding the others eyes. The food was fair, but hot, and they soon finished. Browne got up from the table and walked to the back door, wondering whether to go over to the Dragoon camp. As he stood there, he spied first one, then the other of the two messengers sent south, trotting across the campground towards the tavern.

They reached the back door together. As Browne opened the door, they came to attention. Suspicious, he asked, "Where have you been? You are long overdue."

The shorter man spoke first. "We were just awaiting yourselves to get up, Sir." His fidgeting told otherwise.

Browne concluded they had probably arrived back in camp late at night and had avoided delivering the responses for fear that more messages might have to be carried in the dark.

"Where are the messages for the Captain?"

They both thrust their hands forward. Browne curtly grabbed the messages, dismissed the men and walked back to the table where Morgan still sat. He seemed mesmerized with the flames in the fireplace.

Browne set the two messages down in front of him. Morgan looked up briefly, then tore one of them open. He read it through, then tore open the other one and read it, too. Throwing them both down on the table, Morgan slumped in the chair, his rump at the front edge, his neck supported by the back. He closed his eyes and reached out to finger the messages.

Browne could sense what the messages said: No help from the Commandants to the South. But, why? They could not ignore the importance of what Morgan had said in his messages. There had to be some good reason.

Morgan opened his eyes and looked at Browne. "They each are sympathetic to our needs, but are faced with similar circumstances now that the Rebels have declared independence. The Commandant at New Brunswick is fearful that Washington may send some of his troops to capture the gold stored there, while the Commandant at Amboy is preparing to send his troops south along the East Jersey shore to protect loyalists that are in danger. Neither of them can send us troops or cannon!"

Browne felt an overwhelming empathy with his Captain. Morgan had believed that reinforcements would come to his aid and instead, they were on their own. Browne knew the odds against them in an all-out battle with the Rebels on the hill; they were no match for their repeating weapons. But, he knew what was going through his Captain's mind: honor, dignity and the right of the Crown to govern, must prevail. Even without reinforcements, the Dragoons must attack!

"Damn everyone and everything!" Morgan exclaimed as he sat up bolt straight in the chair. "We will do it! We shall do it! The Rebels will see and feel the might of the Dragoons' and they shall be ours!"

The ferocity of the outburst startled Browne, even though he had anticipated something of the sort. "When?" he asked.

"Today. This morning!" Morgan stood up, examined his uniform and found it not to his liking. He left the table to return to his room and rectify his appearance, calling over his shoulder as he left, "Get the troop ready, we shall attack within the hour!"

Within the hour! Browne could not conceive of the troop being ready to initiate a major attack within an hour. There had to be some planning before starting out. He would seek a delay by asking many questions when the Captain reached the camp.

Browne quickly left the tavern and headed for the camp. He would assemble the troops and await Morgan's arrival.

With the departure of the two Officers from the tavern room, Putnam felt free to speak. "Thanks, keeper. We got quite an earful. Looks like we're gonna have to get word back to Lieutenant Erickson and let him know what's coming off. Sullivan, you get your fanny in gear and get back up the hill. Tell the Lieutenant what we've heard and seen this morning."

Sullivan gathered his rifle and canteen and started down the stairs. "What are you going to be doing?" he asked Putnam.

"When the Dragoons leave their camp, Arnold and I will have a perfect opportunity to go back and look for Hale and MacKenzie again. We'll be OK."

"Piece of cake, huh?"

"Piece of cake. On your way now, and keep low, out of sight."

"Right." Sullivan slipped down the stairs, carefully. No sense running into Captain Morgan, now.

Putnam and Arnold returned to the upstairs bedroom, watching through the window towards the Dragoon camp. A few moments later, they saw Morgan leave the Tavern through the back door, and unmindful of the light rain that was beginning to fall, walk purposefully across the clearing to where the Dragoon troop was assembled in the distance.

Reaching the troop, he mounted his horse, held ready by a Private, and rode slowly up and down the ranks. The rain started falling harder now and Morgan was perturbed. Rain and gunpowder did not mix at all, making an attack at this time out of the question. He slapped his leg with his glove, signaled to Browne to dismount the troop, then turned and rode the short distance to the Quartermaster's hut, where he dismounted and hurried inside. Shortly after, Browne, Sergeant Ramsey, and Corporals McDougall and Thacker joined him to hear the details of his plan of attack.

The rain became a cloudburst. The drops hammered on the pitched roof of the hut, running in great streams down the sides onto the dirt around the outside walls. There it accumulated behind little ridges, until its bulk forced it free to join other ribbons of water, all coming together in four or five great gully-cutting rivulets headed for the center of the camp. Inside the other huts, the Dragoons now sat and waited, knowing that in no time the roofs would become saturated and the rain would start to drop through. It was going to be a miserable morning.

It was miserable for Sullivan, too. He kept slipping and sliding in the mud on the trail, as he forced himself up the hill to the campground. As he cursed Morgan between heaving breaths, he wondered if the rain would halt the attack.

In the Quartermaster's hut, Morgan used a piece of burnt charcoal on a linen cloth to sketch an outline of the terrain leading to the rebel camp. Surrounding him on either side of the table, the others watched in silence as he described a frontal assault, directly up the hill into the Rebel camp! Browne was horrified! He silently prayed for the rain to stay with them for at least two more days to give Morgan time to regain his senses.

As if in response to his prayer, a torrent of rain came down for a full five minutes. But, Browne's luck was fleeting. The rain abruptly stopped, quickly revealing patches of sunlight. He silently swore under his breath and returned his attention to Morgan and the linen sketch.

*   *   *

Sullivan reached the camp just as the rain stopped. At first, it seemed to be deserted, but then here and there, heads began popping out of tents and his comrades were soon out looking for damage. Erickson hurried over to Sullivan as he came into the camp area.

"You're back!"

"Came to warn you." Sullivan took a deep breath and held it for a moment to restore his lungs, then continued. "The Dragoons are planning an attack. They're coming within the hour!"

"How did you find that out?"

"We were in the tavern; overheard Captain Morgan talking to his Lieutenant. He tried to get help from General Howe in New York and some of the British Commanders down south, but they all turned him down. Now he's mad as hell and plans to get us with an attack this morning."

"How long did you say we had?"

"Morgan said he was going to attack within the hour. And, that was maybe fifteen minutes ago."

"Good god! Where're Putnam and Arnold?"

"They stayed in the tavern to watch things. Putnam figures that while the Dragoons are gone, he'll have a good chance of getting into their camp to find Hale and MacKenzie."

"OK. We haven't got any choice, now. Let's get ready for them."

Anticipating an attack similar to the last one, he spread his men around the perimeter of the campground. Handing his binoculars to Sullivan, he told him to keep a watch for the Dragoons, as he moved the rest of Putnam's squad into the trees at the south edge of the camp to blunt any attack from that direction.

Russell moved the mortar into position in the same area, giving the weapon a fairly wide, deep field of fire down the hill. On the north edge of the clearing, Porter, assisted by Lewis, set up the machine gun with a clear field of fire in most directions. The rest of his squad took up positions nearby.

Ten minutes had passed since Sullivan's announcement of the attack. Everyone was ready, waiting; some nervous, some calm, most just trying not to think about it. The ground was still wet from the rain, while in many places large puddles of water stood ready for whatever came. The dripping trees added to the puddles and the men's discomfort. A few birds had returned from wherever birds go when it rains, and the squirrels resumed their hissing and growling. The men remained quiet, straining to hear any sound of Dragoons coming to do battle.

Sullivan's pants were soaked from sitting on the ground at the edge of the hill, while he surveyed the area from the pond to the Dragoon camp with Erickson's binoculars. He saw nothing and wondered what Morgan was up to?

But, beyond his view in the camp below, Morgan had ordered his Troop mounted as soon as the rain stopped. In spite of the earlier predictions, they showed no fear or reluctance for the coming battle.

Purposefully keeping his Troop hidden from the Rebels, he led them far to the east of the Wick House before turning and steadily climbing the hill that would bring them into the open spaces above the Rebel camp. When he finally reached that area, Morgan led the Dragoons through the trees to a point where he could clearly see the Rebel camp below him. Stealthily, the frontal assault that had so horrified Browne had been turned into an assault from the rear!

In the campground, Erickson had reached a decision to do something other than wait, when he suddenly heard the loud, long blast of the Dragoon trumpet behind him! He whirled around in surprise.

The ground rumbled beneath his feet with the beat of horse's hooves as the Dragoons, in massed formation, raced into the American camp! The shouts of men and the sounds of firing rifles, carbines and pistols immediately filled the air with a clamor of reverberating, head splitting, uproar. Caught by surprise, the Americans on the east side of the camp fell back and were quickly overrun. There was no attempt at capture. The Dragoons aimed and shot straight and when their pistols and carbines were empty, charged with vengeance using their sabers. Three men from Porter's squad were dead before any of them could fire a shot.

Porter barely dodged the slash of a saber as he and Lewis vainly tried to swing the machine gun into position. It was jammed on its tripod and wouldn't traverse to the north or the east! Lewis grabbed Porter's carbine and cut loose a full clip, sending two Dragoons and one horse to their maker. Reloading the carbine as he moved, he turned to shoot at more Dragoons, but fired only once before dropping to the ground, dead, a saber stuck through the base of his head.

Russell reacted quickly and moved the mortar around to face the attack. However, after getting off only two rounds, the swiftly moving Dragoons were well past its point of minimum range.

Private Brown stood up to squeeze off a shot at a hard riding Dragoon, but missed. The Dragoon fired his pistol in return, sending the ball into Brown's nose and out through his brain. As his lifeless body fell backwards, the M-l dropped, hitting Private McDougall on the shoulder and face, knocking him out.

The Dragoons were through the camp now, well past the trucks and the kitchen unit. The action stopped momentarily, then resumed with fury as they turned and charged back into the camp again, this time from the southwest. They came around the trucks, yelling and swinging their sabers.

The loss of Lewis stunned Porter. Dropping beside the body, he checked to see if there was anything he could do, and realizing he couldn't, he lost his temper. Jerking the machine gun off its tripod, he cradled it in his left arm and turned towards the Dragoons. Firing without let-up as they started their second charge, he raked devastation across the lead troopers, blunting the charge. Still he held the trigger, spraying the area to the right of the trucks and kitchen unit, catching the next line of Dragoons, and the one behind them, in a torrent of deadly bullets. The dead fell where they were hit, while the wounded screamed, blood spurting over their white and red uniforms, as the remaining Dragoons fought to turn their horses away from the staccato of death.

It was over.

The Dragoons still alive behind the trucks interrupted their headlong dash down the hill only long enough to help the wounded ride with them.

Above the east side of the camp, Morgan and Ramsey struggled to pull Browne's body from under the huge branch that had fallen and killed him instantly – a result of Russell's second mortar round when it exploded high above in the big spruce.

Somehow, his horse had survived the impact and, after pulling his body across the saddle, they retreated from the carnage.

*   *   *

In the tavern below, Putnam and Arnold had seen the Dragoons ride out. They assumed that Morgan would lead his men to the pond and then up the hill, but when he didn't go that way, the two soldiers decided to remain hidden for a while longer. When Morgan didn't return, Putnam decided it was safe to look for Hale and MacKenzie.

As the two men headed down the front stairs of the tavern, Arnold suggested that they check the Officer's quarters to see what they could find. Moments later they looked around the three bedrooms, but finding nothing worth taking, cautiously walked back through the tavern, then out the back door towards the huts of the Dragoon camp.

Worried about Morgan's return, they stayed in the trees as they crept abreast of the huts, then made a short run to the first of them, quickly checking to see if anyone was still inside. Finding no one, and gaining confidence that they would not be discovered, they systematically went from hut to hut seeking the missing Americans.

As they reached the last of the huts, the noise of the battle reached their ears. Arnold went to catch a glimpse of what was going on, but Putnam continued on to the next hut where there appeared to be supplies stored. He approached it carefully, for the door was ajar. Seeing no one as he looked through the front window, he pushed it open with his foot and walked in, carbine at the ready.

On the table in front of him lay the map on which Captain Morgan had shown his plan of attack. Beyond the table, on large shelves attached to the sides and rear walls, were stored the food, gunpowder and day-to-day supplies. Putnam was considering how best to destroy them, when he felt rather than saw another man in the room. Knowing it wasn't Arnold, Putnam swung his carbine around, only to be smashed in the side of the head by the Quartermaster's pistol. In reflex, the carbine fired, ricocheting the .30 cal. bullet off the hard log walls of the hut. He fell, unconscious, to the floor as Arnold, hearing the shot, turned and ran back to where he had last seen his squad leader.

The next shot, coming from the barrel of the Quartermaster's pistol sticking out the door, and the shot after that, fired by the Blacksmith in the hut next to the Quartermaster, convinced Arnold to run for it.

Getting no response to his shouts to Putnam, he headed for the tavern. Once inside, he returned to the rear upstairs bedroom where he laid out his ammunition and prepared his M-1 for defense.

If he were pursued, he would be waiting. In the meantime, he would watch to see what they did with Putnam.

TWENTY

Monday Morning

The carnage had been extensive and the American camp was littered with bodies, mostly Redcoats. Four men from Corporal Porter's squad had been killed too, including Lewis.

McDougall slowly recovered from the blow of Brown's falling M-1, while Durkee nursed a minor wound in the soft part of his right arm, sustained while protecting Molly. She sat on the ground next to him, gently tying a bandage around his upper arm.

Erickson and Bushnell stood amidst the dead horses and Dragoon bodies, counting.

"I make it twenty three," said Erickson, shaking his head. "God, what a waste! That dumb sonofabitch, Morgan! Why did he attack again? Didn't he realize what he was up against from the last time?"

"I don't know," answered Bushnell. "Now, what? What do we do with them?"

"I don't think we have any choice, Sergeant," said Erickson. It won't be long before the stench of death takes hold here. "Pour gas on the horses and set fire to them. We'll bury their soldiers with ours." He looked at the carnage again. The swath cut by Porter and the machine gun had been complete.

"There's gonna be a lot of sick people around here, having to bury all the dead," Bushnell said, with some emotion.

Erickson's look softened. "I know. I know. In any event, it's got to be done. Put together a detail. Bury their guys next to the three we buried on Saturday. Place our guys in a separate area. If we can get out of here, I may decide to take their remains with us for a decent funeral.

"Use the jeep to drag the horses over the north hill. Find a clear area up there where you can start a fire without it spreading. Get it done as quickly as you can." Head bowed, he slowly walked away from the scene, feeling tightness in the pit of his stomach.

He hoped Putnam and Arnold had found Hale and MacKenzie.

*   *   *

Putnam was not doing well at all. He sat on the floor of the prison hut, hands tied behind his back, ankles tied together in front of him. He had been leaning back against the inside wall of the hut, facing the Quartermaster and the Blacksmith, when the Dragoons had returned, badly broken and beaten.

Informed of Putnam's capture, Morgan hurried off to the prison hut in no mood to be trifled with. He wanted answers from this Rebel and he was going to get them! A red-hot loggerhead would help him, if necessary.

"Blow it out your ass!" had been Putnam's first response to the Captain's questions, but now, the sight of the loggerhead glowing in the coals piled in the center of the hut floor caused him to reconsider his rashness. There might be more to be gained from telling the Captain everything he wanted to know, and more.

"Tell you what, Captain Morgan," offered Putnam, whose stomach was growling from lack of breakfast, "cut off these damn ropes, let me get some food in my stomach, and I'll tell you all you want to hear – and plenty more. Bring all the guards you want. I give you my word as a soldier that I'll cooperate and won't try to escape."

Morgan became immediately suspicious of this quick change in the attitude of the Rebel, but was torn between his desire to inflict punishment on him and his need to discover the might of his adversary on the hill. He weighed the alternatives for a few moments, then concluded that he could always do something to the man later. Right now, the Rebel was willing to talk and Morgan would take advantage of that.

"Release him; his feet now and his hands after we reach the tavern. Quartermaster, you have done well in capturing him. You shall have the honor of guarding him. Take him to the Tavern. I will meet you there in a few moments."

Morgan left the hut to find Corporal Thacker, for a plan was taking shape in his mind that would require his services. Finding him, Morgan ordered the Corporal to join him in the tavern.

They soon reached the building and with Thacker holding the rear door open, Morgan marched in. He walked directly forward to sit down across the table from Putnam in the front room. The keeper had already placed food and drink before the American, who was eagerly eating.

Morgan observed his prisoner as he ate. Putnam soon finished and pushed the plate away. "Well, old chap," he started, "if you'll listen while I talk, I think we'll get to the bottom line a lot faster."

Startled, Morgan stared in puzzlement. "What did you say?"

"Sorry. Forgot myself. We've got a language gap, don't we?"

"Gap? You Rebels speak strangely."

Putnam laughed. "If this weren't so serious, it would be damned funny. Anyway, Captain, let me tell you my story."

"Please do."

"I'm from a place called San Jose, California, which you've probably never heard of. Doesn't make any difference though, it's there and I'm here. A week ago, my friends up there on the hill and I, were on a train heading from California to Newark, New Jersey."

"A train?"

"Uh, yeah. It's uh, a form of transportation we use in our time. Runs on steel tracks that lay on the ground. Look, there's gonna be a lot of things I say that won't make much sense to you right off the bat, but bear with me. Maybe the overall picture will make things clearer. OK?"

Morgan just stared at Putnam incredulously.

"Anyway, we were sent back here to take part in my country's celebration of 200 hundred years of independence from Britain." Putnam held up his hand to silence the question on the tip of Morgan's tongue. "Our part of the celebration was to take place over there across the road in Jockey Hollow. We were on that road last Friday afternoon, trying to get into the camp where all our troops were staying, when this dumb-ass Major tells us to get the hell out. He ran us off and we ended up on that hill up there in a nice little park, complete with tables, crappers and water faucets. The next morning we wake up and find ourselves in 1776 instead of 1976, and it's been hell ever since.

Putnam eyed Morgan and took a breath. "We want to get out of here as badly as you want us out of here. We didn't ask to come back 200 hundred years to get personally involved in the Revolutionary War. Although, I have to tell you, there are a few of our guys up there more than willing to fight against you on the side of General Washington. Our weapons are far superior to yours – something I'm sure you've noticed. If you keep pushing us, we're liable to wipe out your whole damn bunch in one fell swoop."

Seeing the reaction in Morgan's eyes, Putnam hastily added, "Sorry, didn't mean to make you mad, just telling you the facts of the situation. We've got one little problem, though. Some of our soldiers are descendants of some of your men. In those little battles we had last Saturday, we killed one of your guys named Hale and another one named MacKenzie. Our Hale and our MacKenzie both disappeared right afterwards. I mean right off the face of the earth! Now, there's a few people up there, like my Lieutenant Erickson and our Sergeant Bushnell who believe Hale and MacKenzie were captured by you Dragoons – but I don't. No sir! In my book, shooting Dragoons means zapping the descendants. But, don't get your hopes up that we'll just give up. We won't. We've got one other problem, too. That's the fact that we don't know how to get the hell back to where we came from. I swear if we knew how to do that, we'd be on our way right now! Well, except that maybe Erickson would still want to know for sure what happened to Hale and MacKenzie? That's why I'm here. We . . . I was sent down here to find out if they were your prisoners."

"Where did the second man go?" asked the Quartermaster.

"What second man?" Putnam dodged the question.

"The man that was with you. The one that got away."

"Damnit man, you hit me over the head, knock me cuckoo and then expect me to know what happened to my buddy? Obviously, he ran back to our camp – to get help. What are you going to do when they come down here in force to get me out?"

The lack of response and the continued look of utter amazement on Morgan's face told Putnam that he was not getting through. "Look, I know it's hard for you to believe what I'm saying. Hell, even Molly can't quite accept it and she's up there with us in the midst of it."

At the mention of Molly's name, Morgan got angry. "You kidnapped her! Let her go and send her back!" He was emphatic.

"No, we didn't! Your non-coms tried to molest her and she ran away with us. She's enjoying the hell out of herself up there, riding around in the jeep with her boyfriend."

"Boyfriend?"

"One of our men. She's taken a real liking to one of the guys in the platoon named Durkee. It's all right, he's a nice kid and they make a great pair."

"We will speak of her later. Tell me about your weapons and these." Morgan removed two brass cartridges from his pocket.

"Those are .30 caliber cartridges. The smaller of the two came from a carbine, like mine. The larger came from an M-1 rifle. Both are semi-automatic weapons, which means they can be fired as fast as the trigger can be pulled. The cartridges are fed into the breech, one at a time. The bolt closes behind the cartridge and when the trigger is pulled, a firing pin hits the silver cap in the center. The cap explodes into the powder in the cartridge, which explodes, forcing the bullet out of the end. It's the same process as is your muskets, only better."

Now he had their attention, even though they did not comprehend what he was saying. "For instance, on my carbine, the reaction of the weapon to being fired causes the bolt to snap back, ejecting the spent cartridge and rearming itself as it springs forward again. What did you do with it, anyway?"

"That odd weapon you carried is still in my store hut," replied the Quartermaster.

Morgan looked up at the Quartermaster. "Bring it here," he said, "I wish to see it."

The Quartermaster trotted off to retrieve the carbine while Putnam continued talking to Morgan.

"What happened up there this morning? I bet they cut you to ribbons."

Morgan looked away. He stared out the window, thinking of his conversation with Browne yesterday. Then he thought of Browne's body, being carried back to the camp across the back of his horse. Morgan tried to reject everything Browne and this man in front of him had told him, but he was finding it harder with every passing moment.

Putnam now remained silent, watching the Dragoon Captain obviously agonizing as the man's thoughts caused his face to screw up one way, then another. The silence was broken by the return of the Quartermaster with Putnam's carbine. He handed it to Morgan.

"We lost many good troopers," Morgan said. "My Lieutenant, Browne, was one of them. He told me of seeing your weapons, but I could not believe him. Now I hold one of them in my hands. I would like to see how it is operated, but I do not trust you not to shoot us. Quartermaster, hold the Rebel here. Corporal Thacker, accompany me out back whilst I fire the weapon."

"Can't I watch?" asked Putnam.

"You may be of some assistance at that. Bring him with you, Quartermaster, but watch him closely."

As they all walked through the kitchen and out the back door, Arnold moved his position from the top of the stairs, where he had listened to the conversation, to the window of the back bedroom, where he could watch Morgan fire the carbine. Peering from the edge of the window, he saw Morgan place the butt of the carbine to his right shoulder and point the weapon towards a tree in the distance.

Closely watched by the Quartermaster, Putnam told Morgan to squeeze the trigger and fire away. He pulled the trigger and immediately jumped back as the carbine fired, ejecting the spent cartridge and snapping a new round into place. Not really believing the Rebel, Morgan pulled the trigger again, thinking the carbine would not fire. Instead, it repeated itself, firing, ejecting and reloading. Two expended brass cartridges lay on the ground.

Morgan leaned over and picked them up. He examined them briefly, then handed them to Thacker.

Raising the carbine to his shoulder again, he aimed at a tree and pulled the trigger. The bark flew off, approximately where it had been aimed. Morgan pulled the trigger again, then again and again, ripping more and more bark away until the clip was empty. The camp echoed to the rapid sounds. Some of the troopers had started over to see what was going on, but Ramsey and McDougall had ordered them to stop since they could clearly see who was doing the firing.

Morgan pulled the trigger several times more, but nothing happened. He looked questioningly at Putnam.

"It's empty," he replied. "It's out of bullets. It has to be reloaded."

"Do you have more?"

"No," he lied.

Handing the carbine to Corporal Thacker, Morgan decided to put his plan into effect. "Take this man to General Howe in New York. Show him this weapon, show him these cartridges." Morgan began to stare straight through Thacker, as his voice became stern. "Then, perhaps, the good General will believe me when I send him messages requesting help. Then, perhaps, the good General will send his apologies for his earlier rash message. Then, perhaps, the good, good General will send the help I have requested, so these Rebels can be disposed of!"

Realizing that he was thinking aloud, Morgan grimaced and concluded his orders to Thacker. "Quickly! Take two men with you. You can yet arrive at Howe's headquarters today."

Morgan left to walk across the camp to find Corporal McDougall. The things Putnam told him had inspired yet another plan.

It did not take Thacker long to locate the two men he wanted and return to where the Quartermaster stood, guarding Putnam. While they waited, the two had chatted briefly about the war to come and the Quartermaster had quickly concluded that Putnam was daft. He would be relieved to be rid of him.

Tying Putnam's hands in front, Thacker took the carbine and led his prisoner over to the horse they had brought for him. He helped him mount and then checked his position in the saddle. Satisfied that Putnam would not fall off, the four-man party rode slowly around the east side of the tavern to the road.

Arnold had seen enough. He raced to the front stairs, jumped down them two at a time, pulled open the front door and ran to the corner of the tavern. He stopped, just as the foursome reached the edge of the road. Slipping the safety off, he raised the M-1 to his shoulder, took careful aim at Thacker and called out: "Hold it right there!"

Thacker twisted around in the saddle. Putnam, too, turned to confirm what he already knew: Arnold had come to his rescue! He half-jumped, half-fell to the ground as the other Dragoons jumped off their horses to grab him. Thacker raised his pistol to fire at Arnold, but his horse, its reins pulled hard to the right from his already contorted position, reared in the air and dumped the Corporal backwards to the ground.

The four men skirmished on the ground, dodging horse's hooves as the frightened animals tried to get away. Putnam kicked one of the Dragoons in the chest and, using his rope-tied fists, hit the other with a hard blow to his Adam's apple. Both lay where they fell. Thacker aimed his pistol at Putnam, but two quick shots from Arnold's M-1 dropped the Dragoon Corporal at Putnam's feet.

"Cut me loose," yelled Putnam, extending his hands and arms towards him.

"I haven't got a knife!" Arnold yelled back. "Grab a horse! Let's get the hell out of here! I'll cut your ropes later."

Putnam ran across the road to where the horses stood, stuck his foot in a stirrup and ungracefully mounted. "Get my carbine," he called to Arnold as he tried to grab the reins and get the horse moving.

Complying, Arnold pulled the carbine from Thacker's dead body as he ran by, stride unbroken. Slinging the carbine over his left shoulder, he awkwardly mounted the nearest horse. Grabbing the reins, he prodded the horse into a gallop. The two horses and riders ran past the Wick house and on towards the pond, Putnam hanging on to his saddle as well as he could. To their left, they saw six mounted Dragoons starting after them.

Arnold and Putnam had picked reluctant mounts. The horses were not used to their larger, heavier bodies, and the voices were strange, giving wrong commands. Nearing the pond, the animals bucked and tried to turn back.

As the Dragoons closed the gap, Putnam and Arnold heard a shout from the willows.

"Over here! We'll cover you!" It was Bushnell.

Straining to turn their horses towards the trees, they heard the thunderous crack of a .45, followed by the harsh reports of several M-1's. The Dragoons, who were now less than thirty yards away, reined in their horses and dismounted. Grabbing their carbines, they fired a quick, wild fusillade at the fleeing pair, but missed as the Americans reached the safety of the trees. Arnold quickly dismounted and helped Putnam do the same. "Got a knife?" he called to Bushnell, without saying how glad he was to see him.

Bushnell produced a sharp pocketknife and Arnold sawed furiously until he cut the bonds that held Putnam's hand together.

Rubbing his wrists, Putnam stuck out his hand to Bushnell. "Thanks. How'd you know we needed help?"

"Christ, it sounded like a bloody war zone down here. Kept hearing a carbine being fired. So, I grabbed Sullivan and Durkee. Got to these trees just as you two rodeo riders came bouncing into view."

The Dragoons fired again, sending the musket balls slashing through the willow branches.

"Come on you guys," urged Arnold, "you can shoot the shit later. Right now, let's get out of here before more Dragoons show up!"

The five soldiers worked their way through the willows to the upper edge of the pond. Electing not to follow the trail for fear of exposing themselves to the Dragoons, Bushnell led the way up the Spruce-covered hillside to the camp. Down below, the Dragoons fired another volley into the willows.

The five soon reached the edge of the campground, where Erickson stood watching.

"I'd ask, 'what happened', Sergeant," he said in an obvious reference to the switch in roles, "but right now we have a problem. Come with me to Lee's tent." His tone was ominous.

TWENTY-ONE

Monday Morning-Noon

Lee heard the gunshots like everyone else. He and Private Thacker were on the burial detail, but the sound of the shots from the Dragoon camp caused them to stop. They tried to see what was happening, but Porter and Russell, overseeing the detail, told them to get back to work.

Reluctantly, they returned to the tedious task of burying the Dragoons and the four Americans. In other parts of the camp, they could see the jeep being used to drag the dead horses over the north hill. Lee and Thacker, perspiring and soon sick to their stomachs, decided that no matter what, they would take a short break.

"Really, Lee," said Thacker, as they sat on the ground near each other, "don't you think it's about time you gave up on this wild tale of yours? I mean, no one believes you but the Lieutenant. And, in his case, it's probably more hope than agreement."

"It happened!" Lee exclaimed, emphatically. "It did! I'm not making it up, it really happened."

"Come on, Lee, you can tell me. You just had a dream, right? It seemed real and you told the others. Now you know different and you're afraid to back off. But, everyone is laughing at you, both to your face and behind your back. May as well 'fess up and stop it from getting any worse."

Lee bit his lip, tearing a loose shred of skin away. He looked at Thacker, trying to figure a way to convince the man he was telling the truth. He liked him and found it hard to accept Thacker's questioning. If there was anyone in the camp that Lee wanted as a friend, it was Private Thacker.

"What can I say to convince you?" Lee asked plaintively. "You're my friend. I wouldn't lie to you. I really did wake up and hit the picnic table. I really did use the outhouse and took a drink from the faucet. I don't know why they weren't there later in the morning when we all got up. All I know is what I saw and did. I wouldn't lie to you."

Thacker just shook his head. He considered Lee a harmless, irresponsible kid and his heart went out to him. He really wanted to help him get over being a kid and join the rest of the adults in the platoon but, Lee's short size and general demeanor kept the others at a distance.

"Lee," he said, "there's such a thing as being dead right. If you're driving a car and come to an intersection, insisting on your right of way at the same time some other guy insists on his right of way – well, you're liable to end up right, but dead. That's the same kind of thing you have right now with the platoon. You keep insisting that you're right and they keep looking at the facts and find they're right. So what have you gained? Why don't you just back off and let everybody forget it as a bad joke? If you admit it, they might even forgive you and your stock would go up a few points."

Lee's eyes blurred up with wetness. Pretending to remove something from his eye, Lee rubbed them both. "Of all the people in this camp, I thought you would believe me." He sniffled and tears began to fall.

Thacker couldn't take much of that. Seeing Lee in tears stirred something inside him, causing him to tell a white lie. "I do believe you, Lee." Thacker reached his arm out and put it around Lee's shoulder. "I do belie . . ."

He didn't finish the sentence. He couldn't. He wasn't there any longer! He just vanished in mid-word!

The echo of Arnold's M-l being fired at the tavern receded through the trees in the campground. Lee was frozen in place, gaping at the place where Thacker had been sitting only a second before! He jerked his head around, trying to find him. But, he wasn't to the right; he wasn't to the left! Lee even spun around, looking behind and everywhere else, but he couldn't see Thacker anywhere!

Slowly, the realization came over Lee that he had actually seen Thacker disappear right before his eyes. Lee's brain began to put together the noise of the rifle firing down in the hollow and Lee *knew* who had been killed by the shots he had just heard. Molly had said there was a Corporal Thacker in the Dragoons. Putnam and Arnold were down near the Dragoon camp. They must have just killed the Dragoon's Thacker! That's why his platoon's Thacker had vanished!

Lee screamed, then vomited. His stomach squeezed itself clean in one gigantic spew, accentuated by the remnants of a gurgling scream. He dropped to his knees and pounded the ground helplessly with his fists. Rolling to his side and then on his back, he continued screaming, kicking his legs and feet in the air. He kept on rolling, first onto his side, and finally onto his aching stomach where he lay kicking and smashing the ground with his hands and feet.

Erickson reached him first. Porter, followed by Russell, came next. Soon most of the platoon was there, watching the incoherent, babbling body on the ground.

Erickson grabbed Lee by the elbow. The words "Thacker" and "van . . . vanis . . . gone" dropped over the edge of his lips in between the rash of unintelligible muttering. The flaying action of his arms, legs and feet finally slowed, then stopped altogether. He lay quiet, face in the dirt.

"Get him to his tent," Erickson ordered.

Russell and Porter each took an end of the prone figure and carefully moved him to the tent.

Someone asked, "What happened?" Erickson, shaking his head, replied, "Don't know yet. I suggest you all get back to what you were doing. Give us a chance to find out."

Erickson followed Russell and Porter to Lee's tent. Inside, he found him stretched out on his back. His breathing seemed to be normal, but his body was rigid as he tried to speak. Eyes slowly flicking open, then closing again, Lee formed, then forced out a short sentence: "Thacker . . . van . . . vanis . . . vanished."

"What?" exclaimed Erickson.

"Thacker . . . gone. Vanish . . . vanished right befo . . . before me."

"When? How?"

But, Lee said no more. His body collapsed into the folds of the sleeping bag, lips silent, ears deaf to all but the screams in his head.

Erickson backed out of the tent and bumped into Dobbs who had come to report more guns firing below. Erickson, so intent on what was happening to Lee, had not heard them and quickly went to the edge of the camp to look. He soon saw Bushnell and the others climbing up the hill through the trees.

*   *   *

"What is it, Lieutenant?" asked Bushnell as he accompanied Erickson back to Lee's tent.

"Lee went banana's on us a few minutes ago. Did the whole bit, kicking, screaming, and vomiting. Russell and Porter carried him over to his tent after he finally quieted down."

"Good grief! What set him off?"

"He kept trying to say something about Thacker being gone."

"Gone?"

"Gone. Lee kept trying to say he 'vanished'."

"Vanished!" Another voice joined in. "Are you sure he said 'vanished'?" It was Putnam.

Erickson and Bushnell turned to him. "Why?" demanded Bushnell.

"Arnold shot a Dragoon while helping me to escape."

"What Dragoon?"

"Thacker. Corporal Thacker. He and two others were taking me to General Howe. Arnold shot him when Thacker tried to shoot me."

Erickson stood motionless, shifting his gaze between Bushnell and Putnam. Settling on Bushnell, he broke the silence that had enveloped them. "Sergeant, get Porter, Russell and Dobbs. You help, too, Putnam. Organize a thorough search for our Thacker."

"I've already got one going, Lieutenant," said Russell, who with Porter, had walked up to join them. "Started it right after you went with Dobbs. Haven't seen him, but we're still looking."

Erickson's words and tone of voice expressed his concern. "OK. Let me know the moment you find anything." Erickson touched Bushnell on the arm and pointed at Lee's tent. The Sergeant crouched and entered.

He backed out quickly. "God, what a stink! He's sleeping there in his own puke!"

"We haven't cleaned him up yet."

"That's for sure."

"We've got to talk to him. Let's see what we can find out."

"That could be above and beyond the call of duty." There was no humor in Bushnell's voice.

"So I'll put you in for the Congressional Medal of Honor. Come on, let's get in there." Erickson led the way this time, crawling headfirst into the tent, followed by Bushnell. They ended up half-sitting, half lying on either side of the Private.

Erickson gently shook him. "Lee, it's Lieutenant Erickson and Sergeant Bushnell. Wake up."

Lee's eyes flicked open for a second, closed again, then opened wide. He jerked up into a sitting position, almost knocking Bushnell over in the process. "Thacker!" he screamed.

Erickson restrained him, gently pushing him back onto the sleeping bag. "Take it easy, Lee. We're here to help. Where *is* Thacker?"

Every muscle in Lee's body tightened up. "Thacker vanished! Right in front of me!"

"When?"

"When the shooting was going on, down below!"

"How did he vanish?"

"He just vanished!" Lee started to cry now. "He was right in front of me, telling me he believed me about the table and the water faucet the other morning." The tears and sobs became more pronounced. "He was my friend, and now he's gone!"

"Did you see it happen?"

"Yes!! One second he was there, with his arm around me, the next he was gone! He just vanished!"

Erickson and Bushnell looked at each other. Their thoughts were the same: Lee was as an exaggerator, a little kid always trying to impress the adults. It was easy to believe this was just another version of a little boy's attempt at center stage. But, something was wrong. While Hale and MacKenzie's disappearance could be rationalized as coincidence, Thacker's disappearance was too closely tied to events. Arnold's killing of Corporal Thacker at the tavern at the same time Private Thacker vanished in their camp pressed them to the very edge of reality.

Erickson signaled with his head for them to leave. Backing out, Bushnell gulped the fresh air. Erickson followed and took a few deep breaths of his own.

"We can't do anymore in there," he said. "Get the Squad Leaders together."

They walked towards the west edge of the camp where Russell, Putnam, Sullivan and a few others were gathering. Russell called out to Erickson as he approached.

"Nothing to report, Sir. We've scoured the whole park and part of the area in the trees beyond. No trace of Thacker."

"Keep looking."

"Sir, we've had three men disappear during the times we've been fighting . . . no, make that killing Dragoons with the same names. I'm no genius, Sir, but they're gone and no matter how much we look, we won't find them."

"You believe Lee, then?"

"I wish it had been someone other than Lee saying they'd seen Thacker disappear. But, that doesn't really change things. Thacker ain't here anymore. Come-on, Lieutenant, we've looked!"

Erickson shook his head with frustration – the kind that comes when a man begins to sense the reality of a situation, even though his intellect keeps trying to tell him something different.

"I know everyone's going to accept the idea now that we've killed these guy's ancestors. But there's something basically wrong with that idea, and I'll tell you what it is: If we've killed the ancestors before they've had any kids, so no descendents exist for them, how the hell did we come to know Hale and MacKenzie and Thacker? Why are we looking for three guys – their descendants – if they never existed? How did we ever get to know them in the first place?"

More men had joined the gathering, intent on listening.

"I don't know how it works, Lieutenant," intoned Russell. "I'm just sure it does."

"Well, it's beyond my grasp," Erickson responded. "I certainly have clear images in my mind of those three. How can that be, *if* they never existed? How *could* they have existed?"

Sullivan fidgeted with his glasses as he entered the conversation. "No disrespect, Sir, but I think you're overlooking something."

"I'm open," Erickson lied. He was afraid of everyone getting into the discussion for fear of how it might result in rash decisions by the men. Yet, he knew they would discuss it anyway, and it would be better if he could try to control the outcome.

"I think the first thing to consider is this: even though we can't explain it, we *are* here in 1776, fighting Redcoats that have been dead for almost two centuries. And the second thing is, *if that's possible,* then anything is possible, including having memories of men who existed for a time, but no longer. It's just that we don't understand the circumstances."

"Hey Sullivan," said Russell. "Are you saying that since we can't explain how we got here, it's not necessary to explain the disappearance of our three guys?"

"No, he's not," said Erickson. "He's saying since we can't explain any of it, all we can do is accept it and act accordingly. That way we don't have to spend a lot of time wondering if the three ever existed or not, or how to explain that we knew them. I guess the real test will come when we get back to 1976."

"How's that, Sir?" asked Russell.

Erickson exhaled then took a deep breath. "Will we, or anyone else remember them? If so, then they existed. If not, how will we know that, since they will not have existed?"

"Maybe they're back in 1976 already, waiting for us to return?" interjected Putnam. The tone of the conversation was getting beyond his grasp and he needed to put it into terms he could accept.

Dobbs joined the group at that moment, jostling Putnam and Russell slightly aside. Erickson jumped on the opportunity to change the subject. "How's the food and water, Dobbs?"

"We got a little water from the pond, but not much. It's too hard to carry up the hill. As far as food goes, I can stretch it to noon tomorrow – no further. Then we better plan to go hunting or raid the Dragoons."

Erickson turned to Russell. "How's our ammo holding up?"

"We really haven't used that much, Lieutenant. I figure there's enough for a bunch of small or a couple of big battles with the Dragoons. But, after this morning, there shouldn't be too many of them left to mount another attack."

"I hope that's true, Corporal. But they can get reinforcements, we can't." Turning to Sullivan, he added, "Speaking of the Dragoons, get back over to the hill with the binoculars and keep a watch, will you?" Then, turning back to Putnam, he went on. "Tell me what you saw down there." It was pointless to ask if they had found Hale and MacKenzie.

"Morgan tried to get reinforcements, but was turned down by both General Howe and the Commandants at Amboy and New Brunswick. I got the impression he was becoming desperate. He lost his Lieutenant in this morning's battle and a lot of other men, too. He was very interested in my carbine. Most of the shooting you heard was Morgan playing with the damned thing. It really surprised me when he ordered me taken to General Howe."

"Why did he do that?"

"I guess so the General could see me up close with the carbine. Probably trying to convince the General that his need for reinforcements was real."

"How about their supplies? Can they wage any more battles?"

"They had me tied up for awhile in their supply hut. They've got lots of powder and balls for their carbines and pistols, but I didn't see that much food or clothing. If Morgan has the guts, he's got the ammo to attack again."

Erickson rubbed his forehead as he considered his options. If he no longer had to find the missing men, he could leave without concern. But, which way to go? Bushnell had said the area to the north of the camp was relatively clear and the trucks could probably get through. But what then? Try for one of the larger cities where they could find food and friendly help? How long would their fuel last? Would they just be jumping from the frying pan into the fire, by running into superior British forces? Hell's bells! His mind buzzed with all the possibilities.

"What *are* we going to do?" Erickson heard himself asking. What had been a thought had suddenly blurted out to no one in particular.

Bushnell took it upon himself to respond. "If the Dragoons attack again, we could have more men disappear. I'd rather move on and take our chances elsewhere."

Erickson thought for a moment. "My concern with that, Sergeant, is that we could be condemning ourselves to live out our lives in the 18th century. Many of us would probably last well into the 19th. It's not a decision to be taken lightly."

"Why do you feel leaving here will lock us into the 18th Century?"

"We came to this place from 1976. This is the place that Lee said he saw the things from 1976 return. How can we leave, when we might pop back into 1976 at any moment?"

"Seems to me we're damned if we do and damned if we don't."

"Yep. The rock and the hard spot get closer together all the time."

In the distance Sullivan suddenly shouted, "Here they come again!" Startled, Erickson and the others ran to look.

Taking the binoculars from Sullivan, Erickson turned to where he was pointing and saw the Redcoats coming out of the west edge of the Dragoon camp. Morgan was in the lead, followed by his trumpeter. Behind him were the remnants of his troops in three columns.

"My god," exclaimed Erickson, "They *are* coming again!"

He quickly ordered his men into defensive positions and waited, not sure of Morgan's intentions. Was he going to surrender? But, there was no white flag or other sign of capitulation. As Erickson watched in fascination, the Dragoons continued their progression, looking fiercer by the moment.

Erickson allowed them to reach the pond before ordering Russell to fire a mortar smoke shell across their path. The 60mm round left the tube with a soft 'whomp' and arced, unseen, through the air to the crossroads near the tavern and the Wick house. Blue smoke burst forth, obliterating the site of the impact.

Just as the smoke obscured his sight of the Dragoons, Erickson saw Morgan raise his saber and push his horse into a gallop. The sound of the Dragoon trumpet reached his ears and his feet felt the pounding of the hooves on the road far below. The trumpet sounded again, just as the head of the first column peeked through the blue smoke.

"Switch to live ammo," yelled Erickson. "Stop them!"

Russell, assisted by Sullivan, started feeding live shells into the mortar. At the rate of one shell every seven to ten seconds, Russell had soon fired eight rounds at the charging Dragoons. The base plate of the mortar dug itself deeper into the soft dirt after each round, slightly skewing the tube down and to the left. The last two rounds landed at the west edge of the tavern, blowing the Officer's wing up in a flying rain of splintered wood and cheap glass. The rest of the tavern shuddered, but stood firm.

"They've turned!" shouted Sullivan, pointing as Morgan jumped the split rail fence of the Wick house, leading the rest of the troop into the trees. A few moments later, Erickson saw him again, on the far side of the tavern, taking the Dragoons back to their camp.

"He doesn't give up, does he?" Erickson said sadly to Bushnell.

"Maybe he can't," he replied, "British pride being what it is in the 18th century. Putnam told us a little while ago that Morgan had the ammunition. Now we know he has the guts, too."

"Don't you mean stupidity?"

"From our standpoint, yes. But, from his, we're the Rebels and we have to be taken. I'm sorry for him."

Erickson looked around at his men, armed and waiting in the campground, and wondered how many more would die or disappear. "I'm not. I feel sorry for us."

TWENTY-TWO

Monday Midday-Evening

It was another disaster! Not at all the way Morgan had planned it!

It had started out as a simple show of force, to show the Rebels he still had to capacity to inflict punishment on them should they decide to attack him.

With Cilly, Browne, MacKenzie, Thacker and perhaps as many as twenty more of his best troopers dead, Morgan was desperate to do something to forestall the attack he knew would come.

He had ordered Ramsey to mount the troop, including the wounded. It was his plan for them to ride out from the west end of their camp towards the pond, make a wide circle behind the Wick house and the far side of the tavern, and then return to camp. He was sure the Rebels would be watching and would see that his command was still there, waiting.

The explosion of the blue smoke had shocked Morgan back to reality. He had forgotten about the Rebel's cannon! His first reaction had been to raise his sword and signal his men to turn and ride away from the explosion. But, the Trumpeter, misunderstanding the signal, had instead sounded the call for charge.

Morgan had been horrified. The exploding shells cut through the center of the columns behind him. Unable to go back, he hastily lead his men over the fence and through the trees near the front of the Wick house, coming out on the road across from the tavern. From there, he regained his original plan, running past and around the tavern, back into his camp.

Morgan could only guess what the tally of additional dead would be because of this latest encounter.

Of one thing, he was sure. He would have to overcome the Rebels with guile, not force. The idea he had conceived this morning after talking to the Rebel Corporal was worthy of further refinement and execution. The Rebels had a weakness and he would exploit it!

* * *

After devastating Morgan twice in the same morning, Erickson felt he would not be back and told the Platoon to take a break. Dobbs fixed lunch.

Durkee and Molly had eaten quickly and walked off into the trees to be alone. They climbed the hillside to the west, walking well beyond sight of the camp. Finding a dry area, they sat down on the ground. Durkee sat close, facing Molly, gently caressing her check with his hand.

"We may leave at any time, now," he said. "Please say you'll go with me. I've never met anyone like you and you've just got to come."

Molly touched his lips with her fingers. "Randy, Randy. You are a lovely person. But, how would I live in your time? I barely get along well enough to live in me own. You do not really know what I am, do you?"

"You're a beautiful girl and I'm falling in love with you. I want you."

"You have had me. You said you enjoyed me last night."

"That's not what I meant. I want you forever. I want to marry you. I want to take you back with me and get married!"

"You are a foolish lad, Randy Durkee. Girls like me do not get married. We stay what we are, or with luck, become the mistresses of men with money. I am sure it is that way in your time, too."

"Hush, now. You're sounding like some sort of street walker, or worse."

"They give me a different name, but the sound of your voice tells me it is has the same meaning. Do you understand?"

He pulled his hand back from her face, slowly beginning to realize what the girl was trying to tell him. Then he touched her face again, as love overcame the knowledge. "I don't care what you are. No one will ever know in my time. Please say you'll come."

"I wish, I wish," she murmured.

"Wish what?" he softly whispered back, running the fingers of his other hand through her brown hair.

"I wish I could go with you. Do you really think it would be possible?"

"Anything is possible. If you want to go, we'll make it happen."

His romantic moment was short-lived though, as he heard his name being shouted in the distance.

"Durkee!" Bushnell shouted at him again. He was standing a good fifty feet down the hill. "Get your ass back to camp! We've been looking all over for you! Christ, the Lieutenant thought you'd vanished, too!"

*   *   *

Durkee's disappearance had caused a few of the men to panic. They demanded that Erickson load up the trucks and leave the campground immediately. But, when Durkee returned, unharmed, they sheepishly cooled down. Sensing an opportunity, others, who had no relatives in the Dragoons, began insisting that the platoon should retaliate against the British with vengeance.

Watching the tensions unfold, Erickson decided it was time to face them outloud. He called the men together. "I know you're all concerned about the fighting and the disappearance of Hale and MacKenzie, and now Thacker. I can understand why some of you want to stay and fight while others want to pack up and leave. But, I want you all to remember two things: we're missing three men and I won't go until I find out what's happened to them; and, this is the place we came to from 1976. What's to say this isn't the only place that'll get us back? Those are pretty big dilemmas and I don't have the answers."

Erickson took a moment and sternly eyed the men standing around him. "I should tell you one more thing. This is not a voting situation and my decision, when I make it, will be final."

He waited a moment, but the quiet acceptance of his resolve assured Erickson that his command of the platoon remained firm.

"Now," he went on, "it's obvious that as long as we stay here, there could be some more disappearances if we fight the Dragoons again. Since Sullivan and McDougall are the ones at risk, I'd like to hear what they have to say about it."

The men turned to stare at the two. Sullivan fidgeted with his glasses for a moment, testing his words in his mind, first.

"My ancestors were British," he said firmly, "and I think one of those Dragoon's down there is probably related to me. I've thought about him being killed and me vanishing, and I don't like the idea – it's scary! Then, I start thinking if he goes, maybe I never existed, so why worry? You may think I'm nuts, but I want to see this thing through, no matter what the end is. I'm a history buff and I find it exciting. Sergeant Bushnell has said he would like to meet his ancestor in Maryland. Hell, I think mine's over that hill and before this is over, I may just go down there and introduce myself."

"You're for staying, then?"

"Yes, Lieutenant. That's right."

"McDougall, how about you?"

"I understand there's a big, mean Corporal down there that's got my name." Laughter greeted his statement. "I'd like to meet him. If he's the one I think he is, I'll give him a punch in the nose for the things he did later on in life to other parts of the McDougall family." McDougall grinned at his comrades, as they laughed even harder. "Besides, I'm not convinced that killing my ancestor means I'm going to disappear, or that I never existed. Hale, Thacker and MacKenzie disappeared, but we all remember them. They must have existed and maybe still do. Based on what I know, you can count me in, Lieutenant. I'll stay."

Erickson looked at Butler, shooting pictures with his camera. "How many rolls have you taken, Butler?"

"Three, so far. I've got pictures of most everything around here, plus a few when we were on the train. Even got some down in Jockey Hollow when we arrived. Got you face to face with that Major, last Friday."

"Wonderful," Erickson replied sarcastically. "That ought to be a good one."

More laughter from the platoon. The mood of the men was improving.

"Did you take any of the fighting?"

"A few during the first attack and a couple during the second."

Putnam jerked around to look at him. "How could you fight and shoot pictures at the same time?"

"I only took them when I could."

"Great, while your buddies are fighting Dragoons, you're shooting pictures!"

"I thought it was important to record the fighting," Butler replied, defensively. "Some day, these pictures will come in handy – when no one believes us!"

Butler had a good point. Erickson looked at him and said so. "Keep taking pictures; as many as you can, when you can."

Butler nodded.

"OK," said Erickson. "Anybody else want to add anything?"

Dobbs spoke up and promptly threw everyone into confusion. "I've been wondering if *we really are here?*" he said. "Or, are we still in 1976 and only think we're in 1776?"

"What do you mean?" demanded Erickson, just as confused as the others.

"Every day and night since we've been in this camp, we've all had food and water from the kitchen unit. All of us, that is, except one person, one time; and that was Lee the night he brought back the water from the pond.

When Lee gave me the canteen next morning, it was half-empty, so we can be pretty certain Lee took a healthy swig from the canteen before he went to sleep. Now, we all know what he said happened to him that night. He got back to 1976 for a while! So . . . are we really here in 1776, or are we still in 1976 having some sort of nightmare induced by the food and water from the kitchen unit?"

Dumbfounded by the thought, Bushnell grabbed Erickson's arm. "My god, Lieutenant! He exclaimed. "It could be!"

"Could be what?" Erickson's mind was racing with thoughts of how this could have happened.

"The food and water. They could be contaminated with something that produces hallucinations."

Erickson shook his head, both at Bushnell and the rest of the anxious faces. "You're grasping at straws, guys. A mass hallucination? Come on. Look at those mounds up there. That's our dead, waiting for a proper burial. If that's not enough, paw through all the dead British, and the ashes of their horses as well. I think we'd be hard pressed to say all that is a hallucination!"

Bushnell wouldn't drop the idea. "Lieutenant, there's got to be a logical explanation for all this. Dobbs has hit on the only thing that is logical. Let's quit eating and drinking from the kitchen unit, then see what happens tonight. I'll bet we end up back in 1976!"

The mood of the platoon echoed Bushnell's request. Erickson looked around at them and felt the overwhelming hope. Sometimes straws to grasp at were more meaningful than anything. "That means delaying my decision. It means staying here – at least until tomorrow morning. What if the Dragoons come back? You know we'll have to fight them, and no matter what's been said, that still puts at least two of our guys at risk."

Heads nodded. They had heard Sullivan and McDougall and knew the risks. It seemed worth it to try Bushnell's idea, if it meant they could get back to 1976.

"All right, let's try it," Erickson exclaimed. "Dobbs, pick some men for a water detail, and then get cracking on hunting us something for supper. You other Squad Leaders give him whatever help he needs." Turning to Bushnell, he added, "You make sure we have enough guards to cover the men when they go down for water."

A sense of relief developed in the camp. There *was* a reasonable explanation after all!

Durkee wasn't at all sure which way he wanted it to turn out. But, if it meant giving up Molly, then he didn't like the idea. Having made that decision,

Durkee made another. He furtively filled some canteens from the kitchen unit and hid them, intending to keep on drinking the water and maintain the hallucination – if he had to.

Putnam gathered all the canteens in camp and led a few men down to the pond to fill them under the watchful eyes of the guards posted along the way. No Dragoons were seen and the filled canteens soon were laid out on the ground near the kitchen unit.

A deer had been sighted and Russell and Butler had brought it down within a short time. Dragging it back to camp, they hoisted it onto a tree limb for gutting. Cursing the yellow jackets and flies clinging to the carcass, Putnam swore they would devour the meat before any of the men had a chance. Seeing the problem, Dobbs found some burlap sacks, cut them open and soon had the cleaned carcass covered.

"Can I use any of the canned goods?" Dobbs asked Erickson. "We need more than deer meat to eat."

"I understand. But, for the experiment to work, no food from the kitchen unit can be used. Be creative."

Dobbs reluctantly agreed and then tried to figure out how to cook the deer.

He had a fire built in the clearing at the center of the camp, while Putnam and his squad assembled a large roasting spit using heavy tree limbs and a length of iron pipe taken from one of the truck benches. The cooking of the deer took on the trappings of a Texas barbecue.

Well beyond suppertime, the meat was finally ready to eat. Tender and good tasting, half the carcass soon disappeared. With no coffee permitted, Dobbs made sure there was plenty of pond water available to drink with the meal.

Sometime later, after the one-dish meal had settled, Molly approached Erickson. "I want to go back down to the tavern, sir. I'm concerned about the damage."

"I'm sorry we blew part of it away, Molly. Is that where you live?"

"Sometimes, sir. Most times I live in Morristown, but the people there don't have much use for me or Beth."

"Who's Beth?"

"Beth's me friend. She spends a lot of her time with Captain Morgan, though. She likes the way he thumps the mattress."

"Oh?"

"If a body likes a body, the color of his uniform should not make it bad or good."

"Ah." Erickson didn't argue. "When do you want to go?"

"Now, sir. If that is all right?"

"Sure. Go ahead."

Molly turned and started to walk away. Durkee immediately joined her.

Erickson quickly called after him. "Hey, Durkee! Where you going?"

"With her, Sir."

"I don't think that's a good idea. There're still Dragoons down there and they won't take kindly to you. Besides, we're in the process of running an experiment up here. I want you with us if anything happens."

"Darn it anyway, Lieutenant! She wants me to go with her."

"Nope. You stay here. Walk with her to the top of the path, if you want; say your good-byes from there."

Angry and with a heaving heart, Durkee walked her to the trailhead, where he held her tightly, kissing her long and tenderly. The moon was rising as he walked back to the campground. There he saw Bushnell posting extra guards with orders to watch for any changes that might signal the return of 1976.

TWENTY-THREE

Monday Night

Standing on the roadway, Molly surveyed the damage to the west wing of the Tavern. The three bedrooms had been destroyed, leaving only the sturdy wall between them and the bar intact. Blackened bits of bedding and piles of odd debris lay everywhere on the ground. Stepping around pieces of broken glass and splintered wood, she walked to the front of the tavern, where she cautiously mounted the steps and entered through the door.

The tavern keeper was behind the bar, sweeping up. He saw her and immediately smiled.

"Molly! Are ya back? I'm happy to see you. Where ya been?"

"With the soldiers on the hill."

"The Rebels?"

"They are not Rebels. They are from another time and are lost. We must help them."

"From another time? Not likely!"

"Please. They want to return to the time they came from."

"And when is that?"

"They say it is 1976."

"They must be liars!"

"No! No, they are not. I have been to their camp and seen the many things they have with them. I even went riding in one of their jeeps."

"What is a 'jeep'?" The voice of the questioner was deep and determined. Molly whirled to see Morgan at the foot of the stairs.

"'Tis a small wagon with four wheels. It holds four or five people and they drive it around in the hills. No horses or mules pull it. The Sergeant made it go one way or the other by turning a wheel on his side of the wagon. It made a lot of noise."

Morgan crossed the floor. "Keeper, get us some more light in here and bring some beers."

The keeper brought out some candles, placed them on the tables in the front room, and nervously lit them before returning to the bar to draw the beers. Morgan had been in an extremely foul mood and the keeper did not wish to annoy him in any way.

"I see the Rebels listened to me and let you go."

"They didn't let me go. I came back on me own. I went with them because your men were hurting me and their soldiers were nicer."

"And you have a . . . uh . . ." Morgan couldn't remember how Putnam described Durkee, and then it came to him, ". . . boyfriend. That's it, you have a boyfriend, up there?"

"There is a sweet lad up there that is very fond of me. I am growing fond of him, too."

"Do you want him to live?"

"Of course I do. What a silly question."

"Then go back up there and tell him to leave. Tell them all to leave. Tell them all to go tomorrow when it gets light."

"I think they shall leave when they are ready to leave, Captain. They are not afraid of you."

"Not of me, perhaps; but, afraid. Some of them have disappeared – their Corporal told me that. They want to go, but are reluctant to leave without their missing comrades. Well, we shall see about returning their missing comrades."

"You have them?"

"I may be persuaded to return them, if the Rebels agree to leave!"

"What will you do if they cannot or will not leave?"

"I have reinforcements arriving tomorrow," Morgan lied. "When they arrive, I shall have sufficient men and cannon to drive the Rebels off the hill and into Hell!"

Molly stiffened. Reinforcements! There would be another battle and Randy could be killed! She stared at Morgan.

"What is it you would have me do?"

"Rest here a while. The keeper will feed you. Then you can return to your . . . ah . . . boyfriend and tell him of the news you have heard from me. Urge him and the other Rebels to retire from the hill, leave this place and go in peace. We will not pursue them if they leave quickly."

"How will they know that to be true?"

"I will send their missing men back to them first. Then they will know that we can be trusted. Then they can leave this place."

Molly looked at Morgan. He *did* have the missing men! He would return them and they could all leave without further bloodshed. She started to get up to go tell Randy and the Lieutenant, but Morgan gently pulled her back by her wrist, insisting she first drink her beer.

Leaving her at the table, Morgan walked out the back door and hurried to find Corporal McDougall. He didn't have much time to put his plan into effect. In fact, he would have to rely on his Corporal's stealth and cunning to produce the results he knew were possible. Finding him, Morgan led McDougall away from the others to speak in private.

"The girl, Molly, has returned to the tavern. She is going to go back to the Rebel camp with a message that we will let them leave in peace. She will also tell them that I will return their missing comrades."

McDougall looked at Morgan in wonder. He knew he had been acting strangely all day, but how could he consider returning the Rebels?

Morgan ignored the look and continued with his instructions. "Take five men and follow her at a discreet distance. Be extremely cautious when you get to their camp. Watch for their guards. When Molly has them distracted with her presence, make good your entry and hide from their sight. I will find out from Molly where they store their uniforms and weapons. Take as many of those weapons and uniforms as you can safely carry back here."

McDougall's eyes opened wide as he stared at Morgan. Go to the Rebel camp? Steal their weapons and uniforms! What madness was this?

"Move with haste. Molly will be leaving shortly. Pick out five men to take with you. Wait for me at the back door of the tavern. I'll tell you where the weapons and uniforms are hidden. Then follow Molly."

Walking quickly back to the tavern, Morgan entered by the rear door and went to Molly.

"I am sorry I left you so quickly. But I wanted to ensure that the Rebel's missing men would be ready to be returned tomorrow."

"Did you see them?" Molly asked.

"They will be ready," answered Morgan. "Before you go, I would like you to tell me more about the Rebel camp."

"What is it you wish to know?"

"The Rebel Corporal showed us his strange weapon. He let me shoot it and I was most impressed. He said they had many more like it at their camp. Do they?"

"Oh, yes; many, many of them. All kinds."

"We keep our weapons put away when not in use. Do they?"

"Yes, sir, they do."

Morgan waited a moment, seeking not to raise suspicion. But, Molly could not contain herself.

"They have many weapons and wagons up there. There is the jeep I spoke about and four big wagons they call trucks. They also have a little wagon that they use to do their cooking. It also carries food and water for them."

"Do they have any other wagons?" Morgan sought the place the Rebels stored their weapons and uniforms.

"Yes, they do. One, but it is smaller than the food and water wagon. They store their weapons and extra clothing in it."

"Extra clothing? Uniforms?"

"Yes."

"Where do they keep *it*?"

"It is attached to the back of one of the trucks."

"Are the trucks still where we saw them when we attacked their camp?"

"I think so. They only moved the jeep, when they let me ride in it."

"Tell me about the jeep and your ride." Morgan wanted Molly's memory of this conversation to be about herself and the ride, not of his other questions.

Molly giggled and told him about the ride in the jeep, up and over the hills to the north of the campground. She tried to explain the noise made by its horn, but did not succeed as he only pretended to listen. Abruptly, he interrupted her. "'Tis getting late. You must get started."

Shaking her head in acknowledgement, she stood up, pushed the beer mug away and walked to the door. As she reached it, she turned to Morgan. "I will tell them of your offer, Captain Morgan. If they accept it, keep your word. They will destroy you if you do not."

Morgan watched her walk down the road, then quickly went to the back door to meet McDougall and the five Dragoons.

"She tells me the weapons and uniforms are stored in a small wagon attached to the back of a large wagon. You should not have difficulty in locating it."

McDougall nodded.

"Take as many of their weapons and uniforms as you can. Take the long and the short guns, the ones you have seen when we attacked their camp. Take complete uniforms, if you can. Now go, catch up with the girl, but do not be seen, or captured!"

McDougall and his men found it easy to follow the young woman as she continued on her way, sometimes skipping, sometimes half-running in the moonlight along the trail. The Dragoons remained quietly behind as she led them to the hillside camp.

Molly reached the bottom of the path and stopped. Looking up, she saw the glow of the campfire at the top of the hill and loudly called out. "Randy! Randy Durkee! 'Tis me, Molly. I'm coming back!"

Peering over the edge, the guards in the campground could see nothing, but heard the girl moving through the ground cover at the side of the path. She shouted again. "Randy! Do ye hear me? 'Tis Molly. I'm coming back!"

Durkee heard her. He ran to the edge of the camp and called out. "Molly? Where are you?"

"I am near the bottom of the path. Come down and meet me."

McDougall had not expected this turn of events. One or more of the Rebels coming down the path? He signaled his men and they moved into the willows at the north edge of the pond. A few moments later, they heard someone running down the path. If they had been close enough, they would have seen the two of them meet, then hug and kiss like they had been apart for months.

Durkee kept his arm around Molly to guide her back. A beam from Butler's flashlight pierced the dark from above, but failed in its attempt to help them see the path any better.

Hearing them move up the trail, McDougall motioned his men to follow. Reaching the path, they quietly and carefully maintained a discreet distance.

On top, Erickson and Bushnell greeted Molly, then escorted her to the center of the campground. Molly was warmly 'helloed' as she sat down to join them.

"What brings you back so soon?" asked Erickson.

"I have good news for you from Captain Morgan."

"News?"

"Captain Morgan says if you agree to leave in peace, he will return the men you are missing!"

Stunned silence greeted her words. Erickson was the first to recover his tongue. "Morgan says he has our missing men? Are you sure he said that, Molly?"

"Yes, he did."

"Did you see them?"

"No. All he said was he would return them to you if you agreed to leave in peace. If you don't, he will come back up here and fight with you again."

"How's he going to do that?" asked Erickson. "After we shelled his troops down there on the road, he probably doesn't have enough men to gather eggs from a chicken coop."

"He said he has reinforcements coming tomorrow. If you don't leave by then, he will attack! He says he will send you all to hell."

"Wonderful," said Russell. "That's one way of getting out of here."

"Where does he expect us to go, Molly?" asked Erickson. "We just can't pack up and leave without somewhere to go."

"He did not say, Lieutenant. He just wants you to go. If you stay, he will attack and kill you all. He has cannon coming with the reinforcements."

The men moved closer, listening to her intently. Erickson wanted more details. "When will he send the missing men back to us?"

"Tomorrow. But, he did not say what time of day. It would be early, I would think, since if you are not gone when the reinforcements arrive, he will attack."

Erickson looked at her and then at Bushnell. "It smells, Sergeant. I don't think he has the men. He just wants us to leave."

Molly, still fearful for Randy's safety, quickly added, "He said he would return the missing men first, before you left. That way, you would know to believe him."

"Well now," said Bushnell, "That gives us some time to think about this. If he has the men, he can bring them up here and we'll know for sure. If he doesn't, then we'll know it's a bluff."

The men had crowded closer to Erickson and didn't wait very long before arguing amongst themselves about trusting Morgan and the affect he might on their experiment. Strong opinions produce strong feelings and they became louder as Erickson let his men have their say.

Corporal McDougall and his Dragoons took advantage of the noise. Silently, they crept into the edge of the camp. Finding the guards were watching and listening to the argument, they cautiously moved behind the trucks and trailers and found the one they wanted.

Unfamiliar with its workings, they had a difficult time in getting the trailer door open. Apprehensive, they started to flee at one point as one of the guards started towards them. He soon stopped and returned to his original position, though, having moved for no particular reason.

The back doors of the trailer finally yielded to their efforts, opening to reveal the shadowed shapes of extra uniforms, rifles, carbines, a flag, ammunition and a bunch of odd-looking helmets. The six of them grabbed as much as they could, dropping one helmet on the ground in the process. It rolled across the ground and clanked to a stop against a rock. Horror stricken, McDougall wanted to run, but pure nerve held him where he stood. The arguments in the clearing continued ever louder and the guards stayed where they were, attention riveted on their platoonmates in the center of the camp.

Looking around to see if anyone was behind them, McDougall signaled his men to put together six sets of the uniforms, helmets and weapons; one set for each of them to carry back down the hill. He wasn't sure what a proper set consisted of, but satisfied that each looked right, motioned for his men to put the rest of the items back in the trailer. Cautiously and silently, they backed away over the edge of the hill and to the trail.

Out of sight of the fire and the guards, he quietly urged his men to go faster. The further away they got, the more his confidence grew that they would get away unscathed. They were soon at the bottom of the trail, easing themselves around the edge of the pond. After another sixty feet, they were free from worry and ran the rest of the way back to their own camp area.

Out of breath, they deposited their loot on the tables in the Quartermaster's hut, where Morgan soon joined them. Looking at the piles of uniforms and weapons, he was ecstatic. "Did you bring the cartridges for these weapons, so we can fire them?" he asked of McDougall.

McDougall nodded, producing a small sack containing a few clips for the rifles and carbines. "I know not which fits what, Captain. I saw these and stuffed them in the sack. I can only hope they are what you wanted."

"They are, Corporal, they are, indeed." Morgan was so gleeful, he danced a little jig. "You have done well, Corporal. I shan't forget this. Tomorrow I will give you the honor of returning the missing Rebels to their Lieutenant. And then we shall see what happens."

Back on the hillside, Erickson could no longer stand the bickering among his men. The constant repeating of their opinions was becoming irritating. Reaching into his pocket, he grabbed his whistle and blew it loudly. The chattering ceased.

"That's enough for now! You're beginning to sound like a bunch of squabbling children, not soldiers. We all know what the alternatives are. It comes down to making a decision, and that's what I'm here for. So, listen up, because I've made one. We started an experiment here today and I expect to see it through the night. Tomorrow morning we'll know whether we've returned to 1976 or not. If we're still in 1776, we'll see if Morgan has our missing men. After that, I'll decide what further actions we'll take."

"What will we do about the missing men, if we return to 1976 tonight?" asked Private McDougall.

"If we're on a hallucinogenic trip caused by the food and water from the kitchen unit, the missing men will be back in 1976 already, since they haven't had anything from the unit for some time now. They'll be just like us, no matter where they are. If we're still in 1776 in the morning, then they may come back to us through Morgan – but I doubt he has them."

Immediately, the bickering started again. Erickson raised the whistle to his mouth again and blew it to quiet them down. "My point is that I don't want you to be disappointed in the morning when the missing guys don't show up. In my opinion, Morgan doesn't have them. He never had them. It's a trick of some sort and we should be prepared for it. Now, I think the best thing to do is get some sleep. I know most of you won't, since you'll be awake all night looking for 1976 to return; but get some rest, at least. No matter what, you're going to need it in the morning."

Reluctantly, the men broke away from the gathering, walking back to their tents. Durkee put his arm around Molly and led her back to his own tent, where unseen by the others, he stopped briefly to remove his sleeping bag and tuck it under his arm. Trailing part of it on the ground behind, he led Molly into the trees and then, hidden from any prying eyes from the camp, walked with her to the area where Bushnell had found them earlier in the day. There he hand-raked together a high, soft pile of needles and leaves and threw the sleeping bag on top. Helping each other undress, they stood clenched together, slightly shivering in the cool night air. The embrace and kissing stopped only long enough for them to crawl into the sleeping bag. By morning, Durkee would have convinced Molly that she should come back with him.

Back in camp, Erickson and Bushnell walked around the perimeter. Bushnell made it clear that he didn't trust Morgan either and was convinced that the missing men would not be returned in the morning. He brought up his relative again, repeating his hope that it would be possible to see and meet him. Erickson understood his feelings and put his arm around the older Sergeant's shoulder, He patted it, wishing in a way that Bushnell could live his dream out.

Seeing the guards still on duty at the south edge of the campground, Erickson asked, "Are you going to rotate the guards soon?"

"Yeah. I may as well do it now." Bushnell knew it would be a long night, but the guards wouldn't be lonely. The rest of the camp would surely be awake too, watching and waiting for 1976 to return.

TWENTY-FOUR

Tuesday Morning

The Tuesday morning sun pierced the branches of the spruce trees of the campground, seeking out the tents, trucks, jeep, and men of the 4th Platoon. The four guards on duty had seen its early glow and were waiting to welcome the fingers of light they knew would soon be sending them warmth.

The camp was quiet, for the collective strain of watching and waiting had worn them all down. One by one, they had fallen into exhausted sleep, until all but the guards had given up the vigil.

The guards had stayed alert, though, and even at this hour still surveyed the scene, looking for any change in the campground to alert their comrades. Seeing none, they checked the status of the ever-strengthening rays of the sun and then returned their watchful eyes to the Dragoon camp.

Wisps of smoke from the morning fires down in Jockey Hollow rose lazily in the air then were gone, only to be followed by more wisps as more fires were started. It was obvious the Dragoons were getting an early start.

Twenty minutes later, Butler blew reveille and the Americans came to life, only to face the disappointment of finding their campground the same as it was the night before.

Erickson walked over to the guards at the edge of the campground. "See anything?" he asked.

"Nothing now," one of them said. "There was some smoke earlier, probably from their morning campfires."

"All quiet up here, I guess?"

"Yes, Sir. Nothing happened." The statement was tinged with disappointment.

Erickson moved off to look around the rest of the camp. Bushnell soon joined him.

"What are we going to do about breakfast, Jim?" he asked. "I don't feel like eating venison."

"Let's find Dobbs. We've got water in the canteens, so we can get some coffee going. The experiment seems to have failed, so why not use the food that's left in the kitchen unit and get a decent breakfast?"

"I'm not sure he has much left. Today's the day he's supposed to run out, isn't it?"

"Yeah, you're right. See him around anywhere?"

"No, as a matter of fact, I don't. But there's Russell, let's ask him." Waving at him, Bushnell called over, "Hey, Russell! Seen Dobbs?"

Russell shook his head no.

"Find him for us, will you?"

Russell acknowledged the request with a high sign. Scanning the immediate area, he trotted off, asking a couple of his men to join in.

Erickson and Bushnell sauntered over to Lee's tent. Pulling open the flap, Erickson looked in to find an empty sleeping bag. Backing away, he turned to Bushnell. "He's gone. Who did you have watching him?"

"No one specific. He was so quiet that we . . . I . . . just let him sleep. I didn't think about assigning a guard to him." Feeling guilty, Bushnell sought to make light of the situation. "Maybe he got up in the middle of the night again and ended up in 1976. Maybe he stayed there this time."

Erickson shook his head with a grimace, then pulled open the flap to take another look inside. Satisfied that Lee was not hidden in the sleeping bag, Erickson said, "Tell Russell to look for Lee as well. But, do it quietly. We don't need anymore missing people and I don't need another panic."

Bushnell ran to catch up with Russell, while Erickson walked to the storage trailer to find the battery-powered megaphone. Its door was slightly ajar and upon opening it, he found a jumble of clothing, weapons, helmets and other items on the floor. He swore under his breath as he dug through the mess to find the megaphone. Closing the door, he wondered if, somehow, Lee was responsible for the mess, but dropped the thought as he walked back to the man's tent.

He was about to raise the megaphone to his lips when a long, terrible scream came through the trees from the northwest edge of the camp! It sounded like Molly! Erickson took off running and soon was joined by Bushnell and Russell heading in the same direction.

They found her standing near a tree, head down, crying on Durkee's shoulder. She was shaking all over. Durkee stretched his right arm straight up and pointed to the tree above him.

Erickson gasped as his eyes spied Lee's body, dangling by a rope from a sturdy branch on the backside of the tree. Within easy reach on either side were branches that could have supported him anytime he wanted.

Erickson coughed, swallowed again and instructed Durkee, "Take her back to camp, get her out of her!" As they moved off, Erickson motioned for Russell to cut the body down. Moments later Erickson heard a moan a short distance away. Turning, he saw Dobbs lying on the ground next to another tree, holding his head. The quiet moaning continued.

"What the hell? What happened?" he asked, quickly reaching his side.

"I'm not sure," Dobbs answered. "He hit me with something big and hard. Knocked me silly."

"Who did?"

"Lee. Saw him go by my tent very early this morning before the sun came up. He went into the back of the trailer and got something out. When he headed off into the trees, I got up and followed him. He must have seen me. I got about here and whammo! I think he hit me with a tree branch. I must have drifted in and out of consciousness. At one point, I saw him take the rope and start up the tree. Next time I saw him was when he let his feet slide off the branch. Molly's screaming brought me around again."

Dobbs hesitated as he tried to stand but couldn't. "Help me up, will you, Lieutenant? I'm not too steady."

"No, I think it's better you stay down there for a bit. I want to make sure you're all right. Did he say anything to you at all?"

"Not a word. Not *one* word. There *was* one thing, though, Lieutenant."

"What's that?"

"You know how he always kinda slumped around when he walked?"

"Yes."

"Well, this time it was different. In fact, that's what first drew my attention to him. He was walking very purposefully, very erect, a real military bearing to him. Kept it up all the time I followed him."

Erickson mulled it over, then asked. "You think he might have decided to go join Thacker?"

"Could be. Thacker's disappearance really tore him up."

As they spoke, Russell gently slipped the boy's body to the ground. It would soon be moved to the edge of the camp where the others were buried.

Lee's death cast a further pall on the camp, where spirits were already depressed over not returning to their own time. To make matters worse, dark gray clouds began to gather to the east. A quick, wet summer shower was in the offing.

After returning to the center of camp, Molly had calmed down and Durkee sat beside her on the ground, digging with his penknife into the bark of a small spruce next to them. Clearing the bark away, he probed the softwood beneath and began carving a heart. When he finished he slowly, methodically carved an 'R' and a 'D' near its top and a 'M' on the bottom left. There he stopped. "I don't know your last name," he said to Molly. "What is it?"

"'Tis Mifflin. I'm Molly Mifflin."

"Hello, Molly Mifflin," he said kissing her on the forehead. He then added a second 'M' to the one already there and proceeded to cut an arrow through the sides of the heart. That done, he leaned back to look at his work of art. "That should last through the centuries. We can come back here in 1976, cut this tree down, and find it again."

She laughed. "Silly lad. Who will ever care?"

"I will. So will you."

Thunder clapped overhead and the downpour started. Sheets of rain swept through the camp, soaking everything before quickly passing on. The warm sun soon returned, causing little clouds of steam to rise.

A few moments later, a guard noticed movement at the edge of the Dragoon camp and called for Erickson to come look.

In the distance, he saw a group of mounted Dragoons surrounding what appeared to be three men walking in the center. Erickson put his binoculars to his eyes for a closer look and easily picked out the three, dressed in combat fatigues, wearing steel helmets against the rain. Two carried rifles. They walked casually, with the distance between them and the mounted Dragoons sufficient for comfort, but not escape. The Dragoons set a deliberate pace, heading for the intersection of the road by the tavern and the trail behind the Wick house.

Erickson's knees buckled slightly. "What the hell? Are those our guys? Does he really have them!?" Erickson handed the binoculars to Bushnell so he could get a look, too.

"I can't tell which is which with the helmets on, but it *could be* our guys," Bushnell replied. "Look at those Dragoons, they're really watching them closely."

Bushnell handed the binoculars back to Erickson who tried to adjust them for a better focus. He couldn't see which of his men they were either, but that didn't make any difference now. They hadn't disappeared; they'd been captured! Morgan *was* letting them go!

Down below as the Dragoons passed by their house, Tempe and her father, Henry Wick watched from the door. The Dragoons waved. Father and daughter waved back, and then stared after them until they reached the pond and started up the path towards the hilltop.

On the hillside, Erickson raised the battery-powered megaphone he was still carrying and called out to the Dragoons, "Is Captain Morgan with you?" His voice boomed down the hillside.

The Dragoons stopped. One moved his horse away from the group, then pulled a sword and waved it in the air. Erickson called Putnam to his side. Handing him the binoculars Erickson asked, "Is that Morgan?"

Putnam adjusted the binoculars. "Yes, Sir," he replied with disdain. "That's him."

"Well, I'll be damned. I didn't think he would deliver them himself." Erickson retrieved the binoculars for another look at his adversary. "He looks tired. His uniform is dirty and his horse needs a good rubdown. In fact, they all look like they're dragging a bit."

"They're beaten, Lieutenant. We beat them."

"Let's not be too sure of ourselves," Erickson replied. "They're still capable of inflicting damage on us. Porter, get the machine gun set up where it will cover the area from the head of the trail into our camp."

"You want the mortar, too?" asked Russell.

Erickson thought about that for a moment. "Put it over in the trees beyond the east edge of the camp. Keep it out of sight, but position it so you can bring it to bear on the trail and the trail down the hill if we have to."

"You want me to disperse the men?" asked Bushnell.

"Take half of them and hide them in the trees to the west, where they can cover the trail and us. Have the rest stack arms in the clearing where they can get them. You and I will keep our sidearms. I want to be protected, but I don't want it to look to Morgan like we're expecting a fight, either. I wouldn't want him to get scared and start shooting at us or the guys he's bringing back."

Erickson looked back down the hill and was startled to see Morgan and the group still standing where he had last seen them. Grabbing the megaphone, he called out, "Come ahead, Captain."

Morgan raised his sword again, swung it back and forth in the air and then pointed it up the trail. The Dragoons moved forward again. Erickson watched as they came up, remembering the day he and Putnam had been stopped by the Dragoon Sergeant and then chased back up the trail, maybe by some of these same Dragoons.

The mounted horsemen briefly disappeared from view before reappearing near the top of the trail. Still fearful of a trap, Erickson unsnapped the cover on his holstered .45 and waited.

Morgan finally reached the top, leading the group into the American camp. The three prisoners had been moved to the rear where two Dragoons guarded them. Morgan saluted with his sword, mistakenly identifying Bushnell as the Rebel leader. Bushnell just pointed at Erickson and Morgan urged his horse towards him. There he saluted again with the sword, in response to which Erickson merely nodded, saying only "Captain Morgan."

As an afterthought, he added a perfunctory salute.

Morgan dismounted and walked over to him.

"I have not had the pleasure, sir."

"I'm Lieutenant James Erickson, United States Army. This is Master Sergeant Thomas Bushnell." Morgan nodded and Bushnell threw him a quick, but perfunctory salute.

Looking around the camp, Morgan saw Molly standing next to Durkee. "I see our Molly has returned to you and, I assume, delivered our offer of peaceful departure."

"Yes, sir, she did. I see you have brought my men back. Will you release them now?"

"In a few moments, Lieutenant. I believe there is a bargain to be made first, is there not?"

"Yeah, there is. You want to be assured that we will leave here just as soon as the men are turned over."

"That is correct, Lieutenant, I want you to put your things in your wagons and be ready to leave. When the men are turned over, you must go! Is that agreed?"

"A moment, please, Captain, while I talk it over with Sergeant Bushnell. I want to make sure we are fully prepared to leave." Erickson knew that they were not ready to leave that quickly. He hadn't planned it this way, at all.

Erickson and Bushnell turned and walked away a few feet so as not to be overheard. As they did, Putnam sauntered up to where Morgan stood.

"Morning, Captain," he said, eyes flashing contempt for the man and enjoying the moment. "Haven't seen you since yesterday."

Morgan's eyes flashed in return. "You! You killed Corporal Thacker."

"Whatja expect me to do? Let him take me off to New York and meet General Howe?" Putnam scratched his leg with the barrel of his carbine. Morgan looked at him and the carbine, then decided that further conversation was unnecessary. He would wait for the Lieutenant and the Sergeant to be done.

Erickson and Bushnell returned. "OK. Sergeant Bushnell will have the men clear out the camp, put our things away in the trucks and be ready to leave. In the meantime, may we talk to our men?"

"No. I do not think you trust me and I do not think I trust you. You may speak to your men after we leave. For now, we shall keep them isolated where they are. Please order your men to stay away from them."

"I'll do that, Captain. And, please order your men to stay where they are, too. A few of my men will watch them, just for good measure."

Morgan nodded his acknowledgement and remounted his horse. Pulling the reins, he guided the horse back to the rest of the Dragoons at the head of the trail. There he sat, straight in the saddle, watching the Americans break camp.

Putnam made a beeline for Erickson. "What's going on, Lieutenant?" he asked. "I thought we would decide whether to leave or not after our men were returned?"

"Hang in there for awhile, Corporal. Something funny is going on."

"Huh?"

"How many of our guys have you seen wearing helmets, except in battle?"

Putnam thought for a moment. "None. They're too hot and heavy."

"And most of our guys blouse their pant legs around their boots, don't they?" Erickson went on.

"Yeah."

"Well these guys – now don't turn around – these guys don't. Something funny *is* going on. I'm going to play the hand out, though. It *could be* our guys over there, giving us some kind of signal. We can't tell yet. Who knows what Morgan has in mind? I don't want to do anything that might set him off and get more of our people killed. We'll wait until the trucks are packed and then see if those guys are ours or not. Pass the word. Tell everybody to be ready for anything."

Erickson moved around the camp, watching the loading of the trucks, as Putnam cautiously and quietly spread his orders and concerns to the men.

The camp was completely cleared and the trucks ready to go within a half-hour. Morgan rode over to where Erickson and Bushnell stood watching.

"Where are your horses and mules?"

Bushnell started to laugh, but Erickson jabbed him in the side. "We don't need horses or mules. Watch!" Erickson signaled the drivers to start the vehicles.

None of the engines, except for the jeep's had been run since Friday night. Starter motors grinding, the powerful truck engines at first refused to catch. Slowly though, they responded to the tramping of the accelerators and the continued turning of the flywheels, finally coughing into life. Bluish black smoke spewed from their exhaust pipes, clouding the air around them and the mounted Dragoons. Apprehensive of the noise and smoke, the Dragoons nervously sought to back away, but Morgan stood his ground and they followed suit.

The motors soon settled down, purring smoothly. Erickson signaled again and the drivers put the trucks in gear and moved forward – out of the ruts they had created with their weight and into the clearing at the center of the camp. There they stopped, engines idling. With the kitchen unit attached to one truck and the trailer attached to another, the only vehicle left in place was the jeep. Erickson walked towards it, followed by Morgan riding at his side.

"Care to go for a ride?"

"In that wagon?"

"Yes. It's called a jeep. Molly rode in it. She really enjoyed herself."

"Thank you, no. Wagons that move without horses or mules must be the work of the Devil!"

"For all the problems they cause back in my time, I'm sure a lot of people would agree with you. Speaking of agreements, we've completed our end of the bargain. Now it's time for you to complete yours."

Morgan mused for a moment, then turned and rode back to his men. Gathering them around, he moved them into the same area the trucks had just vacated. The prisoners stood where they had been left, watching. Morgan eased his horse through his men and stood in front while they lined across behind him. He slowly drew his sword and elegantly raised it in a sweeping salute to Erickson and the Rebels.

Then, replacing the sword in its scabbard, Morgan spoke. "I know we shall not part friends, but, perhaps, with grudging respect. You are not the usual rag-tag we have seen before. You fight well and we have learned much in our encounters with you. Today, I will receive reinforcements and cannon from General Howe. If you come back here, we will be waiting. We will be the victors in the next encounter, of that you can be sure!"

His speech ended, Morgan again pulled and flourished the sword in an elegant salute and pulled back on the reins of his horse to turn. Instead, the horse reared up, front hooves pawing the air! It reared back so far, Morgan was dumped over the rear of the saddle and ended up on the ground, wind knocked out of him. He lay there on his back, trying to recover his breath while the rest of his men scrambled off their horses to help him. Erickson and the others ran to where Morgan lay.

"Are you all right, Captain?" asked Erickson. Morgan moved his hand back and forth in front of his face, indicating that all he needed was air. After a few moments, his men helped him to his feet and then back on his horse. Smiling and nodding a facial salute to Erickson, Morgan again pulled on the reins, this time more gently, and the horse turned a half circle leading the rest of the Dragoons over the west hill, away from the staring Americans. Erickson stood and watched in silence as the last of the Dragoons disappeared from view.

When they were gone, he turned and started to walk back to the jeep. As he did, he looked up and saw the three prisoners, kneeling in a line, pointing two M-1's and a carbine at him and his men!

The man in the center of the kneeling line had removed his helmet, revealing the familiar hairdo of the British soldier. He motioned with his M-1 for Erickson and the rest to halt. "Stay where you are. Do not move. I am Corporal McDougall of the 16th Light Dragoons and you are my prisoners. We will kill you if you do not obey."

"God . . . damn!" sputtered Putnam. "Morgan fell off that horse on purpose, just so they could get into position."

"I'm afraid you're right, Corporal. Looks like we all got taken in." Erickson hoped he sounded convincing, while at the same time wondering how his men in the trees could get clear shots at the three Dragoons.

From his left, Erickson heard a familiar, but demanding voice. "Did you say your name was McDougall? My name is McDougall, too! I had a relative that served in the 16th Light Dragoons, and maybe that's you. His name was Perceval McDougall. What's yours?"

The Dragoon Corporal lowered the M-1 slightly as he looked to see who was speaking. "Aye, my name is Perceval McDougall. You say you are a relative of mine? How is that?"

"You're married to a woman named Judith and have a son named Clyde. The boy was born last month, in New Brunswick. You joined the Dragoons after they got over here from England because you liked riding better than walking. At the same time that your son was being born, you were with a woman named Elizabeth who will also bear you a son. After this war is over, you will become a wealthy man, dealing in land and slaves, but your wealth will all go to the woman Elizabeth and her bastard child. 179 years from now the descendant of your boy, Clyde, will have a son. That's me. I figure I owe you something for the rough life all the generations in between had to lead because you gave your damn money to the bastard!"

His tirade finished, Private McDougall ran across the space separating him from the Dragoon Corporal, grabbed the M-1 from his surprised and distracted ancestor's hands and punched him very hard on the jaw!

The blow staggered the Corporal, who slumped to the ground, dazed and disoriented. The two other Troopers quickly grabbed at Private McDougall, but were overwhelmed by an onslaught of Americans from all directions. Sheepishly, they surrendered, wondering what had happened. Morgan had told them the Rebels would give up peacefully when they saw the Dragoons were armed with the repeating weapons. Now, those weapons were back in Rebel hands and Corporal McDougall lay on the ground, head next to the steel helmet he had been wearing.

"McDougall," Erickson exclaimed, "that was beautiful! Thanks!" He patted him on the back as they walked towards Bushnell.

"Now what?" asked Bushnell. "Will Morgan be back?"

Erickson nodded. "Probably. And, if he does, if anyone so much as sees a Dragoon coming towards this camp, tell 'em to shoot to kill."

As he spoke, Erickson watched the three Dragoons being tied up and placed in the back of one of the trucks. They would stay there until he could decide what to do with them.

The mortar was moved from the trees and repositioned for better use against the road and trail. The machine gun was brought to the center of the clearing and its mounting mechanism checked to ensure full 360-degree coverage. Sentries were sent well out from the edge of the camp, to shout the arrival of any Dragoons.

TWENTY-FIVE

Tuesday Morning-Evening

"How's your head, Dobbs?" Erickson was concerned about Lee's blow to his head with the tree branch.

"Didn't know for a while if I was going to make it or not, Lieutenant. But, I'm OK now. I can see all right and the buzzing has gone from my head."

"Good. You had us all worried."

Erickson turned to Bushnell. "Morgan says he has reinforcements and cannon on the way. He's a determined sonofabitch and I have no doubts he'll take us on as soon as they arrive. I've got to consider the safety of Sullivan and McDougall, no matter how much they say they don't care."

"Well, at least McDougall is safer, now that we have his ancestor tied up in the truck."

"Yeah, but Sullivan's isn't. The problem, is, how do I weigh the risk of having one more disappear, against the three that are already gone? And how much longer can I wait for them to return, if they're going to, before we lose all our options, especially when Morgan comes at us in force?"

"Well, we know one thing, for sure. Nothing happened last night. It sounded good, but Dobbs's theory didn't prove itself out." Bushnell was firm in that conclusion.

"Maybe it wasn't the water and food, after all. There could be a lot of other reasons for being here," Erickson responded.

"Name one." Bushnell was startled at the comment and challenged Erickson.

But, Erickson said nothing, seemingly searching for an answer. Not wanting to press the point, Bushnell changed the subject. "We've got damn little food left. There's some deer meat and maybe enough other food for a light lunch this noon. After that . . . well, we don't know, do we?"

Suddenly switching sides, Erickson perplexed Bushnell even further. "We've got a water supply down below and the woods are full of food from animals and plants. Molly and the tavern keeper can show us which ones are edible and how to cook them. We *can* survive," Erickson replied, authoritatively.

"What are you talking about, Lieutenant? One minute you're ready to leave and the next, stay. What are we going to do, continue fighting? For what? Guys that aren't coming back? A water supply that can't be used when Morgan's reinforcements arrive? Frankly, Lieutenant, I'm tired of the fighting and so are the men. This was supposed to be a summer camp and instead, we've lost a bunch of our troops. Three are buried up there," he said, pointing to the gravesite. "It's time to end it!"

"Look, Tom," Erickson replied in a tone of friendship, instead of authority. "I know I'm vacillating, but it keeps coming back to me – if we leave, is there anyplace else where we can get back home? Is this the only place, or are there others? And, if there are others, where the hell are they? Yeah, I'm vacillating, and with good reason! I know the men were misled when I went along with Morgan, but the risks in us leaving are very high in my mind. If we have to stay, well . . . we're all soldiers, Tom, even if we are summer reservists. I've been lax on discipline at times, because they *are* reservists and we've asked a lot of them. But, don't underestimate them, either. If I decide to stay, they *will* fight if need be. I know we can count on them!"

"Yes," Bushnell replied, slowly. "But, there are other factors at work here! I'm worried about what you said before, about staying and changing the future. We've got some guys that are talking about fighting in the war, not just against the Dragoons, but up to their eyebrows in Washington's army."

"What are you telling me?"

"I hear things. That's my job! That's what I do as a Platoon Sergeant. I also think Sullivan is seriously planning to find his ancestor in the Dragoon camp, now that McDougall is talking to his great, great, great, great, great, great grandfather over in the back of that truck. Problem is, Sullivan will be an easy target to capture, when he does."

"OK, Tom, calm down! Let's not get carried away. Something just occurred to me – Morgan's got to be around here someplace close, waiting for a signal from Corporal McDougall to come back and take us all prisoner. Probably getting antsy by now wondering what's going on. Send a patrol out to look for him. Let's see if *we* can capture *him*. That would put a stop to their attacks and give us some breathing room!"

Putnam, who couldn't help eavesdropping, quickly offered his services. "Let Arnold and me go."

Erickson liked the idea. "Why not? You know him and his troopers best. Take some others with you. When you find him, get back to us, so we can send help."

Russell and Sullivan quickly decided to join them. As the four readied themselves, Private Stewart from the kitchen unit came up and asked if he could join, too. Putnam nodded his head in agreement.

The five quickly moved out, keeping abreast of each other as they cautiously moved up the west hill. Reaching its crest, they moved quietly down the other side, staying well within the trees, avoiding any small clearings. They had gone perhaps a hundred yards when Russell heard and then spotted the Dragoon's horses. He signaled the others to spread out as they worked their way towards Morgan, seated on the ground amidst three other Dragoons.

Putnam anxiously looked around for other Dragoons, but seeing none, decided that Morgan had sent them on to their camp. It was a natural assumption, knowing Morgan's ego: after all, McDougall and the others could easily capture Erickson and his men, and then Morgan, supported by only a few Dragoons could take them all down the hill in triumph.

Realizing he had an opportunity to capture Morgan without wasting time to go back for Erickson, Putnam got the others into position, moving quietly through the trees and undergrowth. The early morning rain did much to dampen the noise of their movements, allowing them to come within feet of Morgan before they were seen.

Startled by the sight of the Rebels, Morgan jumped to his feet and grabbed for his sword, but stopped in mid-reach as Putnam shoved the barrel of his carbine into the soft flesh of his nose. Morgan dropped his hand to his side, expelling an oath under his breath.

The other Dragoons quickly submitted to the weapons pointed at them, as well.

"We meet again, Captain Morgan," said Putnam, with delight. "This time circumstances are in my favor. Why don't you all come along to our camp? I'm sure I can find a loggerhead around that can be heated up for you."

"I used no loggerhead on you! I allowed you to eat breakfast. You returned my favor by killing Corporal Thacker!"

"He didn't kill Thacker, I did," said Arnold coming around to face Morgan. "Thacker was trying to shoot me, so I shot him. Just like I'd shoot you, or any of your men here, if they tried the same thing."

Morgan cast his eyes down at the ground, shrugged his shoulders and motioned for his men to get up. As they did, Arnold, Sullivan and Stewart disarmed them, dropping their pistols, carbines and swords into a pile on the ground. Arnold wrapped them in the blanket the Dragoons had been sitting on and hoisted the load to his shoulder. He would take them back to camp.

Putnam led the way back up the hill, followed by Morgan and the Dragoons. Russell, Sullivan and Stewart came next, keeping guard, while Arnold brought up the rear, carrying his bulky load.

The climb was slow in the wet undergrowth, causing them to slip. Morgan fell down a number of times, staining his white breeches above the knee. Arnold too, slipped, scattering the load of weapons over the forest floor. Telling the rest to go on, he spread the blanket and repacked them, lurching to catch up as the others crested the hill into the campground.

Moments later, Morgan stood in front of Erickson, depressed and surly, as Putnam puffed up the story of his capture by him and the other four. When Erickson and Bushnell moved a few yards away to discuss what to do with Morgan now that they had him, Sullivan impulsively stepped over, seeking answers about the Sullivan in the Dragoons. As he did, though, he bumped into Stewart, jarring him off-balance. Taking advantage of the momentary distraction, one of the Dragoons quickly jumped up, shoved Morgan into Sullivan and Stewart and ran to warn his comrades of the situation.

Putnam, who saw it all, fired a warning shot in the air. "Stop!" he yelled.

Terrified by the sound of the shot, the Dragoon dodged into one of the stacks of M-1's, falling over the rifles as they separated on the ground. In panic, he grabbed one and aimed it at Putnam. Putnam aimed back, but the Dragoon shot first, sending the .30 cal. bullet zinging past him into a tree. Uncertain of the weapon he held, the Dragoon thought about reloading, but caught himself in time to re-shoulder the weapon and aim it again. He was too late – Putnam cut loose a string of four shots.

As the Dragoon fell backwards, dead, Sullivan and Russell let out horrified gasps and muffled shrieks. Morgan, getting up from the ground, reared back, gasped and fainted, while Arnold stood by in cold wonder. Hearing the commotion, Putnam whirled to see what was the matter, but the looks on the faces of his comrades made him stop before saying a word. Russell was bent down in a crouching position. So was Sullivan, a horrified look contorting his face. Staring at them all, Putnam exasperatedly waited for an explanation.

Erickson and the rest of the platoon crammed around, waiting too. Arnold regained his voice first. Attempting composure, he haltingly tried to explain. "It was Stewart. We were helping him back to his feet when Putnam shot the Dragoon. At that instant, Stewart just vanished!"

"What!? What did you say?" Putnam was incredulous at hearing what he'd done.

"He vanished when you shot the Dragoon. One second he was there, letting us help him up. Morgan was even helping. The next second he was gone!"

"My god, that bastard over there was going to kill me! Putnam growled in his own defense. "I *had* to shoot him." That said, he slowly settled to the ground, wrapped his arms around his knees and shook his head, "What have I done?" he asked no one in particular. "What have I done?"

Erickson watched the whole scene, slowly shaking his head from side to side in disbelief. No one had told him Stewart had ancestors in the Dragoons. Why hadn't Sullivan told him? Maybe he didn't know.

"Hey!" Russell yelled, jerking them all back to reality. "The Dragoons are escaping!" He raised his carbine and fired one awkward shot before Erickson bowled him over.

"Put it down! You want someone else to vanish, too!"

Russell sheepishly faced his Lieutenant. "I didn't think. Good, god, Sir, I didn't think!"

Arnold ran over to Erickson, pointing towards the trail. "They went down the hill, probably for help! Maybe even those reinforcements Morgan's been talking about!"

At that same moment, McDougall and Sullivan came running up. "We've changed our minds," said McDougall, with a very serious tone. "Since Sully didn't know Stewart had an ancestor in the Dragoons, there may be others up here we don't know about, too. We think it's time to get the hell out of here, Lieutenant."

Erickson's shoulders slumped for a moment, unable to bear the thought that others in the platoon might be at risk without knowing it. Everyone could be at risk! Nodding his head, he quietly agreed. "All right. We'll go."

Bushnell nodded in agreement, hesitated a second and then asked, "What are we going to do with our dead? They have a right to be buried properly in our time, don't you think?"

"We can't dig them up and take their remains with us. They're still decomposing. Think of the stench and the risks in handling the remains. I know it would be right, if we could, but we don't have the means."

Bushnell acknowledged the logic. "You're right."

Erickson then asked, "How many Dragoons do we still have?"

"Four. Morgan, McDougall and the other two we got earlier."

"Tie Morgan up. Put him in with the others."

Erickson called the platoon together. "All right. We're going. I don't know what will happen, but we've got to stick together. Sergeant Bushnell and I will take the jeep and lead the way. Russell, you and McDougall stay in the truck with Morgan and the Dragoons. I want them guarded. The rest of you Squad Leaders divvy up your men in the other three trucks. And, pick up the mortar and any other weapons still in camp! OK. Let's do it!"

As they hastened to the jeep, Bushnell asked, "Are we going to follow the way I took the other day?"

"Why not? You said the trees were thinner, even gone in places. That seems the way to go." Even as he spoke, Erickson's mind was jumping ahead, wanting to get home and away from it all. The look on the men's faces as they jumped in the trucks, told him they were eager to get home, too. But, was home in this direction? Or, was he taking them away from the only opportunity they would have to get back to their own time?

"Have any idea what's beyond the valley I saw the other day?" Bushnell asked, interrupting Erickson's musing.

"Dover's up there somewhere, maybe a little to the west. Highway 10 should be in our path and so should Interstate 80. That is . . . if we get back. If not . . . well, then there's just more hills and more trees and . . . more Dragoons."

Bushnell got into the jeep and settled behind the wheel. As he started it up, Erickson climbed in the other side and signaled the others to follow them.

*   *   *

The trucks had plenty of room to get through. But, the ground was rough and the terrain hilly, even slick in places from the recent rains, forcing the trucks at times into six-wheel drive. They maintained a steady pace, the jeep moving far in front, scouting for the best course to follow. As the sun settled into a low, afternoon position, Erickson ordered a halt and the men dismounted.

He looked for Dobbs. "Do you have any food left?" he asked when he found him. "In all the excitement back there we forgot lunch and I'm sure the men are getting hungry."

"A little, Sir," he answered, grimacing at the twinge in his own stomach as he realized that he was hungry, too. "I'll go get what we have and spread it out."

"Good. In the meantime, Sergeant Bushnell and I will drive up to the top of that next hill and look around."

Erickson took the wheel this time. They soon reached the top of the hill and stopped. Using his binoculars, Erickson searched a large arc of the area in front of him. The hill they were on sloped down and away to the north, leading to another hill with a crest slightly lower than the one they were on. Beyond he could see a long, wide valley. A distant noise from that direction caused him to cock his ear.

"Listen, Tom. What do you hear?"

Bushnell strained his ears. "Not sure, Lieutenant. Almost sounds like a river. It's a long way off though. What's it sound like to you?"

"A river is as good a guess as any. Here," Erickson said, passing the glasses to Bushnell, "take a look and see if you can make anything out."

Bushnell strained to see, taking the glasses away from his eyes from time to time as he listened closely to the noise. He suddenly jerked around to Erickson with an inspired guess.

"What if I said it's a freeway!? That same kind of steady noise comes from the freeway near my work. I think I can even make out the sounds of trucks shifting gears, climbing hills. You said there was an Interstate around here. Well, I think we've found it!"

Erickson stared at Bushnell, the very words causing his heart to pound in anticipation, but he remained outwardly calm, somehow afraid to believe it possible. "So we've found us a freeway, have we?"

"Here, you take the binoculars and look," said Bushnell, thrusting them back at Erickson. "But, you're got to rely on your senses more than what you can actually see." Getting bold with his conviction, Bushnell asserted himself. "I'll bet my last dollar there's a freeway in that valley! Listen to the noise – it can't be anything else!"

Erickson, dubious, cautious, not daring to share Bushnell's enthusiasm took the binoculars back and put them to his eyes. He could see no Interstate with his eyes, and though he strained, could hear no identifiable modern sounds coming from where he scanned. He continued listening, intently.

Time passed slowly for Bushnell as he stood and waited impatiently in silence.

Somewhere in the distance, the muffled sound of a diesel truck, pulling a heavy load and shifting gears eased its way over the hill and slowly reached Erickson's ears. He listened to it for a few moments before fully comprehending that *that* was a sound *he knew*. Methodically, he took his time, verifying what his mind was telling him. Slowly, he let himself start to believe it, a little at first and then more . . . until it finally swept over his entire body.

He suddenly let out a whoop and grabbed Bushnell's hand, wildly shaking it up and down, before breaking away to the jeep. Climbing in behind the wheel, he waited just long enough for Bushnell to jump in before he roared off down the hill towards the trucks and the rest of the platoon.

The men at the trucks heard the horn and looked up to see the jeep bouncing toward them. Bushnell was standing up in the seat every few seconds, only to be bounced back down again. When he was up, he was yelling and waving his free arm in the air, using the other to grab the windshield to hold himself steady. By the time the jeep got back to the trucks, the men had gathered with unbridled hope and anticipation.

Erickson slammed on the brakes and spun the rear end of the jeep around as he stopped, almost throwing Bushnell off the seat. Jumping out, the two were so excited that they could hardly speak the words. Erickson just kept pointing up the hill and saying three words: "we're going home!"

The platoon erupted with the news. Again, food was forgotten as the men remounted the trucks to leave immediately. Though eager as well, Erickson still took a few moments to check on Morgan and the other three Dragoon prisoners. Satisfied that they were still secure, he started to climb into his jeep when Molly and Durkee suddenly came up.

Durkee put his hand out, touching Erickson's arm. "Sir, Molly has a request to make."

"Sure, what is it?" Erickson, said halfheartedly, irritated at the interruption in getting underway.

"She remembers how frightened she was when I first talked about bringing her back with me to 1976. Now that it looks like we're *actually* going to do that, she thinks someone ought to tell the Dragoons what's going on, so they don't become frightened, too. She'd like to ride with them the rest of the way and explain things, if she can."

Erickson wondered how Molly could even begin to explain to the Dragoons what was going on, but he knew her thought was from her heart.

"That's very thoughtful, Molly," he said. "You go ahead. But first, Durkee, you get Russell and McDougall to check all their bindings to make certain they can't get loose."

"Yes, Sir, and thank you, Sir!" Durkee saluted and walked off with his arm around his girl. He knew in a short while he would have her back in 1976.

A few moments later, Russell and McDougall, satisfied the Dragoons were secure, jumped out of the truck and helped Molly get in. Leaving her alone with them, the two climbed into the back of another truck, as Bushnell, again driving, started the jeep up the hill. The whistling, yelling, shouting and horn blowing coming from the troops and trucks behind made it difficult for him to hear.

The enthusiasm stopped though, when they found over a dozen large boulders blocking their way up the final hill. Grumbling and complaining, the men spent more than an hour pushing the huge rocks out of the way, using the bumpers of the trucks and the jeep. Finally, the last of the big rocks yielded, opening the way again.

Still in the lead, Bushnell led the olive-drab convoy through the final turns before starting down the last hillside. Moments later he and Erickson clearly heard the noise of the Interstate rushing to their ears. After so many days of 18th century quiet, the din and tumult was startling to their ears. Bushnell eased the jeep down the long, final slope, followed by the trucks.

The sun was almost gone now, its last rays glimmering off the scattered, high fluffy clouds to the west, turning them a brilliant yellowish-orange before fading to a finale of purples and reds. In the near distance, they could make out the Interstate. Cars and trucks were speeding along and upon seeing them, Bushnell sped up, the jeep bouncing as it hit ruts and bumps in his path. The trucks remained close behind, bouncing their human cargoes as well.

The slope of the hill started to smooth out in front of him and Bushnell increased speed some more, the jeep now flying across the ground in places, with the trucks still close behind. As the terrain flattened more, Bushnell pushed the accelerator to the floor and the jeep sped up even more, before he finally eased back on the pedal. Erickson's hair blew wildly in the wind.

The Interstate was about 200 yards away when Erickson first saw the fence coming into view in front of them. "My, god!" he yelled. "There's a fence up there!" Bushnell saw it too, and slowed, desperately looking for a place to stop.

The driver of the truck behind them, with Molly and the Dragoons inside, failed to see that Bushnell was slowing; instead holding his speed steady, rapidly closing the gap between them.

Waving frantically, Erickson tried to get him to slow down or turn off, but the driver only thought it was a signal that they were almost there. Hell, he could see that for himself!

Realizing it was too late to do anything but save themselves, Bushnell whipped the steering wheel to the right to avoid the fence. The little jeep lurched, ejecting Erickson across the hard ground. His limp body finally came to a halt near a large rock. With his right arm broken and bleeding, he just lay there.

The driver of the truck immediately slammed on his brakes, dodged the jeep, then crashed through the chain link fence. A hundred-foot section, hooked to his front bumper, dragged him to a halt just short of the highway shoulder and speeding traffic. The other drivers slowed down in time, bringing their big trucks to a stop between the broken fence and the jeep.

Putnam leaped out and ran forward to check on Bushnell. Porter and Dobbs ran to find Erickson, as Russell ran forward to the truck that had pierced the fence, hoping that Molly and the Dragoons were all right.

The jeep had tilted precariously, then settled back on its four wheels as it came to a stop. Bushnell sat in the driver's seat, still holding tightly unto the steering wheel. His eyes were glazed over and his cheeks and tongue were bleeding from the bites he had inflicted as he careened out of control.

Along the shoulder of the Interstate, people poured out of their vehicles to gape at the military truck sticking through the fence and the groups of soldiers standing around on the other side. Erickson's men stood where they were, gaping back. In the distance, a siren wailed and the men could see the flashing red lights coming towards them. Soon, a second siren took up the call and then a third.

Russell reached the door of the truck and jerked it open. Inside, the driver sat bolt straight, arms stiffly holding the steering wheel, foot still jammed down on the brake pedal. Cold sweat poured down his face.

"You OK?" Russell asked.

Staring through the windshield at the edge of the Interstate just feet away, he slowly replied. "I may be. I may not. I haven't made up my mind yet."

Hearing the humor in his voice and seeing no obvious injuries, Russell hurried to the rear of the truck to check on Molly and the Dragoons. He had been riding in the front seat of the truck immediately behind them, to keep an eye on Molly, but as they sped up down the slope, the flaps on her truck had blown closed, shutting off his view. He knew it must have been a wild ride for them, especially since all but Molly were tied up. But, at least no one had fallen out as the truck bounced through the air.

He jerked the flap open. "Everybody all right in here . . . ?" He stared at empty benches! No one was there! Incredulous, he stared for another moment, then dropped the flap and ran back to his truck to grab a flashlight. Returning to Molly's truck, he opened the flap again, shining the light all around, looking for Molly, Morgan, the Dragoons, anyone! They were all gone!

"Anything hurt here?" The Highway Patrolman had approached unseen and was tapping Russell on the shoulder. Startled, Russell jumped back and almost knocked him down.

"Everything's fine!" Russell jammed the words together as he closed the flap. Fear enveloped his body. Where were the Dragoons and Molly?

"You get shaken up in the crash?" The Officer eyed Russell suspiciously.

"Yeah, that's for sure!"

"Who's in charge here?"

"The Lieutenant, over there." Russell pointed to where Erickson was being given first aid by Porter and Dobbs. "His name is Lieutenant Erickson."

As Russell followed the Officer over to where Erickson lay, the Officer turned to him. "You guys with the 4th Platoon, J Company, 76th Special Services?"

"Yep, that's us," Russell replied, somewhat sarcastically. "We're back from the war."

"More than likely you're heading for one. You're in a heap of trouble, you and your friends here."

"What do you mean, trouble?" Russell raised his left eyebrow. "We just got out of trouble like you've never seen before. How can we be in trouble, now?"

"Ever hear of a Major Henry Perkins?"

"Nope. Who's he?"

"Military Police. Says your Lieutenant was insubordinate to him over at Jockey Hollow. And then, you guys went AWOL."

"AWOL!?"

"Yes. When they couldn't find you in the campground he sent you to, they started a big search. After two days, they gave up and declared you all AWOL. I think there are a few other charges pending, too. But I'll let the Major tell you about them after he gets here."

"He's coming here?"

"Notified him as soon as I pulled up and saw the three trucks and the jeep. That's part of the description that's been broadcast on you guys."

An ambulance crew arrived and started working on Erickson. Leaning to see over them, the Officer asked, "You Lieutenant James J. Erickson?"

"Yes." Erickson responded, weakly, wondering how the Officer knew his name.

Eyeing the drooping arm and obvious pain, the Patrolman sought to comfort him. "These guys will take care of you. We'll get you to a hospital as soon as possible." Then, as he backed away to let the emergency crew continue, he added, "What the hell were you guys doing on this side of the fence, anyway? Look at all the chain link you tore out!"

"We were just so glad to get back," answered Russell, "that we got carried away. Roared down the hill and didn't see the fence until it was too late."

"Get back? Where have you been?"

"It's a long, hard story to explain," Russell said, as the siren of yet another arriving patrol car dinned in the background. "You want to hear about it?"

"Save it for Major Perkins. I think that's him that just arrived."

A large tow truck had also arrived and was helping clear the chain link away, releasing the three trucks to pull up parallel to the Interstate. Russell went over to Erickson to tell him about the Dragoons, but was prevented from getting close by the ambulance crew as they continued their work.

Undaunted, Russell tried signaling with his hands, but Erickson was too numb to comprehend. Finally, in desperation, Russell grabbed Porter by the arm and led him away, whispering in his ear as he wildly gestured with his free hand. Together they ran to the truck and checked it again. Still no trace of Molly, Morgan or the Dragoons!

Major Henry Perkins had bounded out of the patrol car and ran as he headed for the group watching the ambulance crew work on Erickson. "One of you Erickson?" he demanded, on arrival.

Dobbs pointed at his Platoon Leader. "There. That's Lieutenant Erickson."

"Oh, yes, I recognize him now." Perkins paused for a moment to take in the scene of the trucks and the accident and then turned back to Erickson. "Lieutenant, I see you're injured, so I'll be brief. I must inform you that you and your whole platoon are under arrest for being Absent Without Leave. Also, you and Sergeant Bushnell are charged with the theft of Government property from Fort MacArthur. You and your men are to be returned to 6th Army Headquarters as soon as possible." Catching his breath, he went on. "I'd sure like to know where you've been. I've had people searching everywhere for you."

Sullivan had joined the group and was standing next to the Major. "Aren't you the same Officer that sent us on our way from Jockey Hollow last Friday?"

"Yes. Who are you?"

"Sullivan, Sir. Private Sullivan. You ever study history, Sir?"

"What?" The MP Major quizzically eyed the Private. "Yes, I have. A lot of it! The Revolutionary War, in particular. That's one of the reasons I was assigned to Jockey Hollow. I – what has history to do with this?"

"A lot, Sir. Can we go some place and talk?"

TWENTY-SIX

Erickson Remembers Something Important

The shape of the porch and the road beyond slowly retook shape as Erickson regained the present. Sitting on the upper step, he realized he was still clutching the envelope in his hands. He toyed with the clasp, wondering if he should open it

It hadn't been easy coming back to the ranch after the Board of Inquiry, but he knew he had to be near his family. His father had welcomed him without question and patiently waited for him to talk about what had happened. His sister and her husband, living just a few miles down the road on their own ranch, had also been supportive, but more curious. Their patience had worn thin upon the death of his father and he knew they blamed him in part for the illness that led to it.

He had no wife. After his return, he hadn't felt the desire for dating in a rural community where everyone knew everyone else's business. He knew about the rumors and he shunned his friends to the point of being reclusive. There was no way he could face having to relive and explain to others what he could never explain to himself.

He had talked to Bushnell once, about a year after the Board of Inquiry. But, it was obvious from the strained conversation, that Bushnell and the others had been discharged from the Army with the same "understandings" that applied to him. The deal was simple, keep it permanently quiet, or be tried for being AWOL, theft of government property and being accessories to the death and disappearance of their comrades.

They were effective threats, since the Army could handle the matter under the Code of Military Justice in any way they wanted. That included hiding it from the public if need be. No, none of them would stand a chance in that environment and he knew that Bushnell and the others had been willing accomplices to maintain their freedom. It was a classic quid pro quo: the Army didn't need the aggravation and the now ex-soldiers didn't need any more hassles as they tried to get on with their lives.

Bushnell had said enough, though, to substantiate the images he already had of what had happened to them after they were separated at the Interstate. Kept in virtual isolation at the Picatinny Arsenal near Dover, they were treated as criminals and repeatedly questioned by a team of Officers. Their personal belongings had been taken and they were not permitted to contact family or friends. After weeks of mental torment, they were suddenly called together and released the next day. He knew what it must have been like for them, because he knew what it had been like for him.

The memories tugged at him to relive that time again, but he abruptly resisted, knowing there were other things to do. Grasping the envelope, he ripped the flap off, reached inside and pulled out the thick, stapled document.

He glanced at it quickly, flipping the pages to get a feel for what it contained. Intrigued, he got up briefly to grab a soft drink from inside the house and then settled back onto the porch swing for some serious reading. It would take him the rest of the afternoon.

He didn't know, and at first didn't care where the report had come from. What he read was enough to send him into a kind of self-righteous indignation at the way the Army had treated him. But, as he read on, he began to contemplate the power of the Leys and Nodes, wondering what part they played in producing his dramatic battles with the Dragoons.

He suddenly found himself wondering why Putnam had told Morgan so much about their weapons and the way they worked? It was unnecessary and the Dragoons were almost successful in using it against them.

His mind stuck on Putnam, as his thoughts shifted back to the night at the campground after they had returned from the Tavern. There he was, showing off the pistols he had taken from the Dragoons. Erickson had relived that scene many times before and in each case, his mental eyes started searching the scene for something – something he knew was there, but couldn't find.

Still not finding the elusive something, yet with gnawing certainty that it existed, he relaxed and let himself go fully into the scene, floating around, observing all. Then the scene quickly changed and there was McDougall talking about the disappearance of Hale and Thacker and MacKenzie. In the background, Erickson saw Butler taking pictures and remembered having asked how many rolls of pictures he had taken.

Jerking back to reality, Erickson yelled it outloud! "HOW MANY ROLLS HAD HE TAKEN?" Good god! That's what he kept looking for in reliving the campground scene with Putnam – only Putnam wasn't the one he needed to see, it was Butler. Butler, taking pictures!

How had he kept that hidden from himself so long? Why hadn't he remembered Butler and the camera before? It might have been the very thing he needed to prove his statements at the Inquiry. He had told them of the tree where Durkee had carved his and Molly's initials, but there was no way, 200 years later, to find the right one.

He had told them about burying the dead, the Dragoons and his own Soldiers, but he couldn't convince anyone to start digging to look for bones and rotted clothing.

It didn't matter, now. He could use those pictures and the Report he had just read, to gain a new look by the Army, forcing them, if necessary with his own threats to go public! Weights were unexpectedly being lifted from his shoulders as vivid thoughts raced from temple to temple in an awakened mind. He was on to something!

*　　*　　*

It took him awhile to get his thoughts organized on how to proceed. It had been a long time since he'd had to face up to making important decisions and the process was a little rusty. In the end, he decided to track Butler down.

Butler, he vaguely remembered, lived somewhere in Santa Barbara, between the ocean and a world famous Morton Bag Fig tree. How he could remember such trivia and at the same time forget the pictures themselves, he didn't know. Hell, he wasn't even sure the trivia about living in Santa Barbara was right, but it was a place to start.

If he'd had a computer, it would have been easy to go into any of the on-line phone directories and look Butler up; but he'd never wanted or even owned one, much less used one. That left only one alternative.

Hoping the library would still be open, he took off in his old pick up truck and reached it in time to get to the reference desk. He pawed through the stacks of phone books until he found the one for Santa Barbara. He couldn't remember Butler's first name, but knew that if he saw it in the listings, he would recognize it.

He found eight Butler's listed in Santa Barbara itself and four more with addresses in the suburb of Goleta. None of the first names were familiar to him, but in desperation, he wrote them all down along with their phone numbers. There was another listing in the small community of Summerland, south of Santa Barbara, which he added to the list, as well.

Returning home, he thought about whether to start calling right away, or wait until tomorrow. Concluding that the Butler he wanted would be working during the day, he decided to start calling that night. Reaching for the phone, he wondered what to say if he found him. Would Butler even talk to him? Did the Army's deal with the enlisted men prevent them from seeing or talking to him at all? He knew he had to be cautious.

Of the first eleven numbers he called, eight had never heard of a "Private Butler of the US Army". The other three numbers had been changed to different persons who didn't know anyone named Butler at all.

The response to the next call sent shivers down his spine!

"Hello." The woman's voice was pleasant, but firm.

"Is this the Butler residence?"

"Yes. If you're a telemarketer, forget it. I don't buy over the phone."

"No, no. I'm calling from Fresno. I'm looking for an old friend of mine from my Army days. Said he lived in Santa Barbara."

"A lot of people live in Santa Barbara. Why call me?"

"Oh, sorry. His name is Butler. Private Virgil Butler." The first name suddenly popped into Erickson's mind as he was speaking.

"I had a nephew named Virgil Butler that was in the Army, but he was killed in an automobile accident many years back."

"I . . . I'm sorry to hear that, ma'am. May I ask, do you recall if your nephew was part of the Bicentennial celebration in New Jersey, back in 1976?"

"Well, I seem to recall something about him going east with the Army on a train around that time. His mother was furious when she found out they had been living in some old boxcars along the way! Anyway, there was some trouble back there and when he came home, he wasn't in the Army anymore. I never did get the details."

"He was a friend of mine. I liked him."

"Do you want his mother's number?"

Stunned for a moment, Erickson recovered and gratefully accepted. "Yes. Please. I'd like that very much. I could call her and offer my condolences."

"She's in Summerland. Do you know where that is?"

"Just south of Santa Barbara, isn't it?"

"Yes. Hang on; I use my automatic dialer, so I've forgotten the number. Let me get it for you from my book." She was away but a moment before returning and giving Erickson the number to call.

"Thanks, so much," he said. "I'm really sorry about your nephew. Please accept my condolences."

"It's been a long time now. We've all had a chance to forget the circumstances and remember the person. He was a fine young man and he is missed. That's what's important, you know."

"Yes, it is." Thinking of nothing else to say, Erickson said, "I'll call his mother. Thank you for your help."

"That's all right. Good night."

Erickson mumbled his "good night," and slowly hung up the receiver as he contemplated what to say when he placed the call to Virgil Butler's mother.

Hesitant to bother her at this hour, he decided to make the call in the morning, but then changed his mind when he realized that Butler's aunt would soon be calling her to find out what was going on. He picked up the phone and dialed.

It rang seven times before she answered, just as Erickson concluded that no one was home. "Butler residence," a woman's voice said.

"Mrs. Butler?"

"Yes. Who is this?"

"Mrs. Butler, I was a friend of your son, Virgil. We were in the Army together." Afraid to say more, he let the last words drop off, waiting for an answer or some recognition.

"Oh, my goodness. Virgil's been gone for so many years now. Who is this?"

Erickson gulped, held his breath for a short moment and then began to say the words that he hoped would not cause her to hang up. "My name is Erickson. Jim Erickson. Virgil was in my platoon."

"Lieutenant Erickson!"

His name thrust from her voice like a piston. This is it, he thought, she knows my name and now she hangs up! "Please, I'd like to talk to you," he interjected quickly. "I'm sorry to hear that your son has passed away. He was a fine soldier and I liked him. I would like to talk . . ."

"I know who you are. My son thought the world of you. Said you always treated him with respect and caring. He said you were a fine man."

"I . . . I thought well of him, too." The conversation had taken an unexpected turn for the better.

"Virgil left a package for you. Said you'd be calling some day for it."

"A package? For me?"

"Yes. He tried to mail it to you some years ago. Had your name on one line and your city – Fresno isn't it? – on another. But, he couldn't come up with the street address in between. He said it was too important to send to just any Erickson in Fresno; it had to get to *you*. Anyway, it's still here somewhere and it's yours, if you want it."

"What's in the package? Did he tell you?"

"No. As I recall, it was fairly stiff, in a big manila envelope."

"Can you mail it to me? I'd like to have it."

"Can you come here, instead? I never met any of the boys he was with that summer. It would be nice to meet you and reminisce about Virgil, if you don't mind."

Erickson was hesitant and his lack of immediate response conveyed his concern to Mrs. Butler.

"Please," she added. "I won't ask questions where I shouldn't. And, if I do, just smile and go on to something else. I'll understand."

So, she did know something. But, what? Erickson wanted to know, and he wanted to see what the package contained.

"I'll be happy to come over and meet you," he said. "We'll open the package together."

*   *   *

The drive from Fresno to Summerland was long and tedious. But, Erickson drove at a steady pace, covering the distance in less than four hours. Summerland was the home of many free spirited residents, content to be near Montecito and Santa Barbara, yet not part of either.

He drove past numerous small, older homes, long settled on tree-lined streets before reaching Mrs. Butler's. With no curb to park against on the narrow street, Erickson pulled his wheels partially on the grass between the street and what served as a sidewalk.

Setting the brake, he smoothed his hair and stepped down from the truck as he eyed the house. He took a deep breath, exhaled slowly and walked towards it. He hadn't taken more than five steps when she appeared in the open doorway, apron at her waist, hand at the screen door, waiting to open it for him when he got to the steps.

He smiled, she smiled and they both knew they would like each other. "Did you eat, yet?" she asked.

"A while back, in Buellton. Bowl of soup, bread and a glass of wine."

"Yes, I know that place. Very famous. Still, I'll get you something to tide you over until dinner."

He went in. The house was small, fitting quite nicely into the neighborhood and like Mrs. Butler, neat and organized. He knew he would not see any dust anywhere in this household.

He held out his hand to shake hers, already outstretched. "Hi," he said, still smiling. "I'm Jim Erickson."

"Call me Helen. Everyone does." She returned the smile and gave the handshake a cordial squeeze. "Come in and don't worry, I won't ask a lot of questions."

She led the way to the living room couch, complete with doilies on the arms, and gestured with her hand for him to sit down. She sat across from him, her back highlighted against the front windows, and offered some quick bits of information to put him at ease.

"Virgil died about a week after being involved in a car accident over in Montecito. No one was to blame, it was just one of those things that happen. Then, you're left with nothing afterwards but a memory. I still miss him. I moved here about a year later to get out of a house filled with the memories of him and of his father." Raising her hand slightly, she added, "Don't say you're sorry. I know you would mean it, but I had them for the time I was supposed to, and I enjoyed them both. My time goes on in other ways now and someday I'll see them again, when I finally go."

Getting up, she reached behind her chair and produced the manila envelope. "Like I told you on the phone, Virgil wanted to mail this to you, but didn't have your full address. Somehow, he knew you'd be by someday, and I kept it for you. It's sorta like a magnet, I knew it would draw you in eventually." She handed him the envelope. "Here, see what it is while I go and fix you some proper lunch."

For the second time in two days, Erickson held an envelope in his hands that caused him dread. Yet, he felt certain it contained information about the platoon; why else would Butler want to send it to him?

The envelope was stiff and did not bend. The clasp was dull from age and the transparent tape used to double seal the flap was old and dried, pulling up in places. It dropped off as he started to peel it back.

The contents peaked through the end, revealing three sheets of grayish paperboard, the same kind used as backing on pads of lined paper. As he slid them out, he could see six color photographs attached to each side. No need to ask Helen if she knew where Virgil's pictures might be, they were here in his hands!

Erickson's hands shook as he carefully separated the sheets, gently prying the stuck photographs from each other. Glancing rapidly at the photos, he saw scenes that he had relived in his mind repeatedly. The campground, the trucks and other vehicles, the jeep with Molly and Durkee, Bushnell and the others arguing over whether to stay or go, the tavern, the trail, the pond as seen from the hill by the campground, on and on, jarring his senses with memories.

As he turned the last page, a sheet of folded, lined paper dropped to his lap. Picking it up, he read the handwritten note, left by Virgil Butler years earlier.

Dear Lieutenant Erickson:

I want you to have these pictures, to use anyway you want. They are the ones I took at Jockey Hollow.

It's kind of strange the way I got them back. The Army took all of our gear when then took us to Picatinny Arsenal. They didn't put us in a stockade or anything like that, but they kept us isolated from everyone while they questioned us day after day. I was scared at Jockey Hollow, but those guys at Picatinny made us all fear for our lives. We all thought they were going to shoot us or put us away in a mental hospital for the rest of our lives.

They used to call us into a small room on the second floor of an old building. Major Perkins was there and so were three other Officers, but we never knew who they were. Major Perkins didn't want any of us, particularly Sullivan, to get out and tell our story to anybody. At one time, there was another Officer, who must have been a shrink because of the type of questions he asked. They even wanted to know what types of drugs we were on. No one believed anything we told them, even though we all told them the same story over and over.

Somewhere along the way, Putnam asked me about the pictures I had taken. He wanted to use them to prove what we were saying. But, the film was still in my duffel bag and we had no way to get them printed or back again. Besides, we all agreed that if the Army found out about them, they would be destroyed and then nobody would ever be able to use them.

We were released in a big hurry one day, after they threatened us with all kinds of things if we didn't keep quiet. We were so scared after all those questions that we all decided to go along with the deal and get away from them.

It wasn't until I got home that I found the rolls of film, right where I put them in the duffel bag. They looked OK on the outside, so I had them developed and printed. Most were all right, and the rest I threw away, because they weren't good pictures.

Anyway, I want you to have them. You'll know what to do with them to help us all the best way.

I'll never forget you and Sergeant Bushnell. It was quite a summer. Too bad we can't talk about it with anyone.

Virgil Butler

Butler's note confirmed what Erickson has surmised from his call with Bushnell. The Army was playing hardball and the men had decided to go along for obvious reasons. Still, Butler had not totally complied, for he had sent the pictures, or at least, had tried to send the pictures, to Erickson.

Now that he had them, he was going to use them! He began looking at them again, more and seriously this time.

"Who's that?" Helen had returned with a sandwich and chips on a plate with a glass of cola. She was pointing to the picture of Durkee and Molly carving their initials in a tree. It was obvious they were not aware that Butler was taking the picture.

"Private Durkee."

"Nice looking girl." The unstated question was equally obvious.

"Part of the Bicentennial crew," Erickson offered. "Dressed for the Revolutionary War period."

"Interesting. How many other women were with you there?"

"A few others, but they were down in the Hollow at the building made up like a tavern. This one came up to be with her friend, Durkee. Want to see the rest?"

"Sure."

He handed her the sheets and she backed up to sit in her chair, holding them in her hand. Settling into the comfortable seat, she put on her glasses and began to examine them in detail. As she did, Erickson skillfully took Butler's note from where it lay on the cushion next to him, and stuffed into his back pocket, out of sight.

"Help me with these, will you?" Helen motioned for him to join her at the chair.

He spent the next 20 minutes cautiously identifying the scenes and the names of the soldiers in them. It went well with Helen accepting whatever Erickson told her without a lot of questions. Once in awhile, she would add a comment or two, mostly to verify and repeat back what she had been told about a previous scene or another picture.

He did not try to explain the pile of burning Dragoon horses, leaving it to her imagination as he quickly passed over that picture. Nor did he dwell on the sight of the freshly dug graves that could have been mistaken for deep pit latrines, had it not been for the bodies lying nearby. When she looked up at him, he merely added a soothing touch with the words, "Isn't the realism they create for these things, wonderful?"

He didn't ask if she wanted a set. If she *had* asked – well, she didn't and that was that.

He didn't stay for dinner, and she made it easy for him to leave, although she was genuinely sorry he was going. It was obvious there was something bigger than the pictures involved and she sensed that he had a terrible craving to do something soon.

Erickson, in fact, had already decided to take the pictures and go to Jockey Hollow. He knew from the report that others had already been there checking on his claims. Now that he had hard evidence, he fully intended to go there and confirm the truth.

TWENTY-SEVEN

Reunion at Jockey Hollow

"Colonel!" General Xetrel's voice boomed through the phone. "Erickson is on his way to Jockey Hollow! Get there first and find out what he's doing!"

An incredulous Lester could only stammer, "How . . . how do you know that?"

"I've had him watched since this thing started. He got a package in the mail two days ago that had to be a copy of the same report you and I got. The next day he went to a place called Summerland and met with the mother of one of the soldiers in his old platoon. Now he's on a plane to Newark. He's reserved a car at the airport and told them he would keep it for a few days. You and I both know he's not going sightseeing. Now I want you to get to Jockey Hollow! Get control of *him* and the situation. Remind him of the deal the Army made and that we can still bring charges against him. Whatever you do, keep him quiet!"

Lester felt like he'd been punched in the head and the stomach at the same time. Erickson on the loose in New Jersey? Heading for Jockey Hollow? Something more than the report must have triggered him. If Erickson was already on his was to Newark, Lester had no time to spare.

He picked up the phone and entered a two-digit code. It immediately rang in an office near the airfield. He gave his requirements, hung up and promptly dialed another two-digit number. Then he spoke ten words: "Find Treppello. Get him to the chopper field in civvies," and hung up. He moved quickly around the office, gathering what he needed for the sudden trip, including a pair of powerful binoculars. He threw on a pair of nondescript coveralls to hide the pants and shirt of his uniform and then ran to his car. Ignoring McNair's posted speed limit, he arrived at the chopper field six minutes later.

A gleaming, refurbished Huey was waiting. Lester climbed aboard just as Captain Treppello arrived and hastily exited the MP vehicle that had fetched him. Eyebrows raised into huge question marks, Treppello grabbed the hand Lester offered and was pulled him into a seat and told to strap in.

"I don't like helicopters, Colonel. They don't like to stay in the air at times."

"That's easy to understand, Captain. Helicopters really don't fly, you know; they stay up only because the earth rejects them."

Treppello laughed, as did the pilots, while they lifted off nose down to gain forward speed before climbing to altitude. Because of the noise, Lester said nothing to his travel companion. The pilots knew where they were going and Carl would soon figure it out from watching the landmarks and traffic patterns below. Lester passed part of the time by replacing his polished shoes with a pair of ankle high field boots. Satisfied that he could now pass for a hiker of sorts, he looked at Carl and was pleased to see that the civilian clothes he wore also gave no clue as to his military position.

In about a fourth of the time it had taken them to drive, the helicopter arrived over the helipad near the National Park Service building at Jockey Hollow and settled down. The two Rangers stationed there remained inside, watching through the windows, but not acknowledging their arrival. The right phone calls had been made in time.

Lester saw the green NPS truck sitting apart from the others and approached it, knowing that the keys would be in the ignition, ready for his use. He motioned Treppello into the passenger side and backed out of the space. Turning west from the Headquarters building, he started for the park up the hill where they had been so recently. The same place where he expected Erickson to soon arrive.

As they climbed the paved road towards the campground, he saw another helicopter arriving. Stunned at his recognition of the distinctive purple and blue colors of the more modern machine, he gunned the truck and swiftly reached the entrance to the campground, where he skidded to a halt. Jumping out, he grabbed the binoculars, ran over to the edge of the hill, and watched in amazement as Admiral Funston climbed into a waiting unmarked sedan. Lowering the glasses, he returned to the front seat of the truck to await Funny's arrival.

He looked at Carl and saw a face full of consternation. Before he could inquire, the sounds of the approaching car diverted his attention. Looking out the rear view mirror of his truck, he saw the familiar face and rotund body of his old boss stepping out of the rear door dressed in relaxed hiking gear. No one would ever know this man was an Admiral.

Funston smiled and gave a little wave with his hand as he started over to Lester's truck. "Nice to see you, again, Colonel," he called out. "Surprised to see me here?"

"Surprised is not the word, Herman. It's more like what toilet did you crawl out of to get here?"

"Careful, Colonel, your talking to a superior officer now."

"Superior, my ass. Why are you following me?"

"Because I'm as interested in what Erickson will do when he gets here, as you are."

Lester looked Funston in the eyes and read the message loud and clear. The Admiral knew as much, if not more, than Lester did about Erickson's arrival.

As Funston's sedan turned around and left the campground, Lester faced him. "All right, what's going on here? You sent me a report, which I read. You maneuvered me into coming up here for whatever reason and I took readings. Now, you show up here at the same time as I do, to watch and see what Erickson does. I don't like this, Herman. We've known each other for a long time and I think you owe me an explanation!"

"I do, too, Ben. Let's sit over at one of those picnic tables and talk."

"Let's do that." Lester started to lead the way and then abruptly stopped. "I'm afraid I've forgotten my manners. Let me introduce you to Captain Carl Treppello, who's been working with me."

"I've known Carl for almost thirty years now," Funston replied. "He's my Nephew."

"What!?" Lester turned towards Treppello with an inner rage that took all of his self-control to keep inside. He'd been had, and he knew it! Cursing inside, he maintained outward control, for he knew that to vent his anger would only add to the mortification he felt.

"Have you guys been working against me as a team, then?"

"Not against you at all," responded Funston. "I think you'll see that it was all in the best interests of everyone – the Army, the Navy, the PRA and the intelligence community in general. And, you've been a big help, just like I knew you would."

"You sonofabitch! So, you admit I was being manipulated. Why?"

"It's an interesting story, Ben. You were part of the beginning and now, you're part of the end – or at least, the beginning of the end. Come on, sit down, and don't be mad at us. At least, until you hear the story."

Lester was an old hand at inter-service and inter-departmental politics and knew that one couldn't win without listening to what the other fellow had to say. Anger had a way of spoiling a lot of victories, but in this situation, it would be better for him if they perceived some anger on his part to help them share the whole story.

"You remember back to the days when we started the PRA, Ben?" Funston asked. He knew Lester did, but he wanted to set the scenario. "We had a lot of fun in those days, testing out the theory of psychic intelligence gathering and practicing our working methods. We had already gotten very good at it by the time you took off with Xetrel to observe the Erickson Inquiry. And, while you were off in Europe, doing whatever you did over there – we continued to develop and advance our methods to the point that our reputations grew and the demands for our services drastically increased. We had no problems with budgets. The were problems everywhere, all the way back to the Russians in Chechnya, the ethnic bust up of Yugoslavia, the Chinese and Taiwan, the North and South Vietnamese after the war, the North Koreans and their on-going nuclear saber rattling, Saddam Hussein, from before Kuwait all the way through the invasion of Iraq, you name it anywhere in the world and we were asked to be there, looking and listening. After 9/11 we were virtually swamped with business!"

"I feel a 'but' coming on."

"You're right! Our biggest problem has always been the dearth of qualified psychic talent to employ. As you well know from your own experiences with us, there are a lot of people out there who think they have the ability to transmit or receive energy on the psychic level. But, the number of those that can repeatedly demonstrate those abilities are damn few. Even fewer can stand the operating pressures we encounter in just one normal pass at intelligence gathering."

Lester remembered, all right. "So you finally went to the Russian system then, using a cage and lasers? When I was there, you concentrated on detecting inbound Soviet intelligence excursions. We didn't have an ability to go out on our own excursions."

"At first, we didn't. But, later, we began to develop our own version of a cage, wrapping the outbound energy in a coherent magnetic field, not unlike how the coherent light of a laser is created and organized. We now transmit that coherent energy across vast regions of the United States utilizing existing power lines."

"I don't understand how that would work," Lester replied. "I mean, the energy that's being transmitted along those lines by the power companies creates its own magnetic fields. I would think those natural magnetic fields would destroy your coherent magnetic fields and the energy being sent by the psychics."

"Yes it would, if we were using the high power alternating current lines, but we use only the low power, direct current lines that make up the bulk of electrical transmission in the U.S. The power companies know that it's cheaper to create and transmit direct current than it is to move high power AC. It's also a big help to us, since the low power DC creates a magnetic field in one direction only and we use it to enhance our own coherent field."

"Where do you send it?"

"Along certain lines from one point to another. It's like a giant antenna system. Instead of a huge antenna tower up in the air, radiating to spokes buried in the ground, we send the energy out along selected lines and then radiate it on command to nearby natural quartz concentrations in the earth. We get the quartz to vibrate at the right frequency, just like a crystal in a transmitter, and it starts radiating into the ionosphere. From there our boys have learned to direct the energy and themselves to the pre-targeted area of interest."

"That's better that beaming it up and around with satellites?"

"Absolutely. Satellites can be tracked. Signals from satellites can be diverted or garbled, even jammed by ground stations."

"OK. I'm impressed." Lester *was* impressed, but his voice couldn't help carrying a slight sarcastic tone. "So what happened to get your attention riveted on Erickson?"

"Well, we're constantly seeking to improve our techniques and methods of operation. Hell the pressure from Homeland Security is on us constantly! Increased range, greater flexibility, more loiter time, you know how it goes in this business – have some successes and everyone wants more. The assignments keep piling up and our spook competitors within the Military and the Government were getting very jealous and angry with us."

"I can understand that."

"Anyway, a while back, we let a few of our best psychics go off on their own, playing out different ideas on how to increase performance. During one of those sessions, one of them stumbled into a retrogression that not only held his attention, but literally drew him into the on-going events. He was terrified at being in the middle of a Sioux war party raiding a Cheyenne camp and tried to get out but couldn't. They saw him, he saw them, they chased him, he ran and ran, right into the wall of the room he was in, just feet from the chair in which he had been sitting!"

"So," Lester added, now caught up in the scenario, "your guy reports this strange event and you organize a search of related information to find out if it has ever happened before. In the process, your people find out about Leys and Nodes and all the related events reported over the years including, eventually, the Erickson thing. And when you hear about that you said to yourself that looks awful similar to the Indian thing."

"That's right. That's what I said."

Lester took a moment before continuing. "Tell me, Herman," he said with a sudden, serious tone to his voice. "Are you trying to use the Leys and Nodes around here as a source of power to transmit your psychic's energy?"

"That's right, Ben. That's exactly what I want to do."

"Aren't you concerned that in using the Leys and Nodes you might end up in situations like your guy with the Indians, or like Erickson with the Dragoons?"

"To one extent, yes. To a greater extent, no."

"That's double talk."

"Not really. Certainly, at first we were concerned that in using the Leys and Nodes, our guys might get diverted into someplace where they couldn't get out. We wanted to know the risks involved and, frankly, we still need to find out more. But then, we decided that maybe we could use the phenomena for our advantage, as well."

"How's that?"

"As I've said before, we don't have enough qualified psychics to do all the jobs that are being assigned to us. But, the Erickson situation suggests we might be able to send plain old everyday, garden-variety intelligence agents to specific targets to acquire detailed information. While my guys are using the energy of the Leys and Nodes to transmit psychic energy for our basic kinds of intelligence gathering jobs, we could send others back, say, to a prior event to understand all the ramifications of its creation. They wouldn't have a schedule to keep as my regular guys would, and think of the intelligence breakthrough that would provide us as a country now, post 9/11."

"You mean, in fighting the terrorists?"

"Sure. Being able to get directly to the terrorists and identify their in-country sympathizers and supporters would give us a significant advantage in the war on terror. We are going to need that ability for many years to come; the aims of the terrorists are deep-seated in centuries of animosity and new fighters imbued with their beliefs are being born every day. Just think of the advantage that would give us!"

Lester nodded his head in understanding, but couldn't quite allow himself to say so outloud.

"And," Funston went on, "an industrial war is also well underway. While our intelligence resources are still going to have to monitor the Russians, the Chinese, and their old friends for military purposes, we also have to watch them and a lot of other countries including the Israelis and the French and the Germans and the British, who are spying on us for technology secrets. All of a sudden, a lot of agencies are working to ensure that the U. S. maintains its competitive edge at the same time as keeping us safe from terrorists.

"We in the PRA feel it already. I'll say it again; we've got more work that we can handle, but we're constrained by the number of qualified psychics that we can find to employ. The jobs that my people do now are recognized within the community for the outstanding professional results they achieve. But, I'm limited in my ability to do any more, and I've concluded that we've got to provide some means for other talent to be employed, to spread the work around."

"Your report said you tried to confirm the energy levels and that you had been partially successful."

"We did and were, as you say, only partially successful. Our equipment wasn't sophisticated enough. We had a bunch of magnetometers, something like what the British used to measure the Leys and Nodes in 1978. The trouble with magnetometers is that they are temperamental, giving a lot of false positive readings because of spurious transients in the earth's magnetic field. We encountered some high readings and one of our guys insisted that the road had disappeared, but the other guy didn't see that happen. We came away disappointed and frustrated. Our guys knew the kind of equipment they needed to conduct the tests for the energy levels, but it was tied up in a warehouse, gathering dust. When we found out who had access to its use, we decided to get them involved."

"Them? You mean *me*, don't you?" It didn't take a psychic to help Lester figure that one out.

"Yes."

"Then this whole thing of digging around the Pentagon, asking questions about Erickson, was just designed to get me and the equipment up here to conduct verification tests?"

"Yes."

"You sonofabitch! *You* sneaky sonofabitch. I'd forgotten how devious you can be. How did you know that I would be assigned?"

"Easy. We targeted Xetrel and made it seem as if the whole General Staff of the Army was involved. You know him; he panics if the Chief of Staff farts. I knew he would turn to you – whom else would he trust this too? Especially after having been with you in Europe, where he trusted you with his life at times. Just as I knew that my nephew would be at the right place at the right time to be assigned as your assistant."

"Good god, Funny, you played us all like puppets."

"Not with any malice in mind, you know."

"I know." Lester realized that a much bigger concern was at the heart of Funny's efforts. What he had heard had softened his mindset. "So, there's no intent to get the Erickson matter before the public?"

"None whatsoever. Oh Erickson will try, but you and I will control him; mainly because he's a decent human being, and will consider the other members of the platoon and what we can do to them."

"Why did you involve him?"

"Two reasons. Pressure on you — because the threat of Erickson doesn't carry as much weight as the reality of Erickson on his way to Jockey Hollow. As it turned out, you came and did your thing before Erickson ever got started for here, so in that respect I didn't need him."

"And the second reason?"

"I wanted to see Erickson at the scene of the crime, so to speak. The Board of Inquiry wouldn't consider coming here. Said it didn't want to lend any credibility, when none was deserved. But, Erickson's testimony never did convey the feelings he and his platoon must have felt at the time. Those will be important to us in creating the right mind set for those we train to use the paths of the Leys and Nodes. They have to know what to expect from an emotional standpoint. Erickson's the one that can give us that insight. Later on we can train our people to work at a higher plane of consciousness, where they act as observers only and not part of what is happening."

"What do you have in mind for Erickson?"

"We'll wait for him to arrive and play it by ear. He's got some pictures that Private Butler took while they were here in 1776. We want to look at those pictures and determine if cameras are a viable option in sending people out on missions using the Leys and Nodes. He will also be full of stories, trying to confirm what happened, trying to clear his name. We owe that to him and will cooperate with him by listening and believing, whenever necessary."

"You seem to know a lot about his plans."

"I've got the best in the business working for me."

"Everywhere, it seems," Lester responded, looking and half-smiling at Carl.

Treppello grinned and finally spoke to the matter. "I wanted to tell you, Colonel. I've enjoyed working with you very much and it was a great experience. I tried to lead you a few times to where we were, but I couldn't come right out and tell you. Uncle Herm . . . uh, Admiral Funston wanted you to come to the same conclusions with us, and I knew you would, when it came down to the bottom line. I'm sorry I mislead you in the meantime."

Lester gestured his acceptance. "Don't worry about it. I know this old rascal and I . . ." He dropped the rest with a nod and a smile at Funny.

*　　*　　*

It was late afternoon by the time they heard the first sounds of a car coming up the hill towards the campground. They had heard many cars in the distance on the road down by the Wick House, as visitors left the Ranger Station and museum to sightsee around the Hollow. None had ventured up the hill, though, for the maps of the area did not indicate anything of historical value up where they were.

It was a quiet arrival. The driver was not in any hurry. It took a few moments before they saw the two-door car turn into the campground and come to a stop on a soft scattering of Spruce needles.

The driver saw them at the table and hesitated for a moment before opening the door. He looked much older to Lester than he had at the Inquiry. His eyes seemed hollowed and darkened and his hair had a tinge of gray around the temples. While Erickson still displayed a certain sprightliness in his step, it was apparent to Lester that a toll had been paid for having been at Jockey Hollow in the first place.

Erickson looked at the three men hesitantly then decided he must know who they were before going about his business. Walking over to the table, he said, "Nice afternoon. Relaxing after taking in all the history down below?"

Funston looked at his two companions. The one thing he hadn't done was to formulate a plan for handling the situation when Erickson arrived. Just how could he get him to talk and share his pictures and the other details? Since the other two only smiled at Erickson in return, Funston elected to go it alone.

"Actually, we're more interested in the history that's been made here in this campground, than anything else. Thought we'd sit here and take it all in."

Puzzled by the statement, Erickson tried to recall the historical information that had been put together for him when they arrived in 1976. "I'm not aware of anything historical happening here," he said, moving to the picnic table where they sat. He certainly wasn't going to volunteer what happened to him and his platoon to a bunch of strangers.

"It's all right, Lieutenant, we're friends and we have a great deal of interest in what happened here. Join us and we'll tell you about it."

Lieutenant! Erickson was instantly apprehensive. Who were these men and what did they want? He calculated the number of steps to his car, but the look on the face of the heavy-set older man had a calming effect that caused him to remain near the table.

"My name is Herman Funston," the man said, sticking out his hand. "My friends call me 'Funny'."

Erickson clasped the hand in a gentle shake, ready to pull back instantly if it was used to hold him.

"You seem to know me, already," Erickson said. "You called me Lieutenant."

Funston ignored the statement. "I sent you the report. I'm with the PRA."

"Whatever that is." Erickson wasn't biting into anything.

"The Psychic Research Agency. We've been looking into several things and one of them is what happened to you and your platoon while you were here."

"You're all with this PRA?"

"Yes and no. This is my nephew, Carl Treppello and this other old geezer here, Ben Lester, used to be part of my organization and has been doing some consulting work for us recently."

Erickson gingerly shook hands with both of them. He took a seat at the table and positioned himself at the end so he could leave, unhindered, if need be.

"Why did you send me the report?"

"Thought you'd be interested. I wanted to talk to you, but knew the Army would have you too worried to tell me what I wanted to know. So I had to dangle some bait and hope for the best."

Warming slightly to the friendly overture, Erickson looked directly at Funston. "What *is it* you want?"

"We're very interested in anything which could prove you and your platoon were here in 1776."

"And if that can be done, then what?"

"Then I may have a job for you, helping others prepare for similar circumstances."

"I don't understand what you mean."

"I'll get to that in a bit. Right now, I'm very interested in what happened to you. I believe you're here to somehow prove to yourself that it really happened, and that when you do prove it to yourself, you're going to try and get the Army to change its mind about the matter and clear your name."

"Yes. That's right, that's what I want to do if I can."

"Then let's cut to the bottom line. You've read our report and you know that we believe you. We also included some pretty solid reasons as to why we reached that conclusion. Ben and Carl were up here a few days ago and confirmed the existence of some extremely high levels of telluric energy that I believe may have triggered what happened to you."

Erickson started to ask a question, but Funny continued with his monologue. "In my considered judgment, and I daresay this will be fully supported by these other two gentlemen – no matter what you prove here – there is no way on this green earth that the Army will change its position and clear your name. Hell, son, there was an action in Congress just the other day where some family in West Virginia was still trying to clear the name of an ancestor that fought in the Civil War, and the Army, the United States Army of today, was still fighting it! If that doesn't tell you how much chance you have, nothing ever will."

"Maybe they won't. But, that's why I'm here; that's what I have to do, for me, for the platoon."

"I'm sorry, son, but what you really have to do, is go on living, and to hell with what the Army did to you. Help us and we'll help you. We think we're on to something very important here and we want your help to prove it. You've got a part to play in a much bigger action and I think it's time we got started."

Still apprehensive, Erickson tentatively agreed. "Let's see how it goes. How do we start?"

Funston gave Erickson the short version of what he had said to Lester earlier about using the Leys and Nodes. When he finished he said, "You've had years to think about it. What are the things you would use to prove you were here?"

"I can think of five. The bones from the dead we buried over there on the north side of the camp. The R D and M M initials carved by Durkee in one of these trees. .30 caliber bullets in a tree behind the tavern fired by Captain Morgan. Spent cartridges that must be buried in the dirt all around this campground."

"That's four. What's the fifth?"

Erickson eyed them all for a few moments then got up and went back to his car. Reaching into the front seat, he picked up the manila envelope and returned to the table. "These," he said, pulling Butler's pictures out.

The three men looked at the pictures as the sheets were passed around. Lester was the first to speak. "These pictures can't be of the same area, look at how different the trees are. And there aren't any tables or restroom facilities, either." He picked up another picture and abruptly asked. "Are these supposed to be your dead?" He was not convinced about the authenticity of the pictures, at all.

Erickson took the picture and looked at it. "Ours and theirs. Mostly theirs. Butler must've taken this when we were getting ready to bury them."

"Where did you do that?"

"Right up there," he responded, pointing to the area on the northeast side of the campground.

"Show us."

Erickson lead them to the area where the dead had been buried. There was no physical evidence of any digging or mounding to the ground. Erickson saw the disappointment on their faces. "Hey. Come on," he exclaimed. "It's been over 200 years. You don't expect to find bones and uniforms thrusting out of the ground, do you? We're going to have to probe and dig. We're going to have to use tools."

Funston looked at him. "You're right." Turning to his nephew, "Go down to the Ranger Station and see if they have a shovel or two we might use."

"Don't!" Lester cut in. "They'll get curious if you do that. We don't need anyone up here seeing what we are doing. Let's go buy what we need."

"That's not necessary," exclaimed Erickson. "I have what we need. I planned for this, remember? I have a pointed shovel, a crow bar, a big saw and an ax. I think there're enough tools for us all to dig around in the ground and the trees for what I'm looking for. Help me get them out of the trunk."

*   *   *

They quietly dug and probed the ground around the camp, looking for any sign of evidence to support what the pictures showed. Erickson insisted that the level of the ground would have risen during the last 200 years, but they couldn't agree on how much. The pictures also mislead them as to position because of the significant growth in the surrounding trees.

They finally selected three trees in which Durkee could have carved the initials. Treppello calculated the estimated growth over the past 200 years, so that they could chop into the bark at approximately the right height in their probing.

"This isn't going to work," he exclaimed as he started to chop, then stopped. "They're going to hear us down below and come up here, asking questions."

"What do you suggest, then?" asked his uncle.

"They go home sometime, don't they? After they've gone, we can start."

"It'll be dark then, Carl. What'll we do for light?"

"The headlights from the car and the truck. We can run the motors if we need to, to keep the batteries charged."

"Good thinking," said Funston. He looked over at Lester for any additional ideas he might have on the subject. "You look concerned," he added. "What's up?"

"We've got to send the choppers away. The pilot's will need their rest for the night, too."

"You're right! I forgot about them. Carl, go down there and have them come back tomorrow morning. At the same time, find out from the schedule on the door of the building what time the Rangers go home for the day."

"On my way." Turning to Erickson, Treppello asked, "May I use your car? I don't want to go down there in their truck."

Erickson tossed him the keys and Treppello quickly drove down the hill. The helicopters left a short time later.

"You realize we're stuck here for the night, now, don't you?" Funston exclaimed. He then raised his eyebrows at Lester, as if to say, *what are we going to do to keep warm?*

"Hey, Funny," Lester replied sarcastically, "no one said it was going to be easy. *You* got this whole thing going, so why didn't *you* bring sleeping bags? We'll stay in Erickson's car if it gets too cool," he added. "Otherwise, I'm going to use my hands and rake up a big pile of leaves and needles to sleep on."

"Are we going to dig into those trees down where the tavern used to be?" Erickson asked, wanting to know what to expect.

"Looking for the carbine bullets?" Funston replied. "Probably, if we find the initials Durkee carved up here. If we don't find the initials, then I won't hold out much hope of finding slugs in a tree down there."

"Agreed," said Lester. "We need food, too. Maybe they have some vending machines down at the Ranger Station."

"I'll send Carl back, when he gets here. One of the advantages of being his Uncle is that, in spite of the fact that he's an adult, I still get to treat him like an errand boy."

They moved to the trees they had selected and examined them, as they waited for Carl to return.

*   *   *

They were not destined to have a successful night. They either had the wrong trees, or were at the wrong height. They found no indication that anyone had ever carved initials into any of the three trees. Nor were they successful at further digging and probing at the site where the Dragoons would have been buried. Hours later, tired, dirty and still hungry, in spite of some vending machine food, they all sat down on the ground in a semicircle.

The car motors and lights had been turned off, but the half moon provided some light through the trees. Funston was exhausted.

"Look," he said, taking a number of deep breaths. "We're not getting anywhere with this, and I've been thinking. The real proof I want is not *in* the ground, or *in any trees*. It's in getting to a place and back that counts. It's in learning how to use the energy of the Leys and Nodes to send us back or forward in time or location. In other words, do I need to create a Synergistic Coupling Effect, with a lot of premeditated work and common goals to move people along the Leys and Nodes? Or, can I just *use* them, by being here when the energy fires up? And, if so, can I just ride along and discover where the paths go, so I can later pick the right starting point to end up at the right ending point? I need answers to those questions, and that's the bottom line of what we're doing here. I know that one of my guys found himself in the middle of a bunch of fighting Indians once and didn't know how he got there. I know that Erickson experienced something like that, on a much more complicated level, while he was here. I know that my people measured something unusual here and that one of my guys saw something unusual here at the same time. In addition, I know that Ben and Carl recorded some phenomenally high-energy readings here. So, this is the place to be, as far as I'm concerned, and the only thing I really have to do, is figure out how to use the energy. So there! Now, if y'all don't mind, I'm going to rake up my outdoor mattress and get some sleep!"

Few words were spoken as they moved back and forth to the outhouses and then settled onto the ground for the night. Erickson knew he was in for a restless night. Above him, an owl hooted softly and glided across the campground towards the hill, searching for a tasty mouse.

They all fell into an uneasy sleep, constantly repositioning for a comfortable position on the leaves and needles they had gathered over the hard ground. It was a long night.

An eeriness in his surroundings and the sound of hooves pounding in the distance awoke Erickson with a start. He could feel an electrical buzzing around him, but it was overridden with the vibration of the ground caused by the beating hooves. Sitting up, he jerked his head towards the sounds, but saw nothing in the morning light but the edge of the hill at the south side of the campground. The men on either side of him awoke to the noise and vibration, too. Funston rolled over and slowly sat up, cocking his ear to identify the source.

Erickson recognized what it was an instant before Sergeant Ramsey led the mounted Dragoons into the camp. Startled and confused, Funston, Lester and Treppello jumped to their feet and moved towards Erickson.

Ramsey looked at the four men and rode over, pointing his saber at Erickson. "Where's Captain Morgan? What have you done with him?"

Erickson couldn't answer. He clasped his hands tightly into fists and tried to answer, but couldn't. The situation overwhelmed him. My god! *He was back in 1776!* He should have known better than to come to this damn campground!

Ramsey pushed the saber into the skin that showed through Erickson's crumpled and dirty shirt. "Where is Morgan? Tell me now!"

Erickson's mind was a jumble and he blurted out the only answer that came to mind. "He went with the others in the trucks. They went over the hill when they left. He and three others; they're in the back of one of the trucks."

Ramsey stared at him, unbelieving, but pulled the saber back because he knew Erickson would not be lying at such a time. "Is he in one of those strange carriages you had here last night?"

Erickson strained to remember what 'last night' would be for Ramsey.

"Yes," he replied. "The same ones we had here for days. Morgan ordered us to leave. You played your trick on us and tried to capture us. We turned the tables and captured him, instead. We have him and we've taken him away." His mind was clearing now, gaining control of the situation. If he had Morgan, he had a bargaining chip to keep the four of them alive.

"Where have you taken them? How long have they been gone?"

"You want him back, do you? Then get off that horse and we'll talk about it."

"I'll not talk with the likes of you. You have killed my men and I do not trust you!"

"Tough it out, buster." Erickson was in control now. "You need me to get him back and I won't help you one bit unless you start being friendly and cooperative. Now get down and let's talk." Erickson started to walk away towards one of the picnic tables, but was jolted back to reality as he saw that none existed. A quick glance around the campground confirmed that none of the outhouses were there, either. He *was* back in 1776.

Ramsey dismounted and came over to where Erickson had sat down on his haunches near a tree. His uniform was as dirty and unkempt as Erickson last remembered seeing it.

"Why are you and these men still here?" Ramsey demanded to know. "Why did you not go with the others and Captain Morgan?"

"Some questions can't be answered easily, Sergeant. We had some tidying up to do, is the best way to answer that."

"What does that mean? I do not understand your words."

"It means that I don't have an answer you would understand. It also means you have a chance to get Morgan back and we have a chance to go. OK?"

"How will Captain Morgan return? Will your men let him go?"

"Yes, I'm sure they will. He's with Molly and the three other Dragoons."

"Molly's with them, too? How will they come back? Will your men bring them in the . . . the . . . trucks?"

"Maybe. I'm not sure yet how I'll have them brought back. First, we want some food and water. Then we'll talk more."

Erickson needed time to figure out what to do and to bring the three others into the decisions he would have to make. They had kept quiet, watching as Erickson and Ramsey had sparred. Now, as the rest of the Dragoon troop moved in around them, and the smell of the horses, coupled with the smell of the unbathed Dragoons themselves filled their nostrils, they waited for Erickson's next move.

It came quickly. "Let's not wait all day, Sergeant. Get some food and water over here so we can start talking."

Ramsey, already off balance because Morgan had not returned with the prisoners he said he would have, decided to comply with the order and signaled one of the Dragoons to bring that which Erickson demanded. The horse and rider left to ride down the hill to the Dragoon camp. "He will return shortly with something for you to eat. While we wait, tell me of my Captain. Is he unhurt?"

"Yes, he is unhurt. His pride has been ruffled, but he is unhurt." Then an inspiration reached Erickson's mind. "Why don't you take your men and go catch up with him? They went over that hill, to the north there. That will save me having to bring him back."

"But your men are still with him, are they not? They have strange weapons and they will surely kill us when we arrive."

"I think not. They do not want to keep your Captain. They only took him to make sure there would be no further fighting here in the camp. I am positive they will give him back to you."

"I think it is a trick to get us to leave. I do not trust you."

"That's what you said before. Leave some of your men here to watch us and take the rest with you. Surely your men are capable of guarding four unarmed men?"

"That they are." Ramsey couldn't say he had no Corporals to leave in charge. But, he had to do something. He thought about taking the rebels with him, but they had no horses and he had no extras on which they could be mounted. However, he could tie them up. He could gain enough information from them as they ate and then leave them behind, tied up, when he went after Morgan.

The Dragoon that had gone down the hill soon returned with a large leather sack carrying the food Erickson had requested. Tied to the side of the saddle was a jug of liquid. Erickson didn't know whether it was water or not, but hoped it wasn't beer. Sullivan had said it was terrible tasting and usually upset the stomach and senses in a hurry. He needed no sick or drunk men on his hands when it came time to get away from Ramsey.

Ramsey took charge of dispensing the food and liquid, which turned out to be water, while at the same time making it clear to Erickson that he wanted more information than just 'they went over that hill.'

Erickson obliged. "They left here in the back of the one of the trucks. They were tied up, but unharmed. The trucks were going to go to the top of the hill over the next rise and then down to the valley beyond. None of my men wanted any more trouble with your men. If you see them, they won't fight unless you force them to. Tell them you want Morgan and the three others back. Tell Sergeant Bushnell, he's in command."

Ramsey eyed Erickson for a long moment and then motioned for two of the Dragoons to come over to him.

Pulling his pistol, he pointed it at Erickson and told them. "Tie them up. We shall leave them here until we return. Do it well, I do not want them to get loose."

Erickson started to protest, but Ramsey stuck the pistol in his face. "You said that your men had tied up my Captain Morgan and that he remained unhurt. We shall do the same to you and if you do not resist, you will remain unhurt."

Erickson understood the logic and the exercise of authoritative power. He, like Lester, Treppello and Funston, reluctantly submitted and soon found themselves firmly bound to a tree, their butts on the ground with legs stretched out in front. Ramsey led his men away without a further word.

Lester was the first to speak. "I don't believe this."

"Welcome to the 18th Century," exclaimed Erickson. "But, I sure don't want to be here when they get back after not finding Morgan."

"I don't recall reading in your testimony what happened to Morgan."

"He wasn't there when we got to the bottom of the hill. Russell was able to whisper that to me as they put me in the ambulance. Morgan, the Dragoons and Molly – none of them were in the truck."

"So, what happened to them?" Lester demanded.

"I don't know. I guess there are no answers. Something about not being able to bring them back to our time, perhaps."

"How are we going to get out of here?" Funston chimed in, his arms aching from being tied up. "They've got me tied up pretty well."

"Well, I'm not," responded Treppello. "I kept my hands and wrists spread. It's not much slack, but it's enough. I'll be free in a bit, so just hang on, Uncle. I'll get us all out."

A 'bit' turned out to be twenty minutes, but Carl finally freed himself, then used a small pocketknife to free his Uncle and the others.

Erickson grabbed Lester by the arm and led him to a young, nearby tree. There he pointed at what he had seen from the ground as he waited to be cut free: the carved initials R D and M M, encircled by a heart. Funston and Treppello came over to see it as well, and then followed as Erickson led them to the northeast side of the camp. There they saw the mound of freshly piled dirt covering what they knew were the bodies of the dead Dragoons and a few American soldiers.

Leading them again, Erickson pointed at the burned mass of horseflesh and blackened hooves. There was now plenty of proof of his having been there. No need to go down to the Hollow, for there certainly would be a tavern and behind that tavern, a tree with slugs in it.

As they returned to the center of the campground, Lester couldn't help kicking up the ground in front of him looking for spent cartridges. He found more than a dozen of various kinds in less than twenty feet. He shook his head in disbelief and acknowledgement of what Erickson must have gone through, both in the campground and later at the Board of Inquiry.

Funston was ecstatic as he settled himself on the ground. "We've done it! We've gone back to another time and place! It's as if we had ordered it. It *can* work! I can use it and we can learn how to train others to use it!"

Treppello smiled at Lester, who could only shake his head in continued disbelief. The Colonel finally blurted out the thing that bothered him the most. "OK, Erickson, somehow or other you got us here. Now, how do we get out?"

Erickson looked at him fully understanding the question. "You mean back to our Century?"

"Of course! This may be 'old hat' to you, Lieutenant, but it's scaring the hell out of me!"

"Look," said Admiral Funston, cutting in, "if we can get here, we *can* get back. Erickson proved that before."

"But at what price?" Erickson interjected. "We were here for days and fought a bunch of battles. People were killed, people disappeared; one even went nuts and committed suicide. There's only four of us and we don't have any weapons."

"True enough, Lieutenant," said Funston. "True enough. But we are all military here and we have the training and skills to overcome matters like this."

"All military here? What do you mean by that?" Erickson demanded.

"In the real world, they call me Admiral Funston. That's Colonel Lester and that's Captain Treppello, both of the Army. No big deal. We're involved in a civilian operation with a lot of military overtones, if you know what I mean."

"I don't care what you mean, Admiral, or Funny, or whatever you're called," Erickson responded sternly. "We're here now and this isn't any joke. If we *do* get back, you're going to have to explain it to yourselves, because I want no part of it. The Army would put me and my men away for life if they found out I was involved with this."

"It's not *if* we get back, Lieutenant," Funston replied. "It's *when*. And, when we do, I have a job for you that's going to keep you busy for a long time to come. This experience will fade away into its proper perspective and we'll all end up having a hell of a great time. Mark my words, Lieutenant, and you too, Colonel and Captain. This is a great start!"

"Tell that to them," Erickson said, pointing to the north hill of the campground, "Sergeant Ramsey's back."

They whirled around to look where Erickson was pointing.

Treppello was the first to call out. "There's a girl with them. She's riding double with one of the Dragoons."

"I see her," replied Erickson. "It looks like Molly; and, there's Morgan, too, on a horse just behind Ramsey. My god! They're all back!"

Amazement interspersed with fear, caused Erickson to stand straighter, watching the group ride slowly down the hill into the upper edge of the campground. One thought kept going over and over in his mind. *What will Morgan do now?*

Lester and Treppello moved towards Funston, and all three clustered around Erickson in desperate concern.

Morgan rode up close and dismounted. "Sergeant Ramsey said you were still here, but I could not believe him. Why did you come back when you had gotten away?" Not waiting for an answer, he strode closer to Erickson and looked right at his face. "What has happened to you since we met yesterday? You look much older and wearier, and your hair has started to gray. Your uniform is gone. Is this really you?"

"Yes. And no."

"Which?" Morgan was in no mood for confusing answers.

Resigning himself to the reality of not being to explain the situation to Morgan now, any more than he could the last time they were together, Erickson said, "I'm still me and you're still you. I don't want to be here and they," he added, pointing at the other three, "don't either."

"I do not recall seeing these men before. Who are they?"

"Friends that have come with me to find some things we left behind. We have found them and are going to leave. We'll say good-bye and mean it. You go your way down the hill and we'll go our way back to our own time."

"You have no vehicles. Your carriages . . . your trucks, and the jeep, as you called them . . . are gone with your soldiers over the hill. They took me with . . . NO! *You* took me with them. You were in the lead. Why are you not with them now?"

"I told you, we came back for some things we left behind. We found them and we are leaving."

"What things?"

Tired of the badgering and angry with himself for even being there, Erickson suddenly exploded in Morgan's face. "Damnit, Morgan! You're really beginning to irritate me! Now back off or as sure as I'm standing here, I'll call my men back and I'll beat your ass all over again until you have no command left!"

Erickson's voice softened for a moment and a slight sadistic smile came across his face, surrounding his next words. "And, when I get finished, I'll nail your carcass to the side of the tavern."

Then, stepping even closer to Morgan so that they were just noses apart, Erickson hammered his invective home with a pointed finger, stabbing each word into Morgan's chest. "So-help-me-god, Morgan! Mount up and take your men over that hill – NOW!"

Morgan reeled back. The man in front of him was insane! Genuine fear reached into his heart and prompted him to remount his horse. There was always another day to deal with the likes of this Rebel. Looking at the four

Americans one last time, he reined the horse around and led his troops down the hill towards their camp in the Hollow below.

Lester, a little pale and slightly trembling turned to Erickson, shaking his head in wonder and relief.

"That was fantastic my boy, absolutely fantastic!" he exclaimed, exuberantly slapping Erickson on the back in proud approval.

Funston and Treppello were less dramatic, the strain of the encounter stifling all but the simplest words of gratitude in a moment charged with emotion.

It was a moment in which reality stood still and then was slowly replaced by a growing sound from the distance – a beating sound which grew louder and louder, and more distinctive as the two choppers returned to the helipad by the Ranger station.

The morning was clear, the sun was out and the birds flitted from branch to branch in the trees above, as Erickson and the others sat down at the concrete picnic table to plan the future.

Edwards Brothers Malloy
Thorofare, NJ USA
February 16, 2015